Stagecoach Road

The Bullies Must Die

A Novel by

DANIEL KAMEN

CCB Publishing
British Columbia, Canada

Stagecoach Road: The Bullies Must Die

Copyright ©2013 by Daniel Kamen
ISBN-13   978-1-77143-045-6
First Edition

Library and Archives Canada Cataloguing in Publication
Kamen, Daniel, 1956-
Stagecoach Road : the bullies must die / written by Daniel Kamen.
ISBN 978-1-77143-045-6
Also available in electronic format.
Additional cataloguing data available from Library and Archives Canada

Photo for cover artwork provided by Daniel Kamen.

Publisher: CCB Publishing
             British Columbia, Canada
             www.ccbpublishing.com

*I dedicate this book to
the William A. Wirt High School class of 1974,
especially to you, Eddy.*

Other books by Daniel Kamen

The Well Adjusted Dog:
Canine Chiropractic Methods You Can Do

The Well Adjusted Horse:
Equine Chiropractic Methods You Can Do

The Well Adjusted Cat:
Feline Chiropractic Methods You Can Do

Preface

I never felt comfortable driving down Stagecoach Road, let alone walking there by myself at night, which I did only once. That was enough.

I was sixteen years old in 1972. I had just got my driver's license and decided to drive to Stagecoach Road to find out, once and for all, if there was any truth to those ghost stories I heard from fellow Wirt High School classmates who swore the road was haunted. Some even said they saw figures at night of people who were dressed like they were from the 1800s.

I remember taking my mother's big old beige 1962 Buick LeSabre, confident I would be OK since it had a full tank of gas, new tires, and just had a tune-up. We lived in a suburb of Gary, Indiana called Miller Beach, just four miles from Stagecoach Road, which is in Portage, Indiana. I figured if I got stuck for any reason, I could always walk back. Little did I know when I started out for Stagecoach Road how prophetic I was.

It was a cloudy and unseasonably cool evening on Saturday, July 1st, 1972 when I got in the LeSabre around 9:30 p.m. We had cool summer evenings before probably due to our close proximity to Lake Michigan which was over the sand dunes, two miles from our house. I tossed a thin spring jacket in the back seat before backing out of our driveway. I slowly drove down Tippecanoe Street then turned onto Potawatomi Trail then finally onto County Line Road, which was flanked by a vast swamp, complete with thick cattails and brown wild ducks. Stagecoach Road was another mile or so ahead over the South Shore train tracks that paralleled Route 12.

Stagecoach Road isn't a main street. It is mostly a deserted country road. If you didn't know it was coming up, you could easily miss the road sign that was partially hidden beneath a hanging oak branch. I knew where it was. I knew only too well. I had a terrifying experience there just two years prior to driving myself on that cool summer night.

When I was fourteen, I made the horrible decision of getting into a car with two guys who introduced themselves as Wirt High School seniors, whom I had never seen before, but befriended me one evening at the after school chess club. They offered me a ride home, "saving my mother a trip." It was a dastardly cold, snowy, winter evening, about 5 degrees, and I was wearing a lightweight wool coat that wasn't designed for the deep freeze.

The seniors seemed pleasant enough, and had more than a passing knowledge of chess. I didn't phone my mother from the lunch room payphone as I usually did on chess night. Instead, I was delighted and grateful to accept the ride home, hoping to surprise my mother who no longer needed to drive through the heavy snow to pick me up.

Chess club was over by 6:15 p.m. The winter days were short, and it was already dark. The two seniors escorted me to the almost deserted school parking lot and into the back seat of their damaged white, 1959 Ford Galaxie with chipped paint and ripped upholstery. I thought nothing of it. Lots of teenagers bought beaters—the only cars they could afford. I forgot their names, but the taller of the two drove while his buddy, sitting on the passenger's side, lit up a cigarette. He offered me one which I politely refused. Then it occurred to me: they never asked me where I lived. They started driving in the general vicinity of my neighborhood, but way out of the way. I could tell they wanted to drive faster, but it was very slippery and the snow drifts slowed them down. I interrupted their conversation to tell them where I lived. The driver weakly acknowledged but continued to drive out of the way. That's when I really felt uneasy. I felt downright terrified when the driver's buddy turned around and asked if I had any money. I told him I only had two quarters on me, enough to make a couple of phone calls. He didn't like that answer and told me I was lying. That's when they headed towards Stagecoach Road.

I tried to compose myself and thought I would bide my time until they stopped at a light. My plan was to quickly get out of the car and make a run for it. They sensed my plan and ran two red lights before turning onto Stagecoach Road. They drove about two blocks down, just before the last house and asked me again if I had any money. I again told them I didn't, except for the two quarters. The driver stopped the car in the middle of the road, turned around and grabbed my shirt near my throat and said he'd drive me home if I paid him twenty dollars. At that moment I had nothing to lose but try to get out of the car. I grabbed the handle with my right hand, pushed the back door open with my shoulder, and monkey rolled outside to the snow below, leaving my books in the car. The guy in the front passenger seat got out of the car and grabbed the back of my neck but slipped in the snow. That gave me enough time to right myself and run a short distance towards the first house I saw. I didn't look back, but I felt I was being chased. The house was ahead, about thirty-five feet in front of me. The snow was deep and I barely slogged another two feet before seeing a thick broken branch poking out of the snow. I picked it up and threw it as hard as I could at the house, breaking a first floor bedroom window. The owner of the house immediately opened the door. I started yelling my head off for him to call the police. That's when the two seniors got back in their car, turned around and drove towards County Line Road.

I got lucky. The owner of the house let me use his phone to call my mother, who had already called the police, thinking I was missing. I don't know what I would have done if those two guys stopped the car five miles down Stagecoach Road, in the middle of nowhere. I might have frozen to death or maybe they would have beaten me. After my mother picked me up she called the police again to report these guys, but they were long gone. I never saw them after that incident. I don't know who they were, but it was clear they didn't go to Wirt. I vowed never to visit Stagecoach Road during winter ever again. When I finally got my driver's license, and in control of my destiny, I decided to get brave that summer evening in 1972 and see what Stagecoach Road was all about during the night.

I still had thoughts of turning back when I reached Stagecoach Road at about 9:45 p.m. But I didn't, and I turned onto that eerie road. I was relieved to see the lights on in the houses as I slowly drove passed the last one and into the dark of the night. I switched on my brights which brilliantly highlighted the gravely pavement below. I knew there were no streetlights along the way, just heavy woods on both sides. Everything looked fine. Normal. When I was about three miles passed the last house my car started making a strange noise—like a clogged fuel line, and then some sort of pinging sound. I kept driving, thinking it was just gravel. Then my headlights suddenly shut off and the engine abruptly went silent, no longer responding to my foot pressure on the gas. I coasted off to the side the best I could, not being able to see a foot in front of me. When I got out of the car I reached down to feel the pavement, making sure I was off the road. There was absolutely no light source of any kind—like I was blind, not even moonlight thanks to the overcast sky. My battery completely died after ten minutes of futile attempts to start the car. There wasn't even enough reserve to work the blinkers. I had no idea what I was going to do. I got back in the car and made one more vain attempt to start the engine. When I knew that was hopeless, I thought I'd find a flashlight in the glove compartment or under the seat, or maybe in the trunk. There wasn't one. I didn't even have any matches or a lighter which I normally carried with me since I started smoking Tiparillos. After closing the trunk, I opened the back door and reached in the back seat for my jacket, locked the door and started walking back towards County Line Road.

Not being able to see, I stumbled every other step, not knowing for sure I was on the road. The night was still. Every animal noise from the woods was magnified fivefold. Some of the animals sounded like small critters such as squirrels and rabbits. Others sounded bigger like coyotes and deer. I heard an occasional distant owl. Surprisingly, I wasn't really scared. I was concerned because I couldn't see my way. I never believed in ghosts, the supernatural, UFO's, ESP, psychokinesis, or anything else that defied the laws of physics. I knew the animals I heard were mostly harmless to people. My mind was just on walking forward and staying on the road, figuring it would take me only half an hour or so to see a house.

I struggled to walk for fifteen more minutes when I heard a car coming from behind. It sounded like it was a block or two away. I turned around and saw faint headlights in the distance that got bigger and clearer for about five seconds. Then suddenly they were gone—like someone purposely shut them off. I heard the motor stop, then dimmer lights reappeared. I ducked into the woods, but was still in earshot of the car and heard at least three men talking and laughing as they got out of the car. I knew there was no way they could have seen me. I also knew they must have seen my car on the side of the road. I wasn't worried about that. I wanted to continue walking towards County Line Road, but was afraid they would hear me.

I stood in one spot in the woods, cold and feeling very vulnerable. Just then the people got back in their car and started the motor. The car was again coming my way. I was only about ten feet into the woods and got a blurry look at the driver as the car drove past. But what got my attention was the passenger in the back seat who was looking out his window in my direction, like he was scanning for something. I stood completely still when the car suddenly stopped again, about a hundred feet up. I heard the people get out then saw two flashlights shining in my direction like they were specifically looking for me.

Scared out of my mind, I had no choice but to walk deeper into the woods and get away from them, frantically and noisily jostling into every tree and branch along the way. My arms were extended, touching every branch, like a blind man feeling his way around an unfamiliar house. I stopped long enough to look behind and saw the flashlights were now even from where I originally stood. I kept going, thinking the woods were at least two or three miles deep until I came out of them. Suddenly, the flashlights were gone. I was a good hundred yards away from the road. I stood completely still, listening for any signs of the people. At that moment I heard the car starting again and saw hazy red lights reflecting against the brush. The beam from the red lights was fanning out wider in the distant trees. The road was too far to make out any detail, but I saw the car slowly creeping backwards, then passed the spot where I was standing a few minutes earlier. I stood in the woods waiting for something else to happen—some other sign of life on the road. It seemed like hours, but it was only ten minutes or so when I heard a lot of noise coming down Stagecoach Road, and getting louder as if a lot of cars were on the road heading in the direction of County Line Road. A few seconds later I saw a car whizz by—must have been doing 60 mph or more. Two seconds later I saw distinctive blue and red strobes going crazy in the trees then four police cars speeding by, chasing the first car. But I didn't hear any sirens. I had no idea what was going on, but I felt a lot safer. I waited where I was for another five minutes before I decided to return to Stagecoach Road and continue my walk to the houses. I thought I only had a mile to go. As it turned out, I was two miles away, but it seemed like fifty. I think it would have been faster walking with a sprained ankle than not being able to see.

After that miserable hour, I finally saw light up ahead. And not just the light from a house, but police car lights, flashing while the squad cars were parked. I was now able to see my feet and jogged the rest of the way to the first house. A small group of onlookers congregated on the lawn in front of all the action. I walked up to the first person I met, a middle-aged man wearing a Bears cap, and asked him what was going on. He said he didn't know for sure, but said it could have had something to do with a high school student who was murdered a couple of days before over a car deal gone bad. The man said there were two other police cars earlier, then left after arresting the three men in the car, which was parked there and empty. I chatted with the man for a minute then told him about my car. He let me use his phone to call home, but instead I called a good friend of mine, Jay Silver, to pick me up, momentarily forgetting my folks would be frantic wondering where I was all this time. Actually, I was afraid to call them. I wanted to show my folks I could handle the situation myself. But Jay didn't mind. He recently got his license like me, and was thrilled I called him. He wanted to see all the excitement himself. And it was a good thing the middle-aged man was listening to my conversation. He wised me up and told me I should also call my folks, which I did.

Jay arrived about twenty minutes later, just as the scene

was dispersing. I told him what had happened with my car and what I just went through. Jay was more interested in finding out why all the cops were there. Everyone found out a few days later that in fact a high school student was shot to death the previous Thursday. One of the guys in the car I saw shot the student. The dead student sold that car for two thousand dollars, but was given a bad check. When he confronted his customer and told him about the bad check, the customer got angry and shot him with a rifle, but kept the car. According to the papers, the murderer drove to Stagecoach Road after the shooting and threw the rifle into the woods, then went back to look for the rifle on that Saturday night.

The LeSabre was towed to our house on Sunday. My folks were more than a little miffed why it broke down so quickly after getting tuned. The mechanic made a house call, looked under the hood and matter-of-factly said the fan belt broke and offered to fix it for free. That was nice of him.

So there you have it. Is Stagecoach Road really haunted? Is it bad luck? I don't know for sure. But what I do know is that I can't shake the uneasy feeling I got when I recently went there to take a picture of the road sign for this novel. I have no plans to go back.

Daniel Kamen
January 4th, 2013

Chapter One

A strange fetid pall mingled with the metallic scent of blood the night of June 14th, 1973. It wafted around Benny. The heat from the idling Mustang and the humid summer night intensified the smell and pain of his injuries. Had he the energy to gag, he would have. But the act of breathing took energy, and he didn't have any left to gag. His mind catalogued his injuries—the cracked skull that seeped warm blood onto the leather seats, his broken legs, and three missing teeth—and rage crept upon him. Rage at the bullies who'd beaten him, at his girlfriend for dumping him on their last night of high school, and at his own stupidity for venturing out to Stagecoach Road alone.

With obstructed vision, he stared out the window and prayed for someone to come by, but only the occasional call of a night animal and crickets interrupted the darkness. An hour passed, and the road remained empty. With each drip of blood, fear padded a little closer. Fear of death. Fear of not seeing his family and friends again. Fear of the once seemingly happy life he envisioned slipping away. And fear he would be unable to resolve this injustice to his satisfaction. To think this happenstance was a result of a banal emotion, jealousy. Four thugs jealous of Benny's new graduation gift from his parents. Jealous of Benny's academic achievements. And jealous of Benny's fulfilling, bright future, destined to elude these four from poor families and alcoholic fathers.

Foggy demons danced around Benjamin Arnold Weinstein's brain as he lay on the sticky upholstery, paralyzed with pain. He pictured each of his four attackers, their faces hollowed with graveyard eyes. Shark eyes. Visions of his past encounters with these school bullies were already deeply etched into his cerebral cortex. Twelve years of terror saw to that. This present act of aggression on Benny's body and soul was meant to be their last. Benny's only thought in his despair was to cheat death for another moment, and to link together as many of these moments as possible. Naivety and innocence were no longer virtues, but lifelong weaknesses, desperately needing to be purged.

Benny was all alone in the midst of this desolate strip of pebbly pavement. A panoramic view revealed just how deserted this road was compared to Gary, Indiana's distant steel industry. Stagecoach Road; an unforgiving stretch of asphalt entwined within a thicket of tall oaks on the outskirts of Miller Beach not far from Route 12. Picturesque sand dunes, a stone's throw away. In the not so distant horizon, orange bellowing smoke, reminiscent of the industry's better days, could be seen emanating from towering smoke stacks hovering over Lake Michigan's icy waters. But Miller's sandy reprieve from the intoxicating sulfur stench was no comfort to Benny that night. His eyelids, all but shuttered by massive swelling from the blows, struggled to open so his mind could form a plan. An escape from his predicament. His mind fixed on a vibration he felt underneath his tires, praying a guardian angel was on the way. Disappointment replaced hope when he realized it was the Union Line rumbling over old, rusty train tracks which crossed over Route 12 just a few blocks away. Stagecoach Road seemed to lead nowhere. But it was about to lead somewhere. Somewhere in Benny's semi-comatose mind were seeds of rage. Rage that was growing for almost twelve years. Rage, like no other, as he slowly started to regain consciousness and began contemplating what had just happened to him.

As that night progressed, Benny realized just how bad his injuries were. He was able to slowly slide his broken fingers to the top of his head, where he felt an open wound and cracked skull, warm blood rhythmically dripping onto the leather seats. His legs were broken. The gap in his mouth felt cavernous from his missing teeth. But he still could see. Thank God, he thought to himself. He couldn't move enough to get help. He had to helplessly and painfully lie there, and wait for morning or luck—someone to drive by and bring him to a hospital.

The minutes turned to hours as he lay there, drenched in his own life fluids, preparing to die. And it was luck. It was the proverbial dumb luck that another classmate and friend of his, Steve Green, just happened down the road on his way to a romantic interlude with Stephanie Shapiro. It was 2:30 a.m. The two had planned this rendezvous the week before. A final fling before each went their separate ways to college.

Steve's headlights shone on the blue Mustang as he negotiated a turn about two hundred yards passed the last house on the road. Not realizing it was Benny's new car, Steve assumed it was someone from the graduation party, and slowly drove alongside—offering some friendly harassment out his window and a 'thumbs up' to the couple he thought must be inside. But it was Stephanie who had the passenger's view of the person in the Mustang. Upon seeing this mangled, bloodied body, Stephanie shrieked. Steve hit the gas. He then turned around and headed back towards the main road, past the Mustang again, and called for help at the Gas 'N Go, the all night truck stop—two blocks passed Stagecoach Road on County Line Road. The police and ambulance arrived within fifteen minutes.

* * * * *

It was only a few hours before that Benny had wistfully entered the graduation party at the Marquette Park Pavilion with his girlfriend, Laura Burns. She was a beautiful, shapely girl with brown hair and gorgeous eyes. Many think she looked like an even more stunning version of Mary Tyler Moore. Maybe they thought that because her name was Laura. Either way, she was a looker, and liked to dress provocatively, as she did that night. They went there in Benny's new car after a family celebration at his house that lasted until 5:00 p.m. He wanted to wish his lifelong classmates and friends good luck. Scott Mathis, Chuck Merkov, and Greg McGee were all there—having a good time and talking about their futures. Chuck often ribbed Benny about how good looking Laura was compared to him. "She must like the Howdy-Doody look," laughed Chuck. Actually, most thought Benny was a good looking guy with his thick mop of red hair, rounded face and handsome nose. He stood about 6 feet tall and weighed close to 180 lbs. Running kept him in shape.

The Pavilion sat atop a hill overlooking the Marquette Park Lagoon. Benny fished there as a kid, and it was his childhood paradise. The lagoon had two old wobbly wooden piers stretching about a hundred feet from shore. It was a typical, spooky body of water—the kind you would see in an old black and white creature movie. During the days before the city cleaned it up and spoiled its charm by replacing the wooden piers with ugly cement piers, the lagoon teemed with all sorts of game and scavenger fish ranging from 5 ounce Sun fish to 15 pound carp—and just about everything in between. It was also at this little body of water where several drownings occurred—mostly Hispanic teenage daredevils trying to swim across without getting tangled in the thick seaweed. Everyone in town seemed to know when there was a drowning moments after it happened. The scene was an all too familiar one—frogmen with space-like masks entering the water and dragging the bottom for the pruned corpse they knew had to be hidden below somewhere—the victim's family standing vigil, anxiously praying for a miracle. But every drowning ended the same tragic way; the body was discovered and the local police chased away the curiosity seekers—kids, mostly.

The Pavilion itself was a little spooky, too. It stands as an old, but solidly built structure that looks strong and marbled like a large city's Capitol building without the dome. While empty, you can hear each of your footsteps echoing in its vast mystical tombs. Knowing the history of the lagoon below adds to its aura of gloom—a place no one would want to visit alone.

But during the night of June 14th, 1973 this old, scary Pavilion was very much alive. About three hundred young men and women were experiencing their first, almost legal, adult party. They finally made it—soon to be catapulted into the real world of work, school, and marriage. The six or so teachers chaperoning the event looked the other way when a few bottles of Crown Royal and a case of Schlitz made it through the front entrance.

Marquette Park was only five blocks from Wirt High School. The Pavilion was the biggest hall in town and every party, from proms to class reunions, was held at this massive building. Behind the Pavilion was a dimly lit and very romantic walkway that led to the moonlit lagoon. It was built some time in the 1920's and was probably never remodeled except for minor repairs to the cracked ceiling and chipped paint. It was at this place where Benny and Laura were to begin another chapter in their young lives.

Laura was Benny's high school sweetheart. They dated for almost three years but Benny sensed she was getting restless and wanted a change. But he never thought the change would occur that night.

The couple arrived at the party at 7:30 p.m. They did all of their talking earlier because as soon as they entered the hall all they could hear was the thunderous sound of the band playing Led Zeppelin, The Doors, Jimi Hendrix, and several cuts from *Hat Trick, America's* latest album. Everyone seemed to be having a good time. People were screaming at the top of their lungs just to make simple conversation. But it wasn't what the band was playing that changed Benny's life. It was the band's drummer, Larry Kroll, who immediately cast a determined stare at Laura as she walked passed. It wasn't your usual stare—not the kind that every guy would make when they see a pretty girl walk by. It was a "she's mine," stare. Larry wanted her.

It wasn't clear to Benny that Larry had designs on Laura. But his suspicions were soon aroused when Laura kept disappearing to speak with a "friend" of hers. She disappeared three times during the first hour. When Laura asked to be excused for the fourth time, Benny quietly followed her. Who was this friend that was so important? Benny didn't even see Larry approach her the first time. It turned out that when Benny went to the bathroom, Larry seized the opportunity to introduce himself to Laura and made his play.

Larry was every nice guy's nightmare. He was a twenty-one-year-old high school dropout, sexually experienced, tall, rugged, a popular musician, and had that dangerous bad boy druggie look that was seductive to the ladies during the post Woodstock days. Benny, on the other hand, was every mother's dream—studious, polite, and non-threatening. And yes, he did look a little like Howdy-Doody like Chuck said, only with casual slacks and open collar dress shirts—a far cry from the hippie culture. To top it off, Benny's and Laura's parents were good friends. So while Benny knew Laura was looking for some excitement, he never thought she would do this about-face. Of all nights. How could she go for this scumbag? How could she even think of it? What were those magic words Larry said to her to make her go home with him that night?

It was about 11:00 p.m. when Benny knew he and Laura were a thing of the past. Laura was now spending all of her time sitting next to Larry as he pounded out the ear splitting rhythms. She flaunted it. The band, by law, had to be out of there by midnight. Benny's friends were trying their best to console him, but to no avail.

Steve Green gave it his best shot. "Benny, you're going to Indiana U in a couple months. The campus is crawling with babes. Don't worry about it."

But all Benny could do was look at Laura, giggling at every remark Larry made and hugging his neck while he played. The night that had so much promise, turned out to be the lowest point of his life.

It was also around that time Benny decided he had enough. Laura didn't need him to drive her home. And he didn't want anyone else to console him. He made his way to the exit.

Steve gave chase and begged him to stay. "We're all going to my house afterward—c'mon, meet us there in an hour."

Benny weakly acknowledged and headed for his new Mustang.

The parking lot was dotted with new cars—mostly

graduation presents from the well-to-do parents. There weren't many people in the lot. Most were still inside, intending to rock to at least twelve o'clock.

It was a pleasant, warm evening. The sounds of late spring filled the air with a steady chirping of crickets. Benny took one last look at the Pavilion, knowing this was going to be a long night, and was imagining the worst case scenario with Laura in Larry's arms, in Larry's apartment. Hell, Benny and Laura never consummated their relationship; almost, but they never did. And the unthinkable; it was going to be Larry, not he, who was going to pleasure Laura that night. Benny was sure of it. He couldn't get those dirty pictures out of his mind; Laura, screaming with ecstasy while Larry fingered her on the floor until he was ready to penetrate her body, letting him steal her virginity that rightfully belonged to Benny. Or worse, maybe once in Larry's apartment Laura wouldn't know how to say no if Larry got so horny he just couldn't stop. At least that was what Benny was thinking. He couldn't stand it. The only thing left to do was get away from that Pavilion. And fast. It didn't matter where. It didn't matter what Benny imagined about Laura in Larry's apartment. He would find out later.

Benny got into his car and sat there for a few minutes, listening to the radio and hearing Bob Cheats, a local DJ, wishing all the new grads good luck and playing farewell tunes.

Sonny and Cher were singing *All I Ever Need Is You* when Benny finally left the parking lot and headed towards Stagecoach Road. And why he headed for Stagecoach Road is still a mystery, even to him. Maybe it was a place where he knew he could be alone. As bad as he felt, though, he wasn't suicidal. He didn't know how the evening was going to end.

Stagecoach Road had a bad reputation. Instead of ghost stories, kids would tell Stagecoach Road stories to scare the hell out of anyone who would listen. These fabricated stories were the stuff of werewolf and slasher movies. A dark, deserted strip where no one would dare venture alone—at least not unless they packed a gun. But that's where Benny was heading. His depression shadowed over any perceived fear he might have had about Stagecoach Road. He just wanted to be alone.

There weren't many stores open late, except for the Gas 'N Go on County Line Road. Benny thought of stopping to get a Coke, but didn't. Stagecoach Road was just ahead, and he wanted to let off some steam by flooring his new car. There were only a few houses on Stagecoach Road, spaced further and further apart as the road narrowed into wilderness. Old, abandoned barns were visible during the day, but a rumor at night. No cops, which made it such a good drag strip. Chances of hitting anyone or anything going 90 were nil. But that's also what made anyone entering the road so vulnerable. Very few people went there, except for the tough guys with fast cars and fast women.

At about 11:20 p.m. Benny turned down Stagecoach Road and slowly passed the houses that flanked him on each side. He had to drive slowly passed the houses since the road was rough and each bit of gravel pinged against his tires—even at 15 miles per hour. Thirty miles per hour would have awakened anyone in the houses.

When he reached the end of the houses, he turned on his brights so he could at least see twenty feet ahead. There were no street lights on the road. He then pushed his foot on the gas and zoomed for a couple of miles, nearly missing a deer. That got his attention. He almost hit that deer. His heart pounded at the near miss. That's when he stopped to turn around and headed back towards County Line Road and then maybe home. Laura was heavy on his mind. He stopped a couple of blocks before the houses, and cut the engine as he looked at the second hand on his watch and counted the ticks which were clearly audible on that still night.

It was fast approaching midnight. The magic hour. The band had to leave the Pavilion by twelve. This also meant Laura would be leaving with Larry and Benny's biggest nightmare would be realized. He didn't want to think about that any longer, but he couldn't talk himself out of it. He tried to think of all the positive things in his life—college, his friends, and how he loved to play the piano. The piano was his best friend. That's how he met Laura. Benny was playing a Chopin Prelude in the school music room when Laura stopped to listen. She was impressed and complimented him on his playing. So even though Laura was no longer his, his music stood by him. They couldn't take that away.

Benny sat in his car for about ten minutes and was starting to snap out of his gloom. He reached for the ignition and turned the key. Still in park, he revved the motor a couple of times before he put the car in drive. He was ready to go home when in the distance he saw another set of brights coming his way. Who on earth could that be, he thought to himself. He wasn't worried because he was in his car with the engine running. But Stagecoach Road was narrow—barely enough room for two cars to ride abreast. He thought he would wait for the oncoming car to pass him before he took off.

The other car, a badly damaged red Camaro with a loud, broken muffler, started to slow down as it approached. As the old hotrod crept closer, it challenged the Mustang by heading straight for it—an uninvited game of chicken. Benny didn't move. The Camaro's brights blinded him for moment and then stopped right in front of his car, headlights to headlights. Benny put his car in reverse and tried to get away. The three passengers inside the heap quickly got out and ran towards the

Mustang. Benny tried to hit his locks but it was too late. One guy was able to open the driver's side. Benny, it appeared, was doomed.

This whole episode was just pure chance. The thugs inside weren't looking for Benny—they were looking for trouble. They thought there was a couple inside and they intended to rape any girl who happened to be in the car. But it turned out to be Benny, the guy these goons bullied since the first grade.

Benny was a sitting duck. He was at the mercy of the four bullies he feared the most: Murphy Spevacek, Frank Stram, Gerald Hill, and Tommy Gunther. He hated all of them.

"Look what we've got here," said Frank, licking his chops like a bulldog with a steak. "Jew boy himself."

Frank was the meanest of the bunch. He had a badly pockmarked face, a blackened front tooth, and the longest rap sheet, burglaries mostly. His hair was dirty blond and oily. He was the tallest of the group, about six-foot-two. All of them dropped out a few months before graduation. They too went to the Pavilion that night but were abruptly escorted out by the security guard. They weren't welcomed there. This added to the already inflamed chip on their shoulders. Not that they needed another reason for their aggression. They were groomed to be anti-Semites even though there was very little anti-Semitism in Miller. What was more convenient than to blame a guy named Weinstein for their troubles.

"L-l-listen guys," Benny stammered. "I d-didn't do anything to you. I just want to go home."

Benny spoke with a slight but embarrassing stutter during stressful situations which was fodder for these delinquents.

"H-h-he just wants to g-go home," mocked Frank. "W-w-well you are home," Frank continued. "This is our home. And what are you doing driving on my r-r-road?"

His buddies got a kick out of that.

There was nothing Benny could say to talk his way out of this horrible situation. Tommy, who was driving Frank's Camaro, got out of the car and joined the other three who were now busy punching Benny in the face. Benny tried to scream but there wasn't anyone around to hear him. By now Murphy covered Benny's mouth and all four started to beat him. They pulled him from his car and kicked his ribs with all their might then began stomping on his legs, then his arms, then two or three kicks to his face and head. Benny felt his teeth crunch then he passed out. Not satisfied, the four beat him for another minute before they picked him up and propped him in his car behind the wheel. They then put the Mustang in neutral and pushed it four feet in front of a large oak tree. The four then took the tire iron out of their trunk and made a bunch of gashes in the tree to make it look like Benny had an accident, rather than the beating of his life. They also had the presence of mind to knock some dents into the front of the Mustang and knock out one of the headlights.

The Mustang continued to idle as the four degenerates hollered some obscenities, tossed a couple of beer cans out the window, got back into their hood-mobile and drove away. It was at this place, in front of the tree, where Benny remained unconscious for a couple of hours until Steve and Stephanie just happened by.

* * * * *

The ambulance arrived at about ten minutes to three. Steve and Stephanie had already called their parents as well as Benny's to tell them what had happened. A couple of squad cars pulled up and within fifteen minutes, there was a small crowd gathered around the scene, including Mildred and Harry Weinstein, Benny's mom and dad.

"Who did this to my son?" screamed Mildred, watching in horror as an officer picked up Benny's broken teeth from the ground.

The paramedics were busy tending to Benny.

"It looks like your boy had an accident," said the cop, pointing to the gouged out tree and the broken headlight.

The attending medic, Harvey Stillwell, examined Benny. "This was no accident," said Harvey. "There's no damage to the inside of the car. But he's still alive."

Benny's jaw was broken, but he was able to talk in short whispers.

"What did you say, son?" asked Harvey.

Benny could barely breathe. His ribs were broken and every breath was a chore.

"The guys did this," he labored.

"Who?" asked Harvey.

Benny couldn't talk any more. It hurt too badly. The medics placed him on a stretcher and rushed him to St. Mary's Hospital. The caravan of Steve and Stephanie, Benny's parents, and the cops followed the ambulance. Benny was rushed into the emergency room. A long period of pain, healing and contemplating was to follow.

Chapter Two

Benny was admitted to the intensive care unit. He had tubes coming out of every part of his body. He wasn't on life support, though he could not breathe comfortably on his own and needed a ventilator. They sedated him, primarily to conserve his energy. The police weren't able to take a statement until two days later. After a long 48 hours, Benny was finally able to give his account of what happened. The police took down the names of his attackers and went to work rounding them up. The first one on the list was Frank Stram.

Frank lived near the housing projects not far from the lake—the tough side of town, but still Miller Beach. The Stram family lived in an old frame house that had seen better days. Much better days. The place was unkempt and in need of repair. It was a white, dirty little house that was situated on Lake Avenue, a busy street with little privacy.

Two officers walked up to the door and attempted to ring the bell. It was broken. They knocked several times and waited for two minutes until a worn out looking woman, Frank's mother, Anita, finally answered.

"No, officers," said Anita, "my husband ain't home. He don't live here no more."

Frank's father, Marty, was always in trouble with the law.

Naturally, Anita thought the officers' visit had to do with her husband.

"No Ma'am," said Lieutenant Mitchell, the burley caucasian head crime detective in Gary, Indiana, "we're not here to see your husband. We're here to see Frank."

"Frank? Why do you want him?" Anita muttered defensively.

"We want to see him about his possible involvement in the beating of Benny Weinstein. He used to go to school with Frank."

Anita took a long drag on her unfiltered cigarette. She hadn't tapped the long ash off the end of it and the glowing butt was nearing her yellowed fingers.

"Frank didn't beat up no kid, man. Go bother someone else."

Officer Mitchell produced a warrant for Frank's arrest and demanded to see him.

"Well, he ain't here," said Anita in a hoarse smoker's growl.

"Do you mind if we look around?"

Anita threw her cigarette on the cluttered lawn and motioned for the officers to enter. They searched her insanely filthy house and saw no sign of Frank.

"Do you know where we might find him?"

"He said he was going out with his friends and he'll be back later," Anita grunted as she forced the door, almost smashing the officer's fingers.

"That's fine," said Lt. Mitchell. "We'll wait in the car for him."

They didn't have to wait long. Anita hurried back in the house and tried to call Frank at Gerald's house. But Frank was already on his way home. The police knew about Frank's Camaro and saw it coming down Lake Street. Frank could see the squad car in front of his house and made a U-turn towards the beach. The officers sped off after him, sirens blaring. They radioed for backup and the chase was on. A short chase at that. Frank ran out of room in the Lake Street Beach parking lot and the cops blocked the only exit. By this time three more squad cars arrived. Frank stopped his car and waited for the officers to approach. With guns drawn, four officers walked towards the Camaro and saw three others in the car with Frank, like a nice neat little package. His buddies, Murphy, Gerald, and Tommy were all inside, planning another night on the town.

"All right," demanded Lt. Mitchell, "everyone get out of the car and put your hands on you heads."

The four friends glanced at each other. Tommy was the runt of that disgusting litter. He looked up to Frank, worshiping his every move. As the hoodlums got out of the car Tommy whispered something to Frank. Frank shook his head and looked straight at the officers.

"I SAID HANDS ON YOUR HEADS!" shouted Lt. Mitchell.

The punks responded and did as they were told.

"What's this all about?" asked Frank, as he quickly glanced at Tommy with a worried expression on his face.

"We have an assault warrant for your arrest. These charges might expand to attempted murder."

"We didn't beat up anyone," Frank grunted.

"Well," continued Officer Mitchell, "we have a young man in the hospital who would strongly disagree with you. He gave us the entire account of the beating."

"You've got nothing on us," said Frank. "I want to see a lawyer."

"You'll need a lawyer. We found two beer cans at the scene. It'll be interesting to see whose finger prints are on them."

Lt. Mitchell read them their rights and the cops hauled them off to the station in separate cars.

There was more evidence than the beer cans, which in fact did bear Murphy's and Frank's fingerprints. Gerald was still wearing the same shoes he had on the night of the assault. There was dried blood on the soles. Evidence like that started to pile up, and since the four thugs were eighteen years old, they wouldn't be charged as minors.

Chapter Three

The Gary, Indiana police lockup was a dingy and badly maintained facility. But it was no stranger to Frank and Tommy, who had the pleasure of spending a few nights there early in their juvenile careers. The lockup was intended to be a one night holding area for criminals on their way to a bigger joint, like the Michigan City Pen. In fact, for a few days in 1972 it was closed down altogether because it didn't pass even the most liberal state inspection. Most of the toilets didn't work. There were rats everywhere, day and night. Feces and urine were never cleaned off the old, decaying mattresses, and there was no food service to speak of—white bread with pancake syrup and bitter black coffee. That was all the prisoners had to eat even though some guys were there for as long as a week. But by 1973 the jail had somewhat cleaned up its act when the health inspector shut it down. At least the prisoners had decent food. The city contracted with the Hardees restaurant across the street to serve hamburgers and french fries three times a day. The lockup also got new mattresses plus the toilets were fixed. Still, it was a holding cell and not a pleasant place to spend a night. The rats continued to squeak.

The police brought the gang there at 3:30 that afternoon for questioning. None of these young men had enough money to hire a good lawyer. One was appointed for them. Only one, Gerald, had a father at home. But they didn't think they even needed a lawyer. They naively clung to their fable of innocence.

The police booked them in the usual manner and each was given their own cell. Gerald's father, Gus, was called. He arrived about an hour later.

Lt. Mitchell had something to show the bullies—snapshots of Benny in the hospital. Mitchell walked to each cell, holding the pictures in his hand and waving them in front of each attacker.

"Does this young man look familiar to you?" Lt. Mitchell said to Murphy.

"No, I don't know him."

"Oh, you don't know him. You didn't go to school with Benny Weinstein since the first grade? Come on, who do you think you're talking to?"

Murphy didn't answer any more questions.

"I'm not going to say anything until I speak with a lawyer."

"That's fine. That's fine," said Lt. Mitchell. "Andy," he continued, "do you have an identity on those fingerprints we got off those beer cans?"

Andy was an old man who worked in the police lab who had seen a lifetime of punks parade past him proclaiming their innocence. That is, until the results were in.

"No, not yet," said Andy. "It's going to take a few more hours."

Lt. Mitchell spoke loud enough for all four boys to hear. This was his subtle method of interrogation.

Gus wanted to speak to his boy. Lt. Mitchell granted him the courtesy, but said he could only be alone with Gerald for five minutes.

"Did you do it, Hamburger?"

Gerald's family and his friends called him Hamburger because his excuse for leaving the house late at night was to get a hamburger.

With his oily skin glistening in the fluorescent lights, Gerald looked at his father and lowered his head to the ground. He didn't have to do any more. Gus knew his son was guilty.

"Hamburger, we don't have the money for a good lawyer. I just got this new job, see, and I'm barely making the house payments now."

"I know, Pop. I'm sorry. It wasn't my idea. We were just going for a ride and that dude was there. You know, all by himself."

"That's no excuse to beat the crap out of him. And if you and the guys are guilty of this, we're going to get sued and you're going to jail for a long time."

Gus walked out of his son's cell and motioned for Lt. Mitchell.

"I'm going to have to borrow some money for a lawyer. What will it take to spring my boy out of here tonight?"

"There's nothing I can do," said Officer Mitchell. "They've been booked and will have to face a judge in the morning. He'll decide that."

The four friends spent a long night in that depressing lockup and appeared before a judge in the morning. The public defender advised them to cop a plea based on the evidence. The evidence was the fingerprints which proved to be Tommy's, the blood on Gerald's shoes, and Benny's account of the crime. The boys were sentenced to three years in the Michigan City Pen and five years probation. They were out in a year and a half for good behavior. That was supposed to be the end of it.

Chapter Four

Most crime statistics go unnoticed by the public. Murders, rapes, armed robbery and such are commonplace in almost any sizeable city. The only ones who care anything about the statistics are the victims themselves—the ones who have to live with the pain. If the victim is lucky, the physical pain will subside and their flesh will heal. But most victims harbor deep emotional scars, reliving the horrible events at night. Some people can get over the emotional hurt with the passage of time. Some can't. In Benny's case, it wasn't just this one night of beating—it was twelve years of mental anguish that culminated in a beating. Twelve years of being humiliated in front of his friends by bullies who punched him in the school hallways just because their paths crossed. Twelve years of those same bullies strong-arming him for his money on the school bus. And twelve years of threats, as Frank warned, "If I ever see you alone, you're a dead man, Christ killer." And dozens of other miseries Benny lived with throughout his school days—regretting that he never had the courage to fight back.

Sure, Benny's body healed and his teeth were fixed. His parents could well afford the best. And yes, Benny entered college that fall and fit in just as he planned. But the real story doesn't begin until almost twenty years later. Like the seventeen year locusts emerging from the ground for a brief appearance to wreak havoc on the crops, only this was nineteen years later. It took this long for the seeds of that beating to take hold, festering into mania. Those seeds were watered by the scars on Benny's body, a constant reminder of that horrific night. Those four thugs were not to be forgotten. Not even for a moment. When Benny jogged, went to sleep, or made love to his wife, the night of the beating was with him. He fantasized about taking revenge for almost twenty years. And during these years he led an exemplary life; a chiropractor with a thriving practice located in a modern, two-thousand-foot stand-alone building on Hohman Avenue in Hammond, Indiana, just 13 miles from the incident. He married his college sweetheart, Marsha Horwitz, also from Gary, and together they had two children, Joshua and Rachel. They were the typical Jewish family. But with the dormant creature inside, awakened from its tortured soul, it was time to take that walk out of the lagoon.

Chapter Five

It was Friday, March15th, 1992. Spring was near and the cold bite of winter lessened with each passing day. Benny was out for his morning jog before going to the office. He only lived three miles from his chiropractic clinic and would sometimes walk to work in lieu of his daily run. He ran not only to keep in shape but as mental therapy. Exercising made him feel good. The endorphin rush kept him sane.

That particular day was a milestone—ten years in practice. His receptionist, Tracey O'Reilly, a slightly plump Irish woman who always brought Mitzie, her mischievous Beagle to work with her, was planning a surprise party for Benny along with a few patients who were more like friends than clients. Benny wasn't supposed to know about the party but found out anyway from Carla Bresloff, a middle-aged patient who had a big mouth and the hots for the affable bone crusher. On a good day she looked like a poor woman's Lucille Ball, but on most days she looked like Ethel. But to Benny, she was Fred.

Benny ran particularly hard that day since he was training for the Hammond Spring Trot, an annual 5K event. As he was making his way back home he stumbled on a discarded morning paper and fell to his knees, scraping his elbow on the pavement. He wasn't hurt badly but as he stood up he noticed a tan cargo van slowly passing by with the words Gunther Tire & Auto Supply boldly painted on the side.

Gunther, he thought. I wonder if there's any relation to Tommy Gunther.

He gathered himself, went home, got dressed and went to the office.

"Morning Tracey," he said when he walked in his store front, noticing big mouth Carla was already waiting for him.

"Good morning Mrs. Bresloff," Benny said. "Gee, it's so nice to see a happy, smiling face this early in the day. Seeing Yasser Arafat in the morning instead of you would be a big improvement."

Carla knew Benny was joking. But she didn't care. She liked him. Oh sure, she was married—to a man whom she hoped would somehow be trampled by a herd of buffalos, leaving her free to roam the prairies once again.

"Benny," she said, "call me Carla. We've known each other this many years."

"Okay, Carla. Right this way. I can see you now."

Carla really didn't have any back problems. She was lonely and bored with life. No kids. Nothing to occupy her time except to feign illness and take care of herself. Her husband, Alex, made enough money as a foreman at a plastic factory so she didn't need to work. They had a marriage of convenience and Alex was numb enough to go along with the status quo.

Carla lay down on the treatment table face up while Benny walked behind her head to adjust her neck.

"Now hold still while I do this move," Benny said. "I don't want to hurt you."

Benny popped Carla's neck and she let out a sigh of relief.

"Thanks," said Carla. "Much better now. And, oh, don't

forget about tonight," she said, winking at Benny about their little secret.

"Don't worry," Benny said, "I'll be here."

Tracey was busy filling out insurance papers while Mitzie was sleeping next to her feet. Benny's office was cozy with a touch of silliness. He had pictures of the Three Stooges hanging on the walls which accentuated his true nature. Out of the thirty or so patients who came in each day, only a handful were actually scheduled. The others just walked in as they pleased. Benny always found the time to treat them.

Benny looked up Gunther Tire & Auto Supply in the phone book and jotted down the address. He took his lunch at one o'clock and decided to take a drive over there. It happened to be located right next to the Gas 'N Go on County Line Road in Miller, about twenty minutes away. Oddly, he never knew about the place even though it wasn't far from his folks' house—in fact, on the way. Subconsciously he blocked out the name on the store's sign, not wanting to revive an agonizing memory. Today he had time. His next patient wasn't until three.

Traffic was light on I-94 and he was able to make it in fifteen minutes. He parked his car, a silver Toyota Camry, at the Gas 'N Go, bought a cup of coffee, and sat there for a few minutes, scoping out the tire center. For the first ten minutes all he saw were a few customers exiting the place and a truck delivering tires in the back. He desperately wanted to go in and see if Tommy, who would have been about 37 or so, was in fact the owner. Then he saw a guy about the age Tommy would have been, smiling while escorting a customer outside to look at his tires.

That could be him, thought Benny as he sipped his coffee. In fact I'm sure of it. He looks older, but he's the same height as I remember. A little less hair. But I think it could be him.

The bastard. Smiling and enjoying life as a business owner. Not a care in the world. Like nothing happened. But I've got to find out for sure. There has to be some way to find out. It can't be that difficult.

Benny couldn't muster up the courage to go into the tire center that day. He was still as big a coward as he ever was. And it was gnawing at him. What did he have to fear now? A confrontation? So he went back to his office to see more patients and to go to his 'surprise' party.

It should have been a happy occasion. Everyone came to the party. His kids, Joshua and Rachel, his wife Marsha, Tracey and her dog, and about forty others jammed into the office and made themselves at home in the waiting and exam rooms, stuffing their faces with all sorts of goodies Marsha bought at the Safeway earlier in the day.

To the outside world Benny was a jolly good fellow. All that was missing was the Mickey Mouse Parade and Annette Funicello. But this was no happy time. Something happened when he stopped at that gas station. Nineteen years wasn't enough time to bury the memories of that horrible June night— forever burned in his mind. Was that Tommy or not?

Chapter Six

Benny simmered all night. He was mostly angry at himself for not having the courage to face the person he thought took part in his beating some nineteen years earlier.

It was Saturday morning. Certainly a tire shop would be busier on the weekends. He could put on a pair of sunglasses, wear a baseball cap and blend in with the rest of the customers. If he could get close enough he knew he would be able to recognize Tommy. No pictures were necessary, although he did glance at his 9th grade yearbook and took it with him just to make sure. He only had two patients that Saturday morning and rescheduled them for Monday. He told Marsha he wanted to go out and look for a new car.

The tire shop opened at 9 a.m. Benny arrived at the Gas 'N Go at 8:30, waiting for the employees to arrive. He slowly sipped his gas station coffee and nibbled on a stale pecan roll as he watched someone walk up to the door. He quickly glanced at the yearbook then up again at the person opening the shop.

"That's him! That's him!" Benny whispered to himself. "That's the motherfucker who beat the living shit out of me.

That's him! That's him!"

Benny started to shake. He nursed his coffee and roll until 9 then started his car and drove to the large office complex across the street, and left it there while he strolled to the tire center—sunglasses and all. He had it all planned that he wouldn't talk much, fearing Tommy might recognize his voice and the familiar stutter. He waited a few minutes until other customers pulled up and went into the store. He casually walked in, inconspicuously inspecting a tire display and caressed one of the Goodyear Radials.

"May I help you?" rang the voice behind him.

Startled, Benny looked over his shoulder and saw Tommy. It *was* him. And there they were, standing toe to toe together after all of those years—with vivid flashbacks: The graduation party. The beating. First to twelfth grade encounters.

Benny cleared his throat, and with a soft, indistinguishable voice said, "No. Just looking."

But he couldn't get those haunting words out of his head, "May I help you?" Benny thought, where was he when I needed help that night in '73? Or in the lunch room at Nobel Elementary School some twenty-eight years ago? Oh, now he wants to help me! Gosh, I see that he turned his life around. That's good. That's real good. I'm glad for him. Real glad. I hope he has a happy family life. Real happy. I hope he has kids. Nice kids. Real nice kids. I hope he has a pretty wife. Real pretty. I hope he has the world to live for.

Frozen for a moment, Benny regained his thoughts, smiled at Tommy, then walked out. For an instant it looked as though Tommy sensed something. He was sure Tommy knew his face even under those dark glasses.

Benny walked back to his car, contemplating his next move. Now what? he thought. So now I know it's him. But that's not enough. Where are the other three? Where's Frank and Gerald and Murphy? How can I find them? I wonder if they ever keep in touch with each other. I wonder how I can find out without anyone knowing I'm looking for them.

Chapter Seven

Finding the other guys wasn't the only thing on Benny's mind. A few years earlier he had found out what happened to Laura the night of the graduation party. Even though Benny was, for the most part, happily married, it bothered him to no end. The bandleader, Larry Kroll, bragged to one of his friends and word got out—in great detail.

The graduation party ended at midnight as expected. That's when the band had to pack up. Larry and the four other members disassembled their equipment and hauled it out to their Volkswagen Van. Laura was helping too, and already was a little drunk from quickly downing four shots of tequila Larry had given her during the last half hour they were playing.

She enjoyed her naughty night watching the band and being the center of attention of such a worldly man. It was much different than her safe, sheltered upbringing which led her to Benny in the first place. And she willfully went along for the ride when Larry asked her if she wanted to join the group for a couple of drinks at the Brass Bomber, a blues bar in Portage about twenty miles away, a block from Larry's apartment. Even though Laura was only 17, Larry knew the manager and could get her in.

Another band member, Mark Holst, did the driving and stopped the van in front of the bar. Larry and Laura got out and the others sped off.

"Where are they going?" asked Laura as he grabbed her arm.

"Oh, they have a gig tomorrow with another band and they have to get home," said Larry. "Come on. Let's have a couple, then I'll drive you home. I live just over there," pointing to a two-story apartment complex.

"I don't know," Laura said in her soft, meek voice. "My parents are going to worry about me. I'd better leave now."

"Alright," said Larry. "My car's just down the road a bit in front of my apartment."

Larry put his arm around Laura's small waist and held her tight as they headed towards his apartment. She was seductively dressed in a white miniskirt and a tight pink blouse that barely held her large, but firm breasts together. Her shoulder length brown hair was adorned by a pink ribbon in the back. The seams in her pulled-up nylons were visible on each of her shapely thighs. Her legs were further shaped by her three-inch red pumps. She smelled of booze and lilac perfume.

Larry fumbled for his car keys as they approached the car.

"I must have left them upstairs," he said as he patted each of his pockets. "I'll get them. This will just take a minute. You can come with if you like."

Laura contemplated for a second and agreed to go with Larry to look for his keys.

As they climbed up the one flight of stairs, Larry gently reached for Laura's hand as they walked down the hall to his door. Larry found his apartment key and opened the door for Laura, letting her in first. He turned on the light and saw his car keys on the kitchen table.

"Are those them?" asked Laura, pointing to the silver

keychain.

At that moment Larry locked the door while grabbing Laura by the hand and passionately kissed her as she tried to get away. She tried to tell him to stop but his mouth completely covered hers as he took her hand and forced it down his pants. She reflexively grabbed his massive, rock hard cock and gently caressed his balls underneath. Larry ripped away the button on her blouse that held her huge, firm white tits together and sucked each of her erect nipples. She pulled on his cock even harder as he reached up to her sweetly perfumed beaver, past her nylons, and felt her moist slit underneath her silk panties, and then stuck his finger in her tight, pink virgin pussy. They fell to the ground with Larry on top with his hand squishing inside her inexperienced young twat as her pink ribbon fell off her head. You could hear her softly say, "No, Larry, don't, don't, don't. I'm still a virrr...."

This made Larry even harder as he pushed his tongue into her mouth until her protests stopped. He then pulled down his pants and she put the tip of his hot organ next to her wet pubic hair as he slowly pumped himself in, not completely able to penetrate her tight pussy at first. She started to moan and he pumped faster and harder until his huge organ was finally completely inside her. Larry's hot, piercing cock popped her defenseless cherry as Laura screamed even louder in ecstasy as he slid in and out her helpless, steamy pussy. She opened her mouth wider and wider with each pump and screamed louder and louder as she continued to stroke Larry's hardened sac. Larry couldn't hold it any longer and sprayed a load of hot white cream in her starving snatch as she cradled Larry's face. He again covered her pink opened mouth with his. He was even harder while cuming in her and she let out a few more moans before he finished. She grabbed Larry's prick, still firm, and gently milked out the remaining gooey liquid, then put her arms around his neck as they kissed for another minute. After it was over, Laura picked up her panties and ribbon off the floor and fixed her blouse and miniskirt. Larry kissed her as they walked out the door, keeping his hand on her tits the whole way, and hers on his cock as they walked down the hallway and outside to his car. Then he drove her home.

With her virginity taken in one evening by the likes of that nasty boy, Laura knew Benny would never forgive her so she didn't even try to contact him after that. Even though he heard about Laura's encounter with Larry years later, Benny was still furious. It should have been him. It didn't gladden his heart or assuage his anger that he was justified that night when he walked out of the graduation party.

Chapter Eight

The next day was Sunday, March 17th, 1992. Benny planned to spend the whole day with Marsha and the kids. First on the list was Sunday school. The Weinsteins belonged to Temple Beth-El, a conservative synagogue a few miles away. Joshua was almost eleven years old and was doing some early preparation for his Bar-Mitzvah. Rachel was eight and still had a little time before she had to worry about her Bat-Mitzvah. Marsha's mother, Sarah, was coming over at 1:30 p.m., and then everyone was going to the Museum of Science and Industry in Chicago. Benny's job was to drive the kids back and forth from Sunday school while Marsha caught up on the taxes which were due the following month. So Benny had some time to kill after he dropped off his children. He knew just what he wanted to do.

The night before he looked through about a dozen phone books he got from the library. These books covered all of Gary and the surrounding suburbs including East Chicago, Munster and Hobart. He also looked through the Michigan City phone book and as far as South Bend. He also scoured the Chicago directories and suburbs. He was able to locate a Murphy Spevacek on Grand Boulevard in Miller, not far from Wirt

High School. There was a good chance it was the Murphy Spevacek he was looking for. Benny vaguely remembered his family living near there back in the 60s. The address looked like a residential address, a house, and not the nearby housing project. Could he afford a house? thought Benny. If so, he has to have some sort of income—a job maybe.

Benny figured if he left by 8:35 a.m. he could easily be back in time to pick up his kids at noon. He dropped his kids off and headed for 346 N. Grand Boulevard.

Every neighborhood in Miller was familiar to Benny. His childhood memories were just as vivid, especially the traumatic ones. As he made his way through the winding sand dunes on his way to Grand Boulevard he passed his old piano teacher's house on Martin Road. Miss Hutchens taught piano on her Steinway Concert Grand in her immaculately kept study. Her house was about a mile and a half away from Benny's, as the crow flies, just over a series of large sand dunes that led to his backyard, and more often than not he would walk through the dunes to his lessons except during the winter.

* * * * *

One day in the fall of '69, during the 9th grade, Benny starting walking home from his piano lesson at around 4:45 p.m. It was deep autumn, and daylight savings time hastened the darkness. As he made his way down Martin Road he noticed a bunch of guys following him. They looked familiar but they were about a block away and he couldn't quite make out their faces. Martin Road ended at a large dune. Just over that large dune were the woods that led to the back of Benny's house—a good half mile away. He had a choice: Should he climb the steep sand dune and cut through the woods or should he take the long way by following Deerpath Road to his left?

There weren't many houses at the end of Martin Road and there was nobody else in sight. The four guys were gaining on him and were finally close enough to recognize. It was Murphy along with Frank Stram and two other guys from a different school. They started running after Benny then shouted, "Hey look, B-benny the Jew. Let's get him!"

Benny had no choice but to climb that hill and run for his life. Clutching his piano books, he bolted up the hill as fast as he could. The guys were about half a block behind him but were more athletic. Out of breath but determined, Benny made it to the top of that steep hill and ran through the dark woods. Only now, the guys had reached the top of the hill themselves and chased after him. Benny knew he couldn't outrun them. His only option was to hide on the ground in some thick leaves and hope they wouldn't find him. So he dove into a gulley of leaves and brush and kept very still. The four punks were now in earshot.

"I think he went that way," said Murphy. "I know where he lives. Just over the hill a ways."

As Benny lay on the ground, he heard them come nearer and was sure they would see or stumble over him. He heard the crunching of leaves with each step they took. They were as close as three feet away. Miraculously, they ran by and headed towards his house, thinking they would catch up to him. It was pitch black in those woods, which made Benny feel a little safer. Any wild animal, a fox or a coyote, was nothing compared to the animals that were after him.

Benny waited in that gully for ten minutes, making sure they didn't backtrack. He picked up his piano books and cautiously walked through the woods, the long way, eventually reaching the back of the houses down the road from his own.

Who knows what would have happened had they caught up to him. They might have killed him or at the very least beat him to within an inch of his life. This was the only time Benny decided to do something about it. The next day in school he went to the principal's office and told Mr. Benson what had happened. Mr. Benson talked to them but couldn't do much more since nothing really happened. This made things worse. Murphy confronted Benny later on that day in the cafeteria and threatened him.

"If you ever tell on me again Jew," as he punched Benny in the shoulder, "you're a dead man."

Benny regretfully kept quiet after that.

* * * * *

But now, nineteen years later, it was Benny who was on the hunt. He reached Grand Boulevard, passed by Wirt High School, and slowed a bit to read the house addresses.

Let's see, thought Benny, as he strained to see the numbers. This one's 330. I can't see that one. Oh, there it is, 346. And there's his name on the mailbox, Spevacek.

The house was small but well kept. It was a single story frame house with a wooden fence surrounding the back yard, a red swing set in plain sight. There was a tan, late model Ford pickup in the driveway and a blue bicycle leaning against the detached garage. There was probably someone home, but from the outside everything looked still.

Benny parked his car across the street and about fifty feet down the road. He sat patiently, reading the Gary Post Tribune and drinking coffee while waiting for some sign of life to come out of the house. He knew he could only wait for about two hours before he had to pick up his kids.

Around 10:45 a.m., someone emerged. Benny spilled the remains of his cold coffee out the window and ducked down a bit. He peered over the steering wheel and saw a man and a young boy, about ten or eleven years old, get into the truck. Benny let them drive a couple of blocks ahead before he tailed them. They didn't go far—just to the 7-11 about a mile away. Benny waited in the small parking lot for a few minutes then spotted the two as they exited the store. The man tapped a fresh pack of cigarettes on his hand as he and the boy got back into the truck.

Sure as hell, Benny thought to himself, that's him! And that must be his kid. He looks like an asshole just like his old man. Same cocky walk. Same smug look. I'll bet that young motherfucker smokes in school just like his scumbag father did. I'll bet that kid is a bully just like his father was. I hope he and his dad get along great, and do everything together like hunt and fish and race motorcycles. I'll bet that kid has a good time. Yeah, I hope so. I hope his old man is married to someone he really loves. I hope they're happy. Real happy. I hope his wife is pretty. Real pretty. I hope they have great sex together. Hot, smok'n sex. Wouldn't that be nice? Wouldn't that be sweet? Real sweet. Yeah, real sweet.

Chapter Nine

Marsha knew about Benny's past but he never let on that it was eating him alive. Only once did they talk about the beating in length, then in passing, when Benny complained of jaw pain. He was left with a chronic case of TMJ (Temporomandibular Joint Syndrome). His dentist fitted him with a bite plate which he wore at night.

Marsha was a pretty girl from a similar background. She had brown eyes and long brown hair that she often wore in a ponytail. Her figure was perfect and shapely. She liked to wear stylish clothes, even to the grocery store. But she was very frugal and didn't spend money on junk. Marsha was the typical suburban soccer mom who liked being busy with the kids and would often help out at Benny's office. She studied accounting in college but decided to become a full time wife and mother after she finished her degree. Marsha had lots of friends with children of similar ages. They would meet for lunch and go out a lot. Benny liked to socialize too, but not as much as his popular wife. He mostly kept to himself after he came home from the office. Sure, he had friends, but preferred to do things alone like fishing, watching television, and betting on the ponies. He was also an accomplished chess player, achieving master status. He was a gifted pianist, and was accepted to Indiana University's prestigious music program. But after a while Benny found it too difficult to play the keyboard since he developed an early case of arthritis in his fingers after they were broken. So he decided to put his talented digits to use as a chiropractor.

It was becoming increasingly difficult for Benny to stay focused on his chiropractic practice while leading a double life as a self-serving sleuth. The most important thing on his mind was finding the other two goons, Gerald Hill and Frank Stram. He went through the motions each day of putting on a chipper face, treating patients, and taking care of his family. Although, he grew less tolerant of pain-in-the-ass Carla. By now she baked something new for him each time she came in for an adjustment. Marsha knew about this, but it didn't bother her. No contest.

At least twice a week Benny would go out by himself, either to the local chess club which met each Tuesday at the Hammond library, or to the nearby off-track betting parlor just across the state border in Illinois. He usually went to the track on Thursday evenings. So he had two convenient excuses to go out at night, and Marsha never asked any questions.

He already knew what Tommy did with his days, and he knew where Murphy lived. But what did he do for a living? Did Murphy just stay in the house all day? Maybe he had a 9 to 5 job somewhere. Benny had to find out.

Chapter Ten

The following Monday Benny decided to get up at 5:00 a.m. and stake out Murphy's home on Grand Boulevard. He thought he might get lucky and follow him going to work. He told Marsha he wanted to try out the fishing at Calumet pier and would be back in time for his nine o'clock appointments. He brought his fishing gear and a change of clothes with him to make it look good.

He arrived at Murphy's house by 5:30 a.m. but didn't see his truck in the driveway. Damn, he thought. He must be working nights somewhere. Or maybe it's in his garage. Either way he was prepared to wait another hour. He made sure he was parked far enough down the street so as to not arouse suspicion.

His wait paid off. At about 6:30 a.m., just as he was about to leave, he saw truck lights coming towards him, which brought back a rush of memories of that night in '73. The truck pulled into the driveway and Murphy got out, wearing some sort of work clothes and boots. It was obvious he had a job somewhere at night. But where? The only way to find out would be to follow him on his way to work. So the following evening, Tuesday night, when he was suppose to be playing chess, he drove to Murphy's house and got there by 8 p.m. There he sat and waited until 9:15 p.m. when he saw Murphy leaving his house, and a woman, about the same age, handing him his lunch box.

That must be his wife, thought Benny. Hey, she ain't half bad. I wouldn't mind doing her myself one day.

Murphy started driving south on Grand Boulevard as Benny followed the best he could without being noticed. Murphy headed towards Lake Street as he passed the old housing projects on the right. That's where Benny's old seventh grade girlfriend, Twila Fairfield, lived. Her parents were really poor but she was the sweetest girl you ever wanted to see, not to mention a little on the trashy side. Twila was brought up rough, and more often than not, had to fend for herself. She had long, natural blond hair, blue eyes, a very pretty face, and the most radiant smile. Oh, and the world's sexiest heart-shaped tush. Twila was also well endowed for her age which got everyone's attention, that, and she spoke with a hint of a southern accent. She was one of only a handful of white girls in an otherwise black neighborhood. Benny and Twila were more like friends than boyfriend and girlfriend. He wasn't that advanced to think of her any other way. Didn't even cross his mind. But it crossed Murphy's.

It was like driving down memory lane as Murphy led Benny to Route 12 and headed west. Most of the locals referred to Route 12 as 12/20 since it converged with Route 20 before hitting the pits of Gary. Through Gary, U.S. 12/20 runs westbound on 4th Avenue, and eastbound on 5th Avenue. Driving west from Miller, Lake Michigan was on the passenger's side, but was obscured by the industrial buildings. Visible were the white foam peeks atop the vast blue water as the waves from the great lake crashed into the distant shore. It was a very familiar scene to Benny. He and one of his best childhood friends, Albert "Al" Fredericks, used to go squirrel hunting just off of Route 12. Al was a great shot and went there often to be near his dad who worked in the parts department at the nearby Chevy dealer.

As Benny continued to follow Murphy, he sensed he was heading for the steel mills. Of course, he thought. Why didn't I figure that out before?

That's just where Murphy was heading. It was very dark outside, but Benny was clearly able to see the brightly lit U.S. Steel sign as Murphy entered the gate and showed the guard his pass. Benny didn't have a pass and decided to park his car in the small public parking area which was on the same side of the entrance, but still had a clear view of everyone who pulled in. He parked there because he had a hunch. Maybe, just maybe he might see another familiar face or two going to work. He knew it was a long shot but as long as he was there, he wanted to wait at least an hour. The night shift, he figured, probably started at 10:00 p.m.

A lot of cars started to pull in all at once and formed a short line to the guarded entrance. It was almost impossible to see anyone's face, especially with the bright lights reflecting off the windshields. Benny decided to go home, satisfied that he at least knew how Murphy spent his days. His plan was to go back to the mills in the morning, about 5:45 a.m., thinking the night shift let out at 6:00 a.m.

The next morning he gave the old fishing story to Marsha and headed for the mills. He parked his car in the same spot, but this time he brought a pair of binoculars. The sun was just coming up and people started to drive out of the lot. Benny must have seen a dozen or so cars and trucks drive out until he spotted Murphy. One by one he examined the drivers and passengers as they made their way out. All of a sudden, Benny's blood froze. "That's him," Benny muttered to himself after getting an eyeful of the guy who savaged him that night some nineteen years ago. "My God! That's Frank Stram and the guy next to him looks like he could be Gerald Hill! God help us, they're still buddies!"

Benny's hunch paid off huge. He got three for the price of one. Murphy worked the night shift and the other two during the day. Now all he had to do was follow that dented, burnt amber pickup Frank was driving.

Chapter Eleven

Benny didn't exactly like bad neighborhoods and was hoping he was being led to a decent side of town. He had a few close calls when he drove his bike to the projects as a 7th grader to visit Twila. For starters, Benny was milky white and didn't quite blend in. But he had an ally who lived there, a 10th grader, Edward Clifford Moss. Eddy's family was just as poor as anyone else's in the project but he was one of the nicest guys you'd ever want to meet, not at all resentful of those who had more. His mother, Joanna, was proud of her son for being such a good student and for the way he treated others. Everyone liked Eddy. He was athletically built, good looking, tall, about 6' 2", had a closely cut Afro and an inviting smile. He also had a little edge, but in a nice way. There was nothing he wouldn't do for his friends. But if you pissed him off, watch out. He'd lay into you like a steamroller.

Eddy and Benny used to play chess after school in the lunch room, and on several occasions Twila sat and watched even though she didn't play. Afterwards, Eddy would walk Twila home. At first they were just friends. But by the time Twila was in 8th grade, Eddy really liked her and she liked him. He wanted to be more than friends. Much more. Twila's mom, however, didn't approve of her innocent daughter dating a black guy. She wanted her only child to stay pure at least until she graduated high school. A bigger problem started when Murphy made a play for Twila.

Towards the end of 8th grade, about the middle of May, Eddy and Benny were finishing a chess game in the lunch room when Murphy and Frank walked in. Twila was sitting next to Eddy. She was wearing a tight fitting T-shirt with no bra underneath, her nipples almost poking through the material. Maybe she couldn't afford a bra. And she had on a snug pair of jeans which made her heart shaped ass look even juicier.

Initially, Murphy and Frank pretended to be interested in the game. "Let's see," Murphy said as he pointed to the chess board as Frank looked on. "If you move your queen there and he takes your pawn with his rook, then you can trap his bishop."

Eddy, Benny and Twila tried to ignore him but he wouldn't stop.

"Then," Murphy continued, "if he moves that horse over here," as he touched the knight, "you can rip off his other pawn like this—zap!" Murphy said as he knocked over the pieces, to Frank's great amusement.

Benny got mad and got up so say something. Murphy quickly pushed Benny in the face with his palm as Frank flung the vinyl board off the table. Benny was too afraid to fight back. He was humiliated, especially in front of Twila who did her best not to notice. Eddy stood up and made a motion at the two losers.

"What's you gonna do, NIGGA?" shouted Frank, as Murphy grabbed Twila by the arm.

Benny just stood there, disgusted with himself that he didn't have the courage to defend her.

"Hey, let go of her," shouted Eddy as he pushed Murphy's

arm off of her.

"Look at that, the nigga's got balls. Is that why you like him so much?" Murphy said as he looked at Twila. "Or do you like his big African dick?"

Eddy got mad and took a swing at Murphy. Frank jumped in and tried to help his buddy, but Eddy could take them both—they knew it, and backed off.

"Hey sweet thang," Murphy shouted to Twila as he and Frank trotted for the exit, "why don't you come home with me and I'll show you things to make you forget your jungle bunny hero!"

With that, Eddy ran after Murphy, pushed him down and kicked him in the balls as hard as he could. Frank was already outside, not wanting to tangle with Eddy. After all, *he* didn't say anything.

Murphy shrieked in pain as he staggered out the heavy glass doors. "You wait, NIGGA," Murphy threatened. "I'm gonna lynch your black ass if you ever touch that white bitch." The two took off running.

Benny was too mortified to continue playing. Eddy tried to make Benny feel better but it was useless. Twila, at this point, was more interested in Eddy anyway and asked him to walk her home.

"See you tomorrow?" Eddy asked Benny as he dejectedly made his way outside.

"Yeah sure," said Benny, acknowledging Eddy's concerned gesture.

It was about 4:30 p.m. The school was just about empty. All the teachers and yellow buses had left, and there weren't any extracurricular activities that day. The only people left were the evening janitors. Everyone, including Eddy, knew the janitors' routine. They first buffed the floors upstairs and cleaned the bathrooms before they did the classrooms. That took a couple of hours. Then onto the first floor. Eddy, who never made a move on Twila, wanted to sneak some alone time with her before he went home.

"Did you ever see the old gym they have downstairs?" Eddy asked Twila as she pressed her books next to her chest, getting a better grip.

"Maybe once last year before the new gym opened," replied Twila. "Why do you ask?"

"It's a really cool place," said Eddy. "Sometimes they leave the back door open at night and me and my buddies go there to shoot some hoops. I have a locker down there where I keep an extra set of clothes and some shoes. I was going to pick them up before I went home. Wanna come with?"

Twila thought for a moment. She liked and trusted Eddy, and she was attracted to him, but wasn't too sure going downstairs with him was a good idea. But she went anyway.

"Sure Eddy, I've never seen a men's locker room," she said, giggling at her own comment.

Eddy put his hand on Twila's shoulder as they walked down the long hall to the basement door. He opened the door for her as they walked down the narrow flight of stairs.

"This way," said Eddy, still holding her shoulder as he pointed to the locker room.

It was quiet and empty in the old gym. Each step echoed against the walls. They walked up to Eddy's locker in the men's bathroom. Eddy worked the combination on the lock and grabbed his clothes. Twila marveled that such a nice big gym was going to waste.

"They could hold church meetings in main gym area," Twila said. "Did you see all those bleachers we passed?"

Eddy was silent. He stared right into Twila's beautiful blue eyes as she stared back. She knew what he wanted.

"Eddy, I don't know," she said as he dropped his clothes

and put his arms around her waist as her books fell to the floor. "What would my momma think?" she said as he kissed her and lowered his hands to her curvaceous bottom.

"You're embarrassing me, Eddy," Twila said, thinking she saw someone walk passed the window above.

Eddy kept on kissing her, then reached up her T-shirt and placed his large brown hand on her big, white firm tits and gently squeezed each one. Then he lifted up her shirt and put his mouth on her rigid nipples. Twila was turned on and kissed him back, placing her hand over his zipper and squeezing his huge hard dick through his jeans.

"Oh Eddy, are you sure it's safe?" Twila whispered as he pulled down her pants and slowly worked his finger in her young, tight pussy. "I'm only 14."

"Don't worry, baby," Eddy whispered back as his pants fell to the ground. "And I'm almost 17. Let me show you the way."

Twila was even hornier than Eddy while she lay on her back as he placed his enormous dick up to her hot virgin box. Twila reached back and grabbed his ass and pushed on his firm cheeks so she could be penetrated for the first time. He slowly worked his way in, breaking her taut juvenile cherry with his ebony bayonet.

"Ow, Ow!" cried Twila. "You're too big. Oh, stop, stop, stop."

It was too late. Eddy slid in the rest of the way, pushing all nine inches of his thick, hot black meat deep into her blond bush.

"Oh Eddy! Oh Eddy! Oh Eddy!" Twila moaned as Eddy pumped harder and deeper as she felt her brain explode with her first climax. "Oh no, Eddy! Oh no, Eddy! Ahhhhhhh!"

Eddy pulled out and turned Twila over to do her doggy style. She liked that even more. After a few minutes he pulled out again and came on her back between her plump crack.

"Baby, I don't want to get you pregnant," Eddy said, breathing heavily and exhausted from the experience.

Twila stretched out on the floor after it was over. She looked totally relaxed. Then, as long as they were in the locker room, they got up to take a shower, sudsing each other up and kissing while they rinsed off.

"We've got to do this again and soon," Twila said to Eddy. "What took you so long?"

Chapter Twelve

Benny managed to get off work early the next day. Frank was driving east down U.S. 20. Gerald, it appeared, nodded off quickly, slumping his head to the side. Benny kept a healthy distance behind the truck, dodging the numerous potholes along the badly maintained stretch of road. At least we're heading east, thought Benny. I'm familiar with this part of town.

About three miles down, Frank made a sharp right down a dark street, Tyler Road, and parked his truck in front of an old, two story wooden house about a hundred feet from U.S. 20 . Benny cut his lights and didn't make the turn. Instead, he stopped short of the street and waited at the corner. Frank nudged Gerald, who woke up with a start, then Gerald opened the passenger door and got out. There weren't any vehicles in front of the house or in the driveway. Benny assumed, for the moment, that Gerald probably lost his driver's license— probably too many DUI's.

Frank was there less than a minute before he made a U-turn and headed back towards the main road. Benny mistakenly anticipated Frank was going to continue east on U.S. 20, but instead he crossed over Route 12 to the other side of Tyler. As

Frank was crossing, Benny saw Frank momentarily glance at him, probably wondering why a strange car was parked so close to the corner. This concerned Benny, as he waited until Frank's truck was out of sight to start his car. He figured this was Frank's daily routine, and could always follow him home another day. Instead, Benny used that time to examine Gerald's house.

The sun was straining to reach the sky as Benny drove down that dark street. Tyler Road, as it turned out, was only three blocks long south of U.S. 20 and came to an abrupt dead end at the small, shallow pond next to the woods. It looked like a forgotten section of town. None of the dozen or so old houses on Tyler were maintained. Many of them were boarded up. Benny knew he had to be careful, so he only took a quick peek around the grounds. The air was crisp and extremely quiet. He could hear the subtle patter of squirrels walking on the dry leaves. He parked his car in front of a debris laden vacant lot and got out, quietly walking towards Gerald's house. Before he could walk five feet, he heard the sound of a pickup truck slowing down on U.S 20. Then, to his horror, the truck abruptly turned down Tyler and sped towards him. Frank was back.

Holy fuck, thought Benny as he bolted to his Camry. *I hope he just forgot to give something to Gerald.*

That wasn't the case. Benny started his car and spun around, barely missing being sideswiped by the dented amber truck. As Benny reached the corner, he gunned his motor, almost rolling over while making the right turn onto U.S 20. He pushed the accelerator all the way to the floor as his tires screeched on the gravely road and tore out of there.

Frank did the same. In his rearview mirror, Benny saw Frank's headlights getting bigger and bigger as the chase was on. The traffic thickened as Benny, now doing 70 on the 50 mph road, was driving for his life. He was quickly approaching a stoplight that had just turned yellow. With half a block to go Benny decided to take his chances and run the light. The end of his car just made it passed the intersection as the light turned red. He glanced in his mirror and saw Frank, in full pursuit, running the light as the oncoming cars slammed on their brakes to avoid him. An unmarked police car was among those who were forced to stop. The cop turned on his siren and pulled Frank over. Benny got lucky.

He couldn't have known it was me, Benny thought as he headed back home. He must have thought I was someone else.

Chapter Thirteen

It was Thursday, April 2nd, 1992. With their kids home for spring break, Benny and Marsha decided to take them along on a weekend trip to Michigan and visit Mackinac Island, Marsha's favorite getaway. Joshua and Rachel had been there before and were eager to go again. Benny planned this escape for a couple of weeks and told Tracey not to book any appointments until Monday, April 6th.

The family headed out, driving east down I-94 towards Detroit. It was slightly overcast and a little chilly to be walking outdoors for very long. But the forecast was sunny and warm for the rest of the weekend.

About fifteen minutes into the ride, Benny turned off onto Highway 50 to get gas at the truck stop. There were long lines at each pump so he pulled out and drove towards County Line Road to try his luck at the Gas 'N Go.

"We're not that short on gas," said Marsha, wondering why Benny was going so far out of his way.

"I know," Benny said, "but I have to pee. Maybe the kids do too."

They arrived at the gas station a few minutes later. Benny pulled up to one of the pumps and filled the tank. Afterward,

Benny took Joshua to the urinal while Marsha and Rachel walked around the mini-mart before using the lady's room. A short time later they all met back at the car, all set to take off.

"Are we finally ready?" Marsha sarcastically asked as she fixed her hair in the visor mirror.

"Not quite," said Benny, as he put on a pair of sunglasses and his Cubs cap. "I want to take a look at some tires next door. I'm thinking of buying them when we get back."

"Now?" asked Marsha, thinking it was a little weird Benny put on sunglasses on a cloudy day.

"Yeah," Benny said as he pulled into Gunther Tire & Auto Supply. "You can come with if you like. I'll just be a minute."

"No," said Marsha, looking a little nervous as she turned her face away from the tire store. "I think I'll stay here with the kids."

Benny really didn't want any tires. He just wanted to make sure of something. Was that Tommy Gunther he saw his first visit to the store? Was it really him?

No sooner did Benny reach the door when he saw Tommy walking out, a pencil tucked between his teeth and clutching a notebook. It was definitely him. Benny walked in the store and looked out the big front window and watched Tommy, apparently heading for Benny's car. But he stopped short, and walked to a different silver Camry in the lot. But that wasn't all. It looked like Marsha completely ducked down to hide herself when she noticed Tommy walking towards her.

Benny pretended to be interested in a tire, looked at the price tag, then left. Marsha hit the automatic unlock button to let him in.

"Did you see anything you like?" asked Marsha, still looking a bit shaken.

"Don't know," said Benny. "We'll stop here on the way back. I think you can use a set of new tires on your van as well. Unless you want to come in now."

Marsha didn't look well. Like she's seen a ghost.

"Why here?" Marsha asked as she handed the kids some M&M's. "What's wrong with the tire places around us?"

"Nothing," said Benny. "But why not here?"

Marsha didn't say anything and Benny didn't think there was really anything wrong. How was he to have known?

Chapter Fourteen

The Weinsteins had a great time on the island and completely forgot about stopping by the tire center on their way back. After a packed day seeing patients on Monday, including Carla, Benny bought something he was meaning to buy for the past month—a gun.

On Tuesday evening, instead of scouting out his past assailants, he drove to a pawn shop in the pits of downtown Gary, disguised in a White Sox cap and a thinner pair of sunglasses. Double J's Pawn & Loan was located on Broadway, about 4300 South. There he bought an old Colt .45 M1911 and paid $468.00 cash for this semiautomatic with a 7-round capacity. He gave another $200.00 cash to J.J. Davis, the septuagenarian proprietor, to forego the paperwork and background check. J.J. was a short, plump, bald man who bore more than a passing resemblance to a black version of Danny DeVito, complete with a little of that 'Taxi' smart-ass attitude. He could get you anything. Anything at all. He wasn't your friend, but he wasn't your enemy either, so long as you paid him. The more you paid him, the faster the service and the tighter his lips were sealed.

Benny had never owned a gun. The only time he fired one was when he went squirrel hunting with Al Fredericks, and even then he only shot it twice, missing his prey each time with the .22. He needed practice and knew exactly the right spot—a place where he could go at night and fire off a hundred rounds if he wanted, where no one would notice—Stagecoach Road.

That Thursday evening, Benny drove to the road he feared most. A place so terrifying in his mind, he wasn't sure he'd be able to turn right onto Stagecoach Road and drive more than a block down. He had to confront his fears. But as he left his house at 9:00 p.m. and drove down I-94, making his way to that daunting street, he experienced an eerie, almost satanic coincidence. He turned on the radio to calm his nerves, but instead, he heard Bob Cheats, now the FM 102.8 Oldie Station DJ, playing Sonny and Cher's *All I Ever Need Is You.*

Benny got scared and pushed the button to change the station, but the song continued on FM 108.9 just where the other station left off.

Benny didn't believe in the supernatural or anything associated with unexplained phenomenon like ESP, mental telepathy, or ghosts. But this was a little too weird. He never even thought about going back to Stagecoach Road before that night. The last time he heard that song was back in '73. The last time he heard Bob Cheats was back then as well. Why now? Why tonight?

The night was dark as could be at 9:28 p.m. on that cool evening. A large wispy cloud hid half the full moon in the otherwise clear, starry sky. As Benny turned right onto Stagecoach Road his hand gravitated to the passenger seat, feeling his newly purchased pistol, reassuring himself he wasn't alone. He drove fast at first, passing the houses that flanked both sides. Then he eased his foot off the gas as he drove passed the last house. There was nothing except desolate road up ahead surrounded by thick woods, the same as he remembered it almost twenty years before. He drove for another two miles, his headlights being his only salvation as he crept to a crawl. Suddenly, a deer bolted out in front of him. He swerved to avoid it and narrowly missed hitting a tree as he came to a complete stop, keeping the motor running and his lights on. He sat there for a moment on the side of the road, catching his breath as he looked at the large oak he almost hit. His eyes fixed on that tree for a moment when he noticed something odd. It looked like that tree had some old healed up gashes about three feet up the trunk. He took in a deep breath and covered his mouth in disbelief. It was *the* tree! The same tree assaulted by Frank, Tommy, Murphy, and Gerald that fateful night.

Benny grabbed his .45, making sure he had a full clip. He got out of his car, slammed the door, and was startled by a wild duck flapping out of the brush, just missing his head. Feeling jumpy, he took his gun and shot at the duck, missing it by a mile. The shot echoed in the silent air and woke up a distant coyote. He then took his hand and inspected the old gashes on the tree.

Memories of that '73 night of terror immediately rushed to the front of his consciousness as he walked away from the tree and stared south towards County Line Road. With heightened senses, but a lucid mind, he vividly brought himself all the way back to that June 14th night. He thought back to the graduation party, with that image of Laura playing up to Larry, crystallized in his mind. He saw his buddies, Chuck Merkov, Scott Mathis, Greg McGee, and his close friend, Steve Green trying to console him as he left the party. But most of all he remembered the beating. The pain was real as he recounted his teeth being cracked, his fingers broken, and his skull bashed in. He became more enraged just standing on the road where it all happened so long ago. Time had stood still as he looked back at the tree, so unfazed, it seemed, by the passage of time. But he was fazed. He was bothered. And it was killing him.

Benny reflected for another couple of minutes, walking slowly down the road, when all of a sudden he saw car lights coming towards him. He hid in the woods and lifted his eyes over a branch to see who was coming. He could hear the loud rumble of a broken muffler rushing towards him. Sweat poured down his face as he nervously gripped the gun in his right hand and pointed it at the road, waiting for the now visible old pickup truck to pass by. Benny was convinced he had been followed by at least one of his high school attackers. Maybe all of them. As the truck got closer, he saw faint images of four men inside, laughing and drinking. He couldn't make out their faces. Then, in an act of courage that even surprised him, Benny bolted from the woods and onto the road, gun still in hand. The truck made a dead stop and four men got out. Each was holding a baseball bat as they walked towards Benny. One of them yelled out a profanity as another maniacally declared, "Look what we've got here!" as they continued towards him. Benny blinked his eyes, thinking he was hallucinating, but when his eyes opened, he saw the men were still coming towards him. With pent up determination, Benny steadied his shaky right hand with his left and raised the gun, aiming it at the closest target. He rapidly emptied all seven rounds at the oncoming men, thinking he had hit them all. When it was over, he went to inspect the carnage. But no one was there. He *was* hallucinating.

Benny, now soaked with perspiration, lowered his empty gun and headed back to his car, knowing that he had shot a phantom. He knew he couldn't be trusted with a loaded gun and worried that this sort of thing may happen again—maybe around his kids. So without reloading, he put the gun in his trunk underneath the spare tire. At least that way, he thought, it would be harder for him to make a mistake.

Chapter Fifteen

Steve Green and his wife Stephanie, formerly his high school sweetheart, came over to visit the Weinsteins on Sunday, April 19th, 1992. Benny and Steve planned to watch the Cubs play the Cardinals on television that afternoon while their wives went out with the kids. The Greens had one son, Isaac, ten, a year younger than Joshua. Even though Benny and Steve were friends since the first grade, Benny never confided in him. Nothing too personal, anyway. In fact, Benny never confided in anyone, not even Marsha. Especially not Marsha. He always sensed there was something amiss about their relationship. Maybe she was keeping something from him. He didn't know.

Marsha and Stephanie left around noon. The guys were anxious to watch the game—Benny more so than Steve, who was a Sox fan. And because Steve was such an ardent Sox fan it didn't make sense why he was so bent on watching the Cubs that Sunday.

"Do you think Maddux will win 20 this year?" Steve asked.

"Maybe," said Benny, as he poured an entire package of Lays into a bowl.

"What about Castillo?" asked Steve.

Benny brought out a big bottle of generic diet pop and put it on the family room table.

"Since when did you become a Cubs fan, Harry Caray?" Benny said sarcastically as he placed two glasses with ice next to the chips.

"I've got to tell you, Benny—Marsha asked me to talk to you. She said you've been acting different. And she's worried."

"Yeah?" Benny said, as he almost knocked over the whole bottle of soda. "What exactly did she tell you?"

"Not a whole lot, other than she knows you haven't been to chess club on Tuesday nights or the OTB on Thursdays."

"Yeah? What made her say that?" Benny asked as he handed Steve his glass.

"You can tell me. Are you schtooping someone?"

"Am I schtooping someone?" Benny asked in surprise. "Hell no! I'm not even schtooping Marsha! Ha. Ha."

Steve was a personal injury lawyer and sent a lot of accident cases Benny's way. Steve also prided himself on being quite the interrogator, the lawyer in him, and he wasn't buying Benny's story.

"Benny," Steve continued, "we've known each other almost all our lives. We've shared everything together. I told you about that time I copped a feel off Heather Glusac in the fifth grade."

"Yes, I know," said Benny. "You wanted to bang her even then."

"I told you about how I caught my dad kissing the rabbi's wife the day after my Bar Mitzvah. And it wasn't to say Shalom!"

"You mean your mother never found out?"

"And I told you when Stephanie finally gave me that blow job in 10th grade."

"Does she know you told me?"

"Benny—who are you schtooping? It's driving me crazy. It's not one of your patients, is it?"

"Of course not," Benny sternly said, pretending he was offended at the insinuation.

"Holy shit!" shouted Steve. "Is it Cathy Price, that new injury case I sent you last month? She said she liked you."

"She did?" Benny said with a smile on his face. "Then it must be her."

"Really? You're doing Cathy? I wanted to fuck her!"

"No, not really. I'm not doing Cathy. Really? *You* want to fuck her?"

"Then who is it?"

Benny turned on the television and saw Stoney, the Cubs' commentator summing up the lineup. He had enough of this questioning and just wanted to relax and enjoy the game. He knew he couldn't fool Steve. What else could it be if it wasn't another woman? Benny had to tell him something believable.

"If you must know," said Benny, "I'm taking karate lessons on Tuesdays and Thursdays. I've always wanted to learn how to defend myself. I didn't want Marsha to know because she might think I'm in some sort of trouble."

"Karate lessons, eh?" Steve said, nodding his head in approval. "You sure could have used those growing up."

"Don't I know it," Benny said as the game started.

Chapter Sixteen

Steve got Benny worried. Marsha might buy the karate excuse, but the fishing story was getting less believable. She never knew him to go fishing every morning for a week. But that's exactly what Benny needed to do to follow Frank and the rest of the guys.

The following Sunday morning, April 26th, 1992, Benny arrived home with some expensive new fishing equipment. Hitched to the back of his Camry was a trailer carrying a used 14-foot aluminum Jon Boat and a 3hp Evinrude outboard motor. He found it in the Gary Post Tribune classifieds and paid the owner just under a thousand dollars cash for the entire package. Marsha was less than impressed, but Joshua liked it and thought his dad was pretty cool.

"Oh man! That's real slick!" said Joshua as his eyes lit up when he saw the boat in the driveway. "Can we go fishing today?"

Marsha shook her head in disapproval. Rachel wanted to side with her mother, but was just as eager as her brother.

"You're wasting all kinds of money on this little hobby of yours," Marsha uttered. "You'll use it three times a year, then it'll sit in front of our house the rest of the time."

"You're wrong about that," countered Benny. "Now that I have a boat I'll be using it all the time. During the winter I'll keep it in back behind the shed. No one will know the difference."

"I'll know," said Marsha. "We'll see how long this fling of yours lasts."

Benny took Joshua and Rachel fishing on the boat that afternoon. They drove to the Marquette Park lagoon, Benny's childhood fishing haunt. They parked at the Pavilion, unhitched the boat, and slid it down to the water below. By that time it was about 1:30 p.m.

"It's not going to be this easy pushing it back up the hill," Benny said to his kids, as they went back to get the motor and the rest of the gear.

Benny filled the motor with gas, attached it to the back of the boat, and made sure everyone put on a lifejacket. Joshua wanted to row instead of using the motor.

"Wait until we're out a ways before you use the oars," said Benny as he pushed the starter button.

Benny was thrilled the motor started so effortlessly as he grabbed the throttle and headed out on that beautiful spring afternoon. Joshua and Rachel were clearly enjoying the ride, the wind in their hair, as their father navigated the small vessel past the small Chinese bridge, making their way to the much larger lake area on the other side.

"You used to come here when you were my age?" Joshua asked as he tied a hook to his line. "Did Bubby Mildred let you take a boat out here?"

Benny looked at his son fixing the line, wishing he could go back and be his age again, knowing what he knows now.

"Yes," Benny replied to Joshua. "But it wasn't my boat. My friend Al Fredericks lived just a block from the shore over there and we used to take his parents' boat."

"Oh, I remember your friend Al. You haven't seen him in a while, have you?"

"No, and I should," answered Benny. "He used to be a good friend, and he only lives in Portage. I'm going to give him a call later this week."

Benny opened up the throttle a little more, speeding up to avoid the wake from a larger boat that just passed by. They headed towards the main body of the lagoon and were quickly approaching the Lake Street Bridge. Benny and Al had somewhat of a traumatic experience there during a fishing outing in their last year of high school.

"Did I ever tell you what happened to Al and me the last time we were here?" Benny asked as he pointed to the big bridge.

"No," replied Rachel. "What happened? Did Al fall in?" She chuckled.

"Worse than that," said Benny as he gazed back as they passed the bridge, slowing down to a crawl. "Al and I rowed all the way down the lagoon to that narrow area about a half mile down. You'll see what I'm talking about when we get to it. We didn't have a motor and took turns rowing. On our way back home we noticed a bunch of guys, about our age, leaning over the railing and waiting for us to row by. Al noticed them first and knew what was going to happen. 'They're going to throw rocks at us,' he said. And sure enough, as soon as we got close enough they pelted us with a barrage of rocks, like they were saving them up for when we passed by. I shielded our heads with the life preservers the best I could, but the rocks just kept coming. About a dozen of them hit us. Many more splashed next to our boat, like little torpedoes. One of the larger rocks hit Al on his arm and caused a bad bruise. Those kids were screaming and swearing and threatening us as they threw the rocks. I don't think they recognized me or Al but I sure as hell recognized them. They were troublemakers and didn't care who they hurt."

Joshua opened up a package of Fig Newtons and gave one to his sister as he heard his father tell the story.

"Then what?" asked Josh.

"Well then Al got mad. After we got far enough away from them, we rowed to the shore and Al had me watch the boat while he went home to get something."

"What?" Rachel asked as she ate one of the cookies.

"His shotgun!"

"His shotgun?" Joshua asked in disbelief. "He wanted to kill them?"

"I don't know about kill them," Benny said, "but at least he wanted to scare them. And I tried to talk him out of it, but Al wouldn't listen. So I foolishly went back on the boat with him as we rowed about 75 feet away from the bridge and near the shore. The guys were still there, waiting for another boat to pass by, when Al took aim and started shooting."

"Did he hit them?" asked Joshua.

"You know it! Al was always a good shot and he quickly got off five blasts. I saw two of the guys holding their faces and screaming bloody murder after the second blast. But Al was really mad and just kept shooting. We were too far away to see any blood, but those guys ran like hell and scattered in both directions. Then Al and I quickly rowed back to shore and dragged his boat through the woods before putting it back into his garage. No one saw us."

"Did you ever find out what happened to the guys he hit?" asked Joshua.

"Sort of. They went to our school and everyone was talking about it. Apparently the police were called when someone reported hearing gunshots and they scoured the area for us, only they didn't know it was us. I was more than a little concerned because I knew who those guys were and they knew me from before. But Al wasn't concerned in the least. He was glad he got back at them."

"He could have blinded them," said Rachel. "Al's a bad man."

"I can tell you that no one was blinded. I saw those guys later on, after graduation, and I can tell you that none of them went blind."

"Were those the same guys who beat you up?" Joshua asked as he put his hand over his mouth, knowing he just misspoke.

Benny went dead silent for a moment when he heard his boy say that.

"When did you find out?" Benny asked as he lowered his head in shame.

"Mommy told us a long time ago," said Joshua. "I'm sorry. I forgot it was a secret."

"That's okay," said Benny. "I'm glad you know. Maybe you can learn something from it. If anyone is bullying you in school, take action now. You'll regret it later on if you don't."

"Do you regret it?" asked Rachel, who was quietly listening as she finished her cookies.

"Yes, I do. Every day I regret not taking action."

"I guess it's too late now," said Joshua as he lowered his line in the water. It was a few minutes passed 2:00 p.m. and time to start fishing.

"Guess so," said Benny, looking away, not wanting to reveal what was inside his mind.

Chapter Seventeen

Coros RV & Boat Storage was located on Cline Avenue in Hammond, not far from Lake Michigan. Benny told Marsha he was going to keep his boat there so he didn't have to haul it through traffic each time he wanted to fish. Of course, everyone knew, including Marsha, that a small vessel like that Jon Boat was way too dangerous to take out on the great lake. The unrelenting winds and choppy surf were just that, even during nice spring days.

Benny had discovered that Frank and Gerald were switched to the night shift, same as Murphy, so early Monday morning, April 27th, 1992, Benny hooked up his boat and headed out, but not to the boat storage—to Tyler Road. He arrived a few minutes before 6:00 a.m. and parked a good two blocks west of Tyler on U.S. 20. Frank won't be looking for a boat, thought Benny as he sat quietly in his car, peeking in the rearview mirror for Frank's amber truck. Benny watched as the digital clock/radio in his car changed to 6:18. No sign of Frank. He waited another ten minutes and decided to leave. Just as he started to pull away, he saw Frank's truck in the mirror. Benny stopped himself from merging onto the road and waited for Frank to drop off Gerald, who was sitting next to Frank, this time, fully awake. About two minutes later he saw Frank cross over U.S. 20 to the north side of Tyler. Benny waited another minute before following Frank.

It looks like they live near each other, thought Benny as he started his car and put it in drive.

Traffic was getting heavier down U.S. 20 as Benny drove two blocks before making a wide left onto Tyler, keeping his eye on his fishing boat in back. He didn't see any sign of Frank, thinking he had waited too long. He purposely crept a few blocks down Tyler, scanning both sides of the street, looking for any sign of that truck. The houses on the north side of Tyler were in slightly better shape than on Gerald's side, but not by much, as they too were sporting a few boarded up houses. As Benny approached the stop sign before Route 12, he spotted Frank's truck which was parked in the alley next to the house on the northeast corner. Probably Frank's house. He quickly drove passed and circled around to U.S. 20 and back onto Tyler, this time parking a block south of the house. Benny put on his Cubs hat and thinner pair of sunglasses as he exited his car and walked towards the old two story wooden dwelling.

The numerous mature, tall oaks with expansive branches and wide leaves provided a broad, shaded cloak as Benny slowly walked down the old chipped sidewalk. It was only 6:24 a.m. which gave Benny at least another half hour to look around. As he neared the house, he heard dogs barking in the backyard, and then running to the front of the chain-link fence which ended even with the façade. There were two dogs, both white Pit Bulls, wearing thick, black spiked collars. They looked aggressive and vicious, just like Benny remembered Frank. If I'm going to do this thing, I've got to find a way to get passed those dogs, Benny thought to himself as he turned right, walking along Route 12 to look at the backyard.

What he saw in the backyard was an oversized doghouse.

No swing sets. No kids stuff. Just a huge doghouse, complete with shingles and a gutter, and numerous piles of dog shit everywhere. There was no real grass to speak of, just tons of tall weeds. The place looked as though it hadn't seen a lawn mower in years. The dogs, however, looked well fed, but the fact they looked vicious was a problem. Benny liked dogs, but he wasn't too fond of Pit Bulls. He didn't hate them. He just didn't care for them.

Satisfied that he knew where Frank lived, on the north side of Tyler, and what he was up against, Benny decided to look around Gerald's house again. He made his way back south towards Gerald's side of Tyler. He drove down to the pond where it dead ended and made the wide U-turn, boat in tow, so he would face U.S. 20 in case of an emergency. He drove his car almost all the way up to the stop sign, then walked towards the pond. As soon as he reached Gerald's house he heard dogs barking. What the fuck! Benny thought, as he stopped in his tracks. Again? More fucking dogs to deal with? And not just more dogs—more Pit Bulls, fenced in the backyard just like Frank's. This time there were three of them. It also appeared that Gerald used the same backyard decorator as Frank. Shit everywhere and an even bigger doghouse, with a fenced-in run leading to Gerald's back door. Why do they have so many damn dogs? thought Benny. Could only be one thing.

Chapter Eighteen

As Benny drove back to see patients that Monday, he started to have second thoughts. There are so many things that can go wrong, he surmised as he contemplated his next move. What if I get caught? What will happen to Marsha and the kids? Yeah, Marsha, he thought. She's a pretty girl. She can always find someone else. And I'm insured. I think I'm insured for a million dollars. More than that maybe. She bought the policy. Yeah, I remember signing something. Who gives a shit? She'll make out OK.

It was almost 6:45 a.m. and the rush hour traffic was heating up. Benny was stuck behind a truck at a long stoplight on U.S 20. He had time to think before he arrived at his office. And he knew what he wanted, and what he had to do. Not just for himself, but for his long lost high school buddy, Eddy Moss. What happened to Eddy bothered him about as much as what happened to himself.

* * * * *

Eddy and Twila became an item after they consummated their relationship in the old high school gym. During the summer before starting his junior year, Eddy got a job at the Lake Street Beach as a lifeguard. Eddy loved that job and everybody loved him. He loved sitting atop the lifeguard stand with his bathing suit and whistle, talking to all the kids and listening to the sounds of summer, especially the waves crashing against the shore. People would buy him hotdogs and sodas from the concessions, and he would let them climb up to the top of his perch and look over the horizon and see the faraway ships. Sometimes, when the beach got too crowded, it was all he could do to distinguish the real emergencies from the fake ones when the girls playfully yelled for help as their boyfriends splashed them in the water. One of the coolest things Eddy liked was being able to see the skyscrapers on the Chicago skyline. The Prudential Building, The Pick Congress Hotel, and the Conrad Hilton were as plain as could be on a clear day. Above all, Eddy enjoyed Twila's company as she sunbathed herself in her revealing bikini next to the stand while he stood guard. Everyone knew the biracial couple was dating and they let them be. After all, it was the beginning of the '70s and racial intolerance was passé. Yes, everyone let them be. Everybody, that is, except Frank and his buddies.

Late Sunday evening, around 9:30 p.m., August 24th, 1970, the Lake Street Beach was starting to fill up with the night crowd, mostly teenagers from Wirt, as well as several families who made the long trek from Chicago. That's when the beach really cooked. There were bon fires, beer, loud portable radios, and even louder radios from the cars that were parked in the gigantic six-acre lot at the end of Lake Street. Bob Cheats was playing his favorite Beach Boy tune, *Wouldn't It Be Nice*.

It was a beautiful warm summer night, and no one anticipated what was about to happen.

Eddy went home briefly to see his mom and to walk Twila back so she could get cleaned up. The mile walk was a pleasurable one for them as they held hands and talked the whole way. Then, at around 9:45 p.m. as they neared the beach, they saw a group of white rowdies on motorcycles, making a lot of noise and purposely screeching past pedestrians just to hear them scream. This group of thugs was Frank and his buddies. All of them, including Gerald, Tommy, and Murphy. When they saw black Eddy holding hands with milky white Twila, they went berserk.

"Hey white bitch!" Frank yelled, as he menaced his Harley around them.

Twila didn't answer. Eddy and she started walking even faster towards the beach where they thought there would be safety in numbers.

"Hey white bitch!" Frank yelled again. "I'm talking to you."

Twila and Eddy continued to ignore him.

"Hey bitch! Whataya doing with that nigga? You know we don't allow niggas here."

Eddy and Twila were almost at the beach and scanning for a cop.

"Hey bitch!" Murphy shouted, as he too got into the act. "We hear you've been fucking that nigga. A tasty white bitch like you fucking a nigga. My oh, my—looks like Mr. Ray didn't finish his job," making a surprisingly informed reference to Dr. Martin Luther King Jr.'s killer.

Still trying to ignore the mob, Eddy held Twila tighter and started running for the beach. But Frank and the gang would have none of that. Tommy, obeying Frank's command, grabbed Twila and forced her to sit on his bike and sped off towards a dark alley behind a boarded up beauty salon about five blocks away. Frank went with him. Meanwhile, Murphy and Gerald got off their bikes and grabbed Eddy, who was screaming loudly and trying to resist.

"Shut up nigga," demanded Murphy, as he dragged Eddy behind an old beat up house just off the road. "One of those white boys may hear you," pointing to some disinterested passersby, "and call the police."

Eddy did his best to fight them off, but before he could take a swing at Murphy, Gerald hit Eddy over the head with a heavy chunk of asphalt he picked up from the street. Eddy fell unconscious with a busted skull as a river of blood flooded out from his forehead. But the hoodlums weren't satisfied. As Eddy lay there bleeding, they lowered his jeans and cut his belly and penis, nearly severing it off at the base. At that moment they heard the sound of sirens and scattered like cockroaches, leaving Eddy, hemorrhaging to death. The police found Eddy, barely alive, and rushed him to the hospital.

There was no sign of Twila. The police knew she was abducted but they didn't know where. A witness pointed in the general direction, but to no avail.

She was right under their noses, behind that abandoned beauty shop, being assaulted just five blocks away. Tommy held her on the ground, which was littered with rusty nails and yellow crumpled newspapers, while Frank forced his hard, diseased prick in her unyielding dry box. But before Frank completed the assault, he too heard the sirens, and pulled out of Twila. The two cowards hastily kick-started their bikes and zipped away.

With her vagina torn and bloody, Twila got up and screamed as loud as she could as she ran towards Lake Street. An elderly black man who lived in a weathered house nearby, heard Twila scream. He motioned to her as she ran to his house, calling out for a phone. He opened the door as he pointed to his kitchen phone. The police arrived within minutes and took Twila to the same hospital as Eddy, who was now in the intensive care unit following emergency surgery.

The police had no problem finding the young terrorists, who were identified, and found hiding at Frank's parents' house, just down the road. They were arrested and booked for attempted murder, rape and a lot of other charges. But the system failed, as each of the sixteen year olds spent only a year in the juvenile detention facility, and then incredibly, were allowed to enroll for their senior year at Wirt, which they never finished.

After the incident, Twila and her mother moved away to another state, never returning to Wirt again. No one knew for sure what happened to Eddy. There were rumors he had died, but some said he and his mother, Joanna, moved to Nashville where they had relatives. Benny found out later.

Chapter Nineteen

"Carla's in the bathroom," Tracey said as Benny walked into the clinic, saying hello to his new personal injury patient, who just completed the case history form.

Benny walked to his back office and plopped himself down on his swivel chair. He put his hands to his face, resting his elbows on his desk, as he tried to compose himself from his journey to Frank and Gerald's houses. He buzzed Tracey who promptly walked in with a cup of coffee, Mitzie at her heels.

"Do I have to see Carla this early in the morning?" Benny griped as he sipped the coffee.

"She was here before I opened," Tracey said. "Waiting outside."

"Waiting outside? She's getting worse. What's the emergency?"

Tracey left Benny's office for a second and came back with a brown box.

"Look," Tracey said, as Mitzie, Carla's biggest fan, started to salivate. "She baked you an orange cake!"

"An orange cake, for God's sake. What for? It's not even my birthday.

"She wanted to surprise you," Tracey said as she broke off

a piece to give to her anxious Beagle. "Look, you can quickly see Carla and I'll finish up the paperwork with your new PI. Steve called and said this one's a good case."

"Who's the insurance company who hit him?"

"Don't know yet," said Tracey as she went back to her receptionist desk.

Benny walked in the hallway and bumped into Carla.

"Oh, hi Dr. Weinstein!" Carla cheerfully said as she grabbed Benny's arm. "Did you have a chance to sample the cake?"

"No, not yet" Benny said, escorting Carla into the nearest exam room.

Carla changed the headrest paper herself and assumed the position on the electric chiropractic table.

"Just my neck today, doc," she said as she lay there.

Benny stood behind Carla's head as he prepared to adjust her neck.

"You have to stop bringing me all these goodies," Benny said as he patted his stomach. "You're going to get me fat."

Carla waited for the reassuring cracking sound as Dr. Weinstein performed the neck maneuver.

"No you won't!" Carla playfully said, using that opportunity to also pat Benny's belly. "You're in great shape, doc. Are you still running?"

Benny didn't respond. He finished the treatment and raised the table so Carla could get off.

"See you next week," Carla said, as she walked down the hall to the waiting room and booked another appointment with Tracey.

The new personal injury patient finished filling out the forms and got up to hand them to Dr. Weinstein, who was saying goodbye to Carla.

"You have to watch out for this one," Carla said, pointing

to Benny while noticing how pretty Dr. Weinstein's new patient was. "He gives great manipulation!" she continued, tossing out the remains of her depleted reservoir of discretion.

Both Benny and Tracey rolled their eyes in mock disgust as the shapely new patient politely smiled and followed Benny to his office. Carla mercifully left, giving Dr. Weinstein a much needed respite, if only for a few days.

Gail Mercer, the curvaceous injury victim, who couldn't have been more than 18, sat down in front of Dr. Weinstein's desk as he read her case history.

"It says here," Dr. Weinstein said, "that you were rear ended by a motorcycle?"

Gail nodded then shook her long sandy brown hair in an effort to exaggerate her neck pain.

"That's how I explained it to the cops," Gail said as she reached for a picture in her purse. "What really happened was this guy was following me on his bike, an old boyfriend of mine, and a car pulled in front of me so I mashed on the brakes. Kurt, that's my old boyfriend, couldn't stop in time and crashed into me."

Benny jotted that down, trying to hide his eyes as he glanced at her pretty face. "So this guy was stalking you?"

"Sort of. Kurt won't accept the fact that I'm married. I married his best friend two months ago. Kurt still thinks we're going together."

Dr. Weinstein scribbled some more. "Did you tell this to Mr. Green? Did the cops arrest this Kurt guy?"

"No one got arrested," Gail said as she placed the picture on the desk. "I thought I'd spare Kurt the hassle of spending another night in jail. Besides, he was pretty banged up himself. Look at the bike."

Benny studied the picture for a second. "Yeah, looks like he should have been killed."

"He's just getting out of the hospital today," Gail said. "And of all things, Ricky, my husband, went to see him. But I never want to see Kurt again. He's trouble. He's mad that I quit his band and enrolled at the I.U. extension on Broadway. I'm majoring in psychology. But most of all he's mad I married Ricky. You see, they were going to be famous musicians together. I never thought Kurt was that good. Not compared to Ricky. But I'm grateful to Kurt because without him I wouldn't have met Ricky. And Ricky is so, so good to me. He bought me that car and he's paying for some of my tuition. Isn't that nice of him?"

Benny finished the case history and initial exam as he endured her rambling. As Gail left the office, Benny couldn't help but think there was something very familiar about her. That perfume. Her walk. Her inflections. But they never met. And the way she was acting. Not at all like a newlywed in love. And she didn't seem all that angry that her old boyfriend was following her. In fact she seemed rather flattered. But what a space cadet, he thought.

Breaking out of his daydream, Benny was thinking, what difference does it make who she is? A patient is a patient. Steve is going to want a full report when she's released. But she smelled so nice, Benny thought, lapsing into another fantasy as he inhaled deeply through his nose. Snap out of it man, he thought to himself. I've got to see J.J.

Chapter Twenty

It wasn't until the following evening, Tuesday, April 28th, 1992 that Benny decided to head out and visit J.J. Davis' pawn shop on Broadway. That part of town wasn't the best even in the light of day, and at night, perilous. That's when the druggies and gangs really got going. Benny knew this, but that was the only time he could get away without Marsha asking too many questions.

It was almost 8:30 p.m. when Benny arrived at J.J.'s. The shop didn't close until 10:00 p.m., and Benny didn't want to stay there a minute longer than necessary. He parallel parked his Camry next to a meter, about fifteen feet in front of the store. He switched on the inside car light and went through the list of things he needed to buy. Of course, Benny knew J.J. wouldn't have half the things on hand. It was just a quick stop to place his order.

OK, he thought, with his silver Cross Pen in hand as he wrote in a small spiral notebook. Tranquilizer rifle, check. CO_2 cartridges, check. Let's see here…1cc Type 'P' disposable darts 1-inch needle length, check, check. Um, 18-gauge 2-inch hypodermic needle, check. Oh, yeah, Sucostrin (100 mg/ml), check. As much as I can get. I wonder if J.J. knows a veterinarian. Maybe I can buy some powdered succinylcholine chloride instead and make my own Sucostrin.

Sucostrin is not a tranquilizer, but a muscle blocking agent that essentially paralyzes an animal. Under the influence of Sucostrin, the animal is fully awake and can feel pain. They are aware of everything, which causes them much stress, especially in that paralyzed state. It was no accident Benny chose this chemical. It was a calculated decision.

Benny flicked off the ceiling light and got out of his car while putting on his Sox cap and sunglasses. He looked both ways down the sidewalk before he entered J.J.'s. It crossed his mind to shed the sunglasses since it was already dark, but he didn't. There weren't many people walking down Broadway, but there were plenty of people in the store, about five or six. J.J. had some help that evening—a young, handsome, fair-skinned black man they called Rings, around twenty or twenty-two years old. Rings was very tall and thin with a short Afro. He had a small but pronounced scar on the left side of his chin, and another scar just above his right eye. Rings worked the register behind the bulletproof glass. They called him Rings because he was the only one who used the cash register to ring up a 'legitimate' sale. Everything J.J. sold was sold under the table and you paid him in round numbers. Being the only white guy there, it was impossible for Benny to look inconspicuous. No one bothered him, though. The others just wanted to sell their stuff and get some quick cash.

The shop finally thinned out about a quarter past nine, but then another two people walked in. Benny decided not to wait. He walked up to the window and asked Rings if J.J. was around.

"He's talking to someone in the storage room," Rings said. "Is there anything I can help you with?"

Benny only wanted to deal with J.J., even though J.J.

probably told Rings everything.

"It's not really a private matter," Benny said, "but I would like to talk with him."

Rings sized up Benny, who was still wearing those sunglasses.

"You're not the law, are you?" Rings cautiously asked.

"No, I'm not the law," said Benny. "I bought a .45 here a little while ago and I wanted to ask J.J. to get me some other things."

Rings excused himself while the two other customers looked around. J.J. walked in less than half a minute later.

"I seem to recall you," J.J. said in a weak, gravelly voice. "It's the Sox cap and sunglasses that did it for me," he laughed. "All you need now is some brown shoe polish and a boom box pressed against your ear. No one would ever pick you out of a lineup!"

Benny smiled, then pushed the list of items he wanted through the slot under the thick glass. Rings didn't even glance at the list as J.J. examined the order. J.J. told Benny to go outside and meet him in the parking area in the alley behind the store.

"Are you in trouble young man?" J.J. asked as he opened the back door to let the other guy out.

Benny waited until they were alone then walked inside.

"No, nothing like that," said Benny. "I have a varmint problem that I want to handle myself."

J.J. looked at the list again.

"Most of these things you can get yourself," said J.J. But it's not up to me ask why you don't. The tranq rifle is no problem. I can get you the darts too. I can get the CO2 cartridges OK, and the hypodermics. And you want Sucostrin?"

At first, Benny though J.J. wasn't familiar with Sucostrin.

But he was.

"Yes," said Benny. "As much as you can get."

"Well, okay," said J.J. "All this stuff doesn't come cheap."

Benny didn't want to argue price and pulled a huge wad of bills out from his left front pants pocket.

"I have fifteen hundred dollars here," Benny said as he handed over the cash, knowing he just gave J.J. a one thousand dollar bonus. "You might have to get the Sucostrin from a veterinarian unless you have a druggist friend."

J.J. folded the money and put it in his back pocket without counting it.

"Don't worry 'bout where I get the stuff," J.J. said while buttoning up his back pocket. "I know just the vet to call," he laughed while spitting out some phlegm in his handkerchief.

For a moment, Benny thought he insulted J.J. by telling him his business. But the extra grand took care of that faux pas.

"Just be here a week from today," J.J. said as he opened the door for Benny. "Ten o'clock p.m. on the nose, right here in back. Knock hard, twice."

"Ten p.m. it is," Benny said as he scurried to his Camry which was still in one piece.

Chapter Twenty-One

Sucostrin, Benny thought, as he drove home that evening from the pawn shop. That wears off fast. I think just after a few minutes. Hmm, that doesn't give me much time in-between.

It started drizzling. Benny turned his wipers on the slowest speed. The hypnotic back and forth rhythm of the blades put him in a trance as he subconsciously slowed for a stoplight. The rain came down harder—his hand automatically reached for the wiper control to increase the pace.

"Epinephrine!" Benny shouted, startling himself as he approached the last stoplight on Broadway before the turnoff. "Motherfucker. I have to go back and tell J.J. to get me some of that. I can't do this thing without epinephrine."

Benny turned around and headed back to J.J.'s. It was almost closing time and the streets around the shop looked scarier than before. Groups of young drug dealers walked down the street in plain sight only to vanish behind the buildings to conduct business, then quickly emerging after the sale. Benny decided to park in the alley behind the store and wait for J.J. to come out. At about 10:12 p.m. Benny saw the back door creek open but didn't see anyone. The door was left ajar for a couple of minutes before he finally saw signs of life. It was Rings. Benny honked his horn.

"Hey Rings," Benny yelled, seeing J.J. also walk out while locking the door.

"Yeah, what?" Rings yelled back, momentarily taken by surprise.

"Tell J.J. I forgot something."

J.J. was within earshot and walked up to Benny's car.

"Hey, Sox, what did you forget?" asked J.J., giving Benny a nickname. He was more interested in getting home than doing business. "Don't tell me, you need a gold tooth!"

Benny courteously acknowledged that remark.

"Yes," Benny said, humoring J.J. "And I also forgot to order epinephrine."

"Sure thing. How many viles do you need?"

Benny pulled out three hundred dollars from his wallet.

"As many as you can get with this," Benny said, as he handed J.J. the cash.

"Alright," said J.J., stashing the bills in his front shirt pocket. "See you next Tuesday, Sox."

Benny wrote a few things in his spiral notebook as he watched Rings and J.J. drive off together. They seemed comfortable around each other. Almost like family. Rings had a mature way about him for a young man. People liked his easy manner. J.J. was more streetwise, and hardened by life, but with a sense of humor and humility.

So now Benny had a whole week to get everything else he needed. With the wheels in motion, his resolve was stronger than ever. Nineteen years is long enough, Benny thought, as the wipers lapsed him back into a trance, for Frank, Tommy, Gerald and Murphy to live in peace. It's my turn. They have no idea what's coming. And no one is ever going to find out. Those pieces of shit. They've got jobs. They got homes.

Tommy has his own business. Looks like a good one. Murphy seems to have a family. That's nice. His bitch isn't bad looking. I'll have to do something about that. Yeah. I've got to do something about that. She has a nice rack with pointy tits. Yeah. Murphy has a nice looking bitch. I've got do something. Yeah, I've got to do something. Man, I bet he fucks her all the time. And I bet he enjoys it. I've got to do something about that. I'll bet she sucks his cock. Yeah. I'll bet she does. I've got to do something about that. I need to get a large dog cage. I wonder if that'll be big enough and strong enough. I wonder if the pet store has anything bigger.

Chapter Twenty-Two

The next day, Wednesday, April 29th, 1992, started off like all the other normal days at his office. Dr. Weinstein had a full schedule, and without Carla. He was glad of that. He was also glad that his new injury case, Gail Mercer was coming in for her second appointment. Her face, figure, perfume, and even manner of speech were on his mind.

Dr. Weinstein walked into his office at 9:10 a.m., a few minutes late. There was a long line at the Dunkin' Donuts where he bought a large regular coffee for himself and a small decaf for Tracey. There was no need to buy donuts—too much of Carla's orange cake left. Gail wasn't expected until 11:00 a.m., which was fine. There were ten other patients to see. Tracey walked into Dr. Weinstein's office and handed him an arm load of files.

"Looks like we're having a good month!" Benny said, as he thumbed through each one.

Benny then jokingly pulled out Gail's file and sniffed it from top to bottom. "Hmmmm, Ahhhh," Benny sighed as Tracey was watching.

"You like her, don't you?" Tracey said, pretending to scold her boss.

"You know it," Benny said. "And for the life of me I can't figure out why she seems so familiar? Was she here before? Like maybe when she was a kid?"

"I don't think so," said Tracey. "But I'll look. What was her maiden name?

Benny looked at Gail's file.

"It doesn't say. Oh, what does it matter? Who's my first patient?"

"Another injury case," said Tracey. "In fact you have three in a row. All from Steve. Lucky you have him as a friend. Last year he gave you over a hundred grand worth of patients. I betcha this year it'll be twice that."

"Yeah, I'm lucky to know Steve. He's helped me through a lot of things in my life. He's been good to me. That's why I work with him when the cases are ready to settle."

"I know," said Tracey. "Last week he had you shave off eight hundred from Mr. Willoughby's bill."

"Don't care," Benny said as he sipped the last of his coffee. "I still ended up with two grand. Let's get rolling, eh?"

Dr. Weinstein saw a steady stream of patients for a couple of hours. Eleven o'clock rolled around and Gail walked in, looking more stunning than ever.

"Go right back," said Tracey as she pointed to the last exam room.

Gail walked to Room 3 and saw Benny waiting for her next to the chiropractic table. She didn't start holding her neck until she saw Benny.

"Ow, my neck and shoulders really hurt today," Gail said as she lay face down on the table. "Can you massage me first before the adjustment?"

Dr. Weinstein was only too happy to oblige. This would also give him some time to find out if they ever met. There was a soft knock on the door.

"Dr. Weinstein," Tracey said, "I'm taking Mitzie to the vet. I'll be back at 2:00 p.m. You don't have any more patients until then."

"Okay, I'll see you at two."

Dr. Weinstein put his hands on Gail's neck and started to work out the tight muscle spasms.

"Hmm," Gail sighed with each stroke of her back. "That feels great!"

Dr. Weinstein worked his hands a little further down her spine just short of her waist, then back up to her neck. Gail was sighing louder and deeper with each stroke. Benny had a hard time concentrating on his work. But Gail was fully clothed and the doctor-patient relationship, thought Benny, had to remain intact.

"Wouldn't it be easier for you to get to the muscles if I took off my blouse," Gail said as she started to push herself away from the table.

"No," said Benny. "That's only necessary when a masseuse uses oil."

"Then why don't you!" Gail said as she let out a flirtatious giggle.

Dr. Weinstein composed himself and let that last comment go. He was more curious about Gail's past.

"Were you ever here before?" Dr. Weinstein asked as he worked his thumbs into Gail's tight Trapeziums.

"Ooo, ahhh!" Gail moaned. "What did you say?"

Dr. Weinstein took his hands off her shoulders for a second.

"I can't help but thinking I know you," Dr. Weinstein said. "You never babysat for my kids, did you?"

"Oh, don't stop," Gail pouted. "Um, no, I don't think so. I never had any babysitting jobs."

"Do you mind me asking your maiden name?"

There was a five second pause before Gail answered. Dr.

Weinstein's hands froze on her neck when he heard the name.
  No, it can't be! he thought to himself.

Chapter Twenty-Three

The following Tuesday, May 5th, 1992, came around very fast. Benny knew he had to be at J.J.'s at 10:00 p.m. He finished work early that afternoon and thought he'd spend some of the evening playing baseball in the backyard with Josh. Since Benny was going to be home for a few hours, Marsha thought she'd take Rachel out shopping, and didn't even ask why Benny didn't go to the chess club. Marsha got home about 9:00 p.m. and Benny immediately put on his brown bomber and grabbed his car keys. He told Marsha not to wait up.

"I'm going to watch the end of the tournament at the club then go to White Castle with the guys."

Since Benny was a vegetarian, he only ordered coffee and fries while the others had sliders. But he had no intention of going to the hamburger stand that night. He used that excuse before and kept an empty White Castle coffee cup in his car in case Marsha needed evidence.

It was a cool, drizzly spring evening with light traffic. Benny took it slow and got to J.J.'s around a quarter to ten. He parked his Camry about twenty feet from the shop and went over the list of things he was to pick up. He had another list of items he had to get the next day at the pet shop in Michigan City, namely a large animal cage. The biggest one they had.

At 10:00 p.m. Benny drove to the alley in back of J.J's and waited for his stuff. A few minutes later he saw Rings and J.J. walk out empty handed. Benny lowered his window.

"Hey guys," Benny yelled as J.J. quickly lifted up his eyes.

"Oh, there you are, Sox," said J.J. "I thought you were going to meet us inside. I forgot."

"That's quite alright," said Benny. "Were you able to get everything?"

"I think so," J.J. said as he motioned for Benny to get out of his car and come in the shop.

Benny turned off the ignition and applied the parking brake, something he never did. In the back of his mind he had the paranoid thought someone may tow his car while he was away.

J.J. and Rings escorted Benny to the storage room, an organized mess. No one except for Rings or J.J. could find anything in that pile of junk. But there, sitting on a wooden egg crate amidst boxes of old watches and gun parts was Benny's order all bagged up—like he just bought his weekly groceries from the A&P. The only things missing were the celery stalks.

"Wow!" exclaimed Benny as he softly caressed the tranquilizer rifle, darts, CO_2 cartridges, sucostrin, and syringes. "Oh, *there* it is," he continued, as he found five small bottles of epinephrine.

J.J. and Rings looked at each other as they saw Benny inspect the goods.

"You got everything?" J.J. asked.

"Looks like it," said Benny. "You guys are the best!"

"Good. Real good. 'Cause I got to go," said Rings, cutting off any of J.J.'s chitchat. "My mom is waiting for me at the home."

Benny was able to handle both paper bags by himself and loaded them into his trunk. Pleased with the service, he waved and smiled at J.J. and Rings as he pulled out of the lot.

"I might be back for more stuff next week," Benny shouted as his front wheels bounced over the curb making his way onto Broadway.

As Benny started to make his way back he couldn't help thinking about Rings. What did he mean by 'the home'? How old was his mother? She certainly couldn't be old enough to be in an old folks home. Maybe she was infirm. Crippled somehow, either mentally or physically. Didn't matter. Benny had his stash. And he needed to practice up on some new skills.

It was approaching 10:30 p.m. and the night couldn't have been darker. The temperature dropped to about 45 degrees with the wind kicked up noticeably. The rain had all but stopped, just enough to moisten the windshield. The rearview mirror was slightly fogged. Benny switched on the defroster, turned up the heat and set the wipers on low. There was barely a soul on the road as Benny headed down U.S. 20 on his way to Stagecoach Road.

Benny turned left onto County Line Road and noticed the streetlight was broken next to the Gas 'N Go. That was the same light that illuminated Gunther Tire. He filed that observation in the back of his mind as he turned right onto Stagecoach Road. He drove passed the now familiar houses and parked a couple of miles down the road next to the oak tree where the beating took place so long ago. It was here, again, where he had to confront his fears if he was going to carry out his plan. He took off his baseball cap and rubbed the top of his head with his right hand to smooth out his hair. Then he looked at his face in the rearview mirror to make sure he wasn't hallucinating this time. Benny doubted his own senses. How could he be sure he wasn't dreaming any of this? Pain, he thought. I know I'm not dreaming and you can't really experience pain when you're fully asleep, that is, unless you're drugged. Benny took out his cigar lighter from the front pocket of his jacket and pointed the flame on the back of his hand, singing the fine hair on his wrist. "Ow, ow," he softly screeched. "I'm awake!"

Yes, he was awake, very awake. And scared. This was one emotion he had to overcome. Or was he more angry than scared? The tree brought back the familiar flood of horrors he endured almost twenty years before.

Benny sat, idling in his car for a few moments to gather his thoughts. Satisfied with his plan, he cut the engine and opened the door. Every noise was magnified fivefold in the quiet, cool darkness as he got out of his car and walked to the trunk to get his new gear. The trunk key made an irritating metallic sound as he pushed it into the lock. Like it squeaked in. Maybe it was the moisture in the air. He opened the trunk then grabbed the tranquilizer rifle along with the darts, CO_2 cartridges, syringes, and sucostrin. He already had a bottle of water he kept under the driver's seat. It was too dark outside to mix and measure the solution, so he brought everything back into the car where he made up his first batch of darts and loaded one into the rifle. He then got out of his car, tranquilizer rifle in hand along with a small flashlight, and started walking down the pitch black deserted road, looking for something to shoot. A deer, if he was lucky.

It was about a quarter past eleven. He took each step slowly, his running shoes crunching the wet pebbles underneath. There wasn't a soul in sight. There was nothing in sight. But he could hear the sound of small animals in the woods running through the dry, brown leaves, remnants of the cold winter. If I could only find a raccoon, a rabbit, a possum, anything. A two hundred pound deer would be better, he thought. I loaded enough solution for that I think. Just then he heard something big scurry in the woods. Its footsteps sounded like it was very big. What the hell is that? he thought as he lifted up his gun and pulled back the slide, ready to shoot. The rustling stopped, then started just as fast. "Holy fuck, it's a buck!" Benny exclaimed to himself, admiring the rhyme. The 14-point beast was about fifteen feet away, the same distance he expected to use the rifle for its intended purpose. Perfect, he thought as he looked through the sights and took aim at the frightened 300-pound animal. Benny steadied his arms as he pulled the trigger and heard the sudden, almost muffled blast of the CO_2 cartridge as it discharged. "I think I hit him," he said softly. "I'll know soon enough," he whispered to himself as he loaded another dart, preparing for another shot. But the deer kept on moving, though not as fast. Benny followed the game into the woods, stumbling on some branches, but kept his balance and tried to keep pace. Sure enough, the buck slowed down and staggered some until he fell to the ground. "I must have hit him just right—in his thigh muscle or something."

Benny shone his flashlight at the terrified animal and clearly saw the whites of his eyes, its dark eyeballs almost completely hidden behind the sockets. He heard the poor creature laboring to breathe, but breathe he did which brought a sigh of relief to Benny. "I don't want to kill him. I just wanted to see if this stuff worked." Apparently it did, but the effect didn't last long. After only ten minutes the buck strained to get back on his feet. The fumes from the large animal's nostrils permeated the cold night air, like a mad bull ready to charge. Benny took off running towards his car, not knowing if his victim had the presence to take revenge. Benny made it back to his car and started the engine. Good! he thought, a wide grin appearing on his face. All I need to do is use more and dilute less next time. And next time it's for keeps. That motherfucker can't weigh more than 200 pounds.

Chapter Twenty-Four

Benny didn't go directly home after his jaunt to Stagecoach Road.

Still a bit shaken from his buck encounter, but pleased with the result, Benny decided to make one more stop that night. He drove to the Marquette Park Lagoon.

Benny turned onto County Line Road and set his odometer to zero. He wanted to calculate exactly how long it took for him to drive from the beginning of Stagecoach Road to the back parking lot of the Marquette Park Pavilion. He estimated it would take about fifteen minutes going 30 mph. He was almost on the money. It was exactly 7.2 miles away.

It was about 11:30 p.m. The air was much chillier than it had been just a half hour earlier. He parked his car at the closest spot to the water which was about 25 feet away.

Yeah. Yeah. I think this will do, Benny thought to himself. I won't have any trouble launching the boat from here by myself.

Benny zipped up his leather bomber and put on his Cubs hat then started his stroll around the dark body of water. There wasn't a ghost in sight as his Nikes sloshed through the soft soil that lined the shore. He could hear small critters scampering through the leaves as he walked passed the woods. His breath was steaming from his mouth, chilled by the cold spring night. An old 1920's street lamp lit up a raccoon's eyes in the distance. Benny stumbled on a protruding tree root and broke his fall on his shoulder. The sound of him hitting the ground scared a crow who loudly flapped away, provoking an entire tree of sparrows to disperse in a rush. He got up and started walking again through this twenty year time warp—like it was yesterday.

My God, Benny reflected as he knelt down to touch a clump of grass. This is the spot I used to dig for worms when I was a kid.

Nothing much had changed around the lagoon except for that ugly cement pier which replaced the old broken wooden one. It was dark as hell as he made his way around the perimeter and headed for the Lake Street Bridge—the same bridge where he and Al Fredericks were pelted by rocks by those thugs some twenty years earlier.

OK. Right. Right. The bridge, Benny contemplated. That gives me an idea.

The base of the Lake Street Bridge was about 40 feet from the water. The water, Benny figured, was about 12 feet deep at the center of the bridge and a lot shallower, maybe 4 feet deep, closer to the shore.

This is just what I had in mind, he thought.

Benny took one long last look at the bridge from below then climbed up the hill leading to the end of the bridge. It was amazing how close Lake Michigan was to the lagoon—not more than two hundred yards. In fact if he climbed to the top of the small sand dune next to the lagoon, he could roll down the other side to the shore and keep the dead alewives company.

Just as Benny reached the top of the hill and prepared to

walk across the bridge, he was startled by the sight of two police cars parked in the Lake Street parking lot, just in front of Lake Michigan. And there were other cars there too.

"What the fuck," Benny whispered to himself. "I forgot it was the end of the smelt fishing season. This could change a few things."

Actually, the smelt season was usually over by April 30th. It didn't make sense there would still be fishermen out with their nets that late at night, especially since it was so cold. But there were. This wouldn't be a problem if Benny had a good excuse to stay out until 3:00 in the morning. What was he to tell Marsha? Did it make any difference what he told her? If only he knew then what he was about to find out, it wouldn't have made any difference.

Chapter Twenty-Five

Wednesday, May 6th, 1992 was another shopping day. There was an exotic pet shop at the Michigan City Mall that sold just the right size cage Benny wanted. The cage was about three feet all around, give or take a few inches, and was used to contain dogs of all sizes, parrots and monkeys. It weighed about sixty pounds and had four small wheels. While at the mall, Benny picked up a few other items: a blue lantern flashlight with extra batteries, two rolls of duct tape, a new pair of scissors, black and white print film to go with his old Rolleiflex camera, a backpack, sixty feet of rope, a six-inch hunting knife, a small box of colored stars, a ball of reinforced twine, and a high school G.E.D. study guide he bought at the bookstore. All paid for with cash. He already had other items he picked up earlier including two black markers, a ream of yellow card stock, a box of one hundred latex gloves, and a sewing kit with heavy duty thread. He also had a change of clothes in his trunk, identical to the clothes he was going to wear while carrying out this little exercise of his.

The rest of the week flew by with Benny going over everything in his head he planned on doing Tuesday night, May 12th, 1992. He acted normal at his office, at least normal for him—joking with patients and feigning courtesy when Carla stopped in. He played catch with Josh and listened intently when Rachel played a new song on the piano. Marsha, though, seemed to sense Benny was up to something but didn't ask. That's the way he wanted it anyway. This was Benny's war. His idea. Why did Marsha have to know? She didn't.

First on the list was Tommy Gunther. He seemed like a logical choice. He was closest to Stagecoach Road and had a predictable schedule. It also looked like he had the most to lose. Isn't that nice! Benny thought. He had tons to lose. Then again, Benny knew nothing of his personal life, but he surmised he had someone, a wife maybe—probably kids as well. Tommy's tire business always seemed busy when he drove by. And best of all, Tommy really looked happy. He couldn't have been happier owning a successful business where people sought his advice as an expert plus he made a pretty penny on the retail end. Ah, yes, life for Tommy appeared to be perfect. What a tempting dish that made. And he looked good too, as if he worked out every day. Yessiree— life sure looked good for ol' Tommy boy! Ah, the good life, as Tony Bennett used to sing—in the lyrics to the song *The Good Life*.

And now Tuesday, May 12th. Today was the day. Benny scheduled patients until 3:00 p.m. He told Tracey and Marsha he was interested in buying a used chiropractic table from a practitioner in Michigan City, and for Marsha not to wait up. As if that was a problem.

At 3:00 p.m. sharp he left his office and drove to Coros RV & Boat Storage and hitched his Jon boat, motor, oars, and all, to the back of his Camry and headed for Stagecoach Road. He arrived at Stagecoach around 4:00 p.m. There was light traffic on I-94 so it only took him twenty minutes. Once at Stagecoach he drove to the now familiar damaged tree and unhitched the boat and dragged it in the woods, about thirty feet from the tree, well into the brush. It was still light outside and sundown wasn't until 7:30 p.m.—and somewhat light even then. Benny had time to kill and decided to enhance his experience.

Benny drove to the tire store and parked his car amongst many others. He put on a pair of sunglasses and his Cubs hat. He wore his black leather bomber instead of the brown one, but had the brown bomber in his trunk just in case. He changed into light blue jeans and a beige sports shirt and wore his white Nikes with the red stripes. He entered Gunther Tire & Auto Supply and was immediately approached by a salesman, not the owner.

"Can I help you find anything, sir?" rang a voice from behind.

"Yes please," Benny said. "I bought some tires here a few weeks ago and I forgot to pick up a tire iron. Do you sell those here?"

"We have accessories in that aisle there behind the Goodyear sign," said the young, courteous salesman.

Benny casually walked to that aisle and picked up a 24" tire iron/pry bar made from forged steel with a chrome plate finish.

"Man, this is a nice tool," Benny muttered as he headed to the cashier. "This is great. Just what the chiropractor ordered."

No one paid any particular attention to Benny as the lady cashier with a beehive hairdo placed the iron in a plastic bag and handed him the receipt. Before walking out of the store, Benny looked around for another minute in hopes of spotting Tommy, now 37, like himself.

"There he is," Benny said softly as he spotted Tommy assisting another customer.

Benny walked out of the store with his purchase and sat in his car and waited five minutes, then pulled away. The plan was to eat at the nearby Denny's and come back at 8:00 p.m., closing time. By then it would be dark. He needed it to be dark. Now all he hoped for was for Tommy to be the last one out of the store when it closed.

Chapter Twenty-Six

Eight o'clock was fast approaching. Benny busied himself by going back to Stagecoach Road after he ate, to prepare the darts and the syringes. He also prepared a few epinephrine shots. He knew he was going to need those.

The night air was crisp, about 35 degrees, unseasonal for a May evening. Benny dressed for it. He put on an orange Bears winter stocking cap that covered the top of his head and ears. He kept his sunglasses on, but still could see well enough with the help of the brightly lit streetlights. The wind was mostly calm with an occasional gust of bitter wind blowing at the side of his neck. He wore his heavier brown bomber. He surgically put on a pair of latex gloves, squeaking each one over his large palms. Benny carefully strapped on his bulging backpack and snapped together the side buckle. His tranquilizer gun was waiting for him in the back seat as 8:00 p.m. approached. Benny slowly turned into the tire store's parking lot off of County Line Road. He saw two cars parked in the employee's parking spaces. Just two cars. He then parked his car about 150 feet away from the cars in a remote section of the lot, almost off the lot and under a tall old oak tree—nowhere near the entrance. He waited. And he waited. It was almost 8:20

p.m. when he saw the lights go off in the store. A minute later he saw a woman emerge—the cashier. She lit a cigarette as she walked to her car, then waved at someone, probably Tommy, before getting into her car and pulling away. Benny carefully but nervously grabbed the tranquilizer gun from the back seat. He checked the dart one more time to make sure everything was in place. He quietly slid over to the passenger's side and opened the door leading to the trees at the side of his car. He got out, tranquilizer gun in hand, and crept slowly around the edge of the parking lot until he had a full view of the back entrance. He waited for Tommy. It was a short wait. A few seconds later he saw the brass doorknob turn and the door open. Tommy was wearing only a thin spring jacket as he exited his store then turned his back to lock the door. There wasn't anyone else in sight. Benny was standing directly behind him, about two feet away, as Tommy turned again—facing Benny.

Phhhhooooot! The dart sounded as Benny fired the drug into Tommy's right thigh.

"Hi Tommy!" Benny yelled. "It's my turn!"

Tommy let out a weak scream as he fell to the ground, not fully realizing what was happening.

The drug worked quickly as Benny ran back to his car then pulled up to the store to collect his game. For a moment though, it looked like Tommy was able to get up. Tommy made a vain attempt to get to his car but was only able to stagger a few feet until he dropped like a rock, but was still fully awake, and laboring to breathe. Benny pulled his Camry next to Tommy's helpless but very much alive body, and dragged him onto the back seat and sped away, heading for Stagecoach Road. Benny then pushed a cassette into his tape deck. It was cued to play *American Pie*.

Benny glanced at the back seat.

"Sort of brings back good old memories, doesn't it Tommy?" Benny said as he turned up the volume.

"Them good old boys were drinking and singing this will be the day that I die."

"I said, DOESN'T IT TOMMY?" Benny sternly repeated, knowing full well Tommy was paralyzed and couldn't speak.

Benny turned off County Line Road and onto Stagecoach Road. He lowered the volume on the Don McClean tune as he slowly drove down Stagecoach Road, now completely immersed in thick fog. He passed the final house before entering the dismal asphalt abyss and into the black of night on his way to the tree. Benny turned on his brights which were barley sufficient to light the gloomy pebbled street below. As he headed for the tree he saw a shadowy figure in the distance and slowed even more, just in case it was a deer. Tommy was breathing heavier and heavier as Benny came to a complete stop on the side of the road, finally reaching his destination. That shadow turned out to be a deer that quickly scampered away into the woods.

Benny turned off the engine. There was tomb-like silence as he opened the driver's side door then got out to open the back door, taking the ball of twine from his backpack along with the blue lantern flashlight which he quickly switched on. Tommy's eyes were wide open, and glowed in the lantern's light as he burned a frightened death stare at Benny—just now realizing the identity of his captor.

"Yes, Tommy," Benny said as he unwound a long piece of twine, cutting the end with his six-inch knife as he took off his Bears cap and sunglasses. "I'm exactly who you think I am. Oh, certainly you must remember me. Oh, yes. I'm Benny Weinstein. The Jew. The stuttering fool you used to torment. My high school friend was Eddy Moss. Remember, the nigga? You know, the one with the severed cock," Benny said as he lowered the knife within an inch of Tommy's genitals. "Now you've got to remember me. I would be awfully disappointed if you didn't. Oh, did I forget to mention Twila Fairfield?"

Saliva started running down Tommy's chin, not being able to swallow.

"I certainly remember you," Benny whispered as he flipped Tommy over onto his stomach, binding his hands behind his back—making four strong knots.

Five minutes elapsed since Tommy was shot. Benny grabbed the tranquilizer gun again and loaded another dart—this time a little less potent. Tommy started to grunt.

"Ut, ut," Tommy throated as his left hand started to come to life.

"Oh no, Mr. Gunther," Benny patronizingly said. "You mustn't move." Benny then gave him another dose. Phhhhooooot! This time in the stomach.

"We'll get along just fine," Benny said as he nodded his head. "But you have to stay still. I want to tell you a bedtime story," Benny continued, in full control, as he dragged Tommy deep into the woods onto a waiting pile of dry leaves. Benny then tied Tommy's ankles together and perched the lantern on a stump. There was no escaping.

Tommy wet his pants as he struggled to move his frozen eyelids. Benny opened up his backpack and removed a number of items.

"Let me further refresh your memory," Benny said as he loaded yet another dart into the gun. "About twenty years ago I wasn't feeling so well. I remember a car coming down this road—this very road! And who was in that car? Why it was you, Tommy. It was you! And you brought along some friends. Is your memory coming back? And there I was. I can remember it like it was yesterday. You and your friends. Oh, what were their names?" Benny sardonically said while snapping his fingers. "Ah yes. I think their names were Gerald, Murphy, and Frank. But feel free to correct me if I'm wrong."

Benny saw Tommy's heart thumping through his blue buttoned up shirt. The words Gunther Tire & Auto Supply were stitched above his name. His eyes were wide open in surprise and started to dry out. Benny poured water on them— not to make Tommy more comfortable, but just so Tommy could see him.

"I see you have a nice business," Benny said as he took out the G.E.D. book from his backpack. "You must be the smartest of the four. So I'm going to give you a little test and a chance to free yourself from this horrible predicament you're in. If you pass," Benny said, while opening up the book, "you get to go back to your wonderful life and forget this ever happened. And I'll forget the beating you gave me that night back in '73 that put me in the hospital for several weeks. I'll forget about that. Isn't that nice of me? Now, this could be a little tough since I know you didn't finish up at Wirt. You may have been absent when the fine teachers there went over this material. But I can assure you they did. In fact, in all fairness, I'll let you quiz me after I quiz you. Fair enough?" Benny asked, hogging both sides of the conversation. "But I'm letting you go first. And, oh, you have to pass, otherwise you won't get a chance to test me."

Benny took out a few shots of epinephrine and more darts. He then jogged back to the car to get his newly purchased tire iron he bought at Tommy's store. Gosh, he almost forgot that. Then he hurried back to Tommy's motionless body and wrapped three thick pieces of duct tape around his mouth. He purposely let the last dose of Sucostrin wear off.

"Now," Benny continued, "let's get started with the test."

A raccoon's fluorescent green eyes blazed just a few feet

away as Benny took out a package of colored stars. Crickets were happily chirping on that cold night. Tommy was envious of their unbridled freedom.

"OK," Benny said as he turned to Chapter 8 in the thick study guide. "U.S. history. I think I'll start with U.S. history. My personal favorite. I've always been fond of U.S. history. Tommy, do you like U.S. history?"

The effects of the drug were subsiding. Tommy was able to wiggle his shoulders and managed a few groans. His hands and ankles were still impossibly tethered by the twine. He breathed deeply and deliberately through his nose, the only available life vent.

"Now, I'll start off easy. And I want clear, distinct responses," Benny said as he put on a pair of drugstore reading glasses and clutched a small box of grade school aluminum stars. "And if you don't know the answer, just say so and I'll go to the next question," Benny continued, knowing full well Tommy's mouth was bound by duct tape. "But if you do know the answer, you get a gold star. If you get three gold stars in a row, I'll let you go!"

Tommy managed to shimmy his pelvis a few inches. Benny saw this, grabbed the tire iron and held it over Tommy's head.

"If you don't keep still I'll have to use this," Benny threatened.

Tommy didn't move.

"OK, now I'll have to start again," Benny said, miffed at his hostage. "You know, Tommy, that really chaps my ass. I told you to keep still. And what do you do? You move your pelvis." Whack! Benny hit Tommy's left shin with the tire iron. "Now for the last time—KEEP THE FUCK STILL!"

But Tommy *was* still. He wasn't moving. And he reeked of urine.

"I can see you moving," scolded Benny. "I'm losing patience with you. Now for God's sake—KEEP THE FUCK STILL!" Benny repeated. Whack! Whack! The tire iron picking up speed with each blow. This time harder, on the right shin. Tommy, now able to uses his vocal chords, let out a muffled yell through the tape. This made Benny even madder.

"I did NOT say you could talk!" Benny shouted, admonishing his helpless plaything.

Tommy started blinking his eyes, afraid to do even that much.

"First question," Benny stated, with tire iron in hand. "Who killed Abraham Lincoln?

Tommy pleaded for mercy with his eyes as he desperately tried to make a sound through his fastened lips.

"I SAID," Benny repeated, only much louder this time, "WHO KILLED ABRAHAM LINCOLN?"

Tommy regained the use of his legs and arms, but was unable to walk due to the tight twine. He managed to roll over once. The sight of Tommy trying to get away infuriated Benny, and he kicked Tommy in the head as hard as he could until he stopped moving but was still conscious.

"Let's take this from the top," said Benny. "Now, for the last time, WHO KILLED LINCOLN? And I want you to enunciate. I know you never had a stuttering problem so I expect you to enunciate just fine."

Tommy was powerless as he lay there on his back while Benny parted Tommy's bound legs. Benny swiftly kicked Tommy in his groin five times, as hard as possible, rupturing Tommy's testicles. Tommy, dripping with sweat, tried to scream but fainted from the pain. Benny then grabbed a shot filled with epinephrine and poked the needle into Tommy's right bicep.

"As a chiropractor," Benny said with a smile as he drew the

needle in then out of Tommy's arm, "I know I'm not supposed to be administering any type of drugs to my patients. It's not part of my Indiana chiropractic license. You won't tell anyone, will you Tommy?"

Tommy quickly regained consciousness. Benny then lowered Tommy's pants and pulled out Tommy's little dick, shriveled by the cold air and drugs. He showed Tommy the knife.

"You better get this next question right," Benny threatened as he sharpened the blade on a large piece of gravel. "I'll give you one more chance at a U.S. history question. This one you can't miss."

Benny thumbed through the history section.

"All right. In what year did the United States invade Germany and free the Jews from Hitler's concentration camps? And if you miss this one, I'll make you a little more Jewish than you want to be," he said, pointing to the knife.

Tommy didn't budge as Benny repeated the question.

"What's your answer?" demanded Benny while mouthing the Gestapo siren. "Wha—ooo, ah-oo, ah-ooo, ah-ooo."

Tommy, his lips cemented with duct tape, could do nothing except wait for Benny's next move. Benny then kicked Tommy in the mouth as hard as possible, smashing three of Tommy's front teeth, which made a queasy squish beneath Benny's sneaker.

"Aw! Everybody now—aw!" Benny said while stripping the tape away from Tommy's bloodied mouth. "Did I crack your teeth?"

Tommy's gums were hemorrhaging. The broken teeth stuck to the tape as Benny flung the whole mess to the ground. The Sucostrin was wearing off. Tommy was able to speak in short sentences.

"H-h-h-errr idea. H-h-h-h-rrr idea," mumbled Tommy.

Benny took a hold of the knife and started sharpening it again, not knowing what Tommy meant by *her idea*.

"Oops!" said Benny in a devious tone. "I'm about to commit another illegal act against my chiropractic license. I think I'll do a little surgery, too."

Tommy's pants fell to his ankles and his mouth was now visible as Benny shot him with another tranquilizer dart. Phhooooot! Tommy's vocal chords were again paralyzed as was the rest of his body. He was still able to feel and hear everything with great intensity.

"Boy, I'll tell you," Benny said, shaking his head as he finished scraping the blade, now razor sharp. "Where are your friends now when you need them? They don't appear to be around anywhere. They sure were around about twenty years ago. And what happened to you? Where's that brave man I once knew who beat the living shit out of me so long ago? What happened to him? Oh, there he is!"

Benny put the knife down for a second and grabbed his cigar lighter from his bomber jacket.

"How 'bout a little fire, Scarecrow?" Benny laughed, borrowing a line from his favorite childhood movie as he flicked on the flame and lit it under Tommy's dwindling prick.

The flame quickly singed the hair off of Tommy's ruptured sac as more saliva streamed from his mouth. Tommy again lost consciousness. Benny reached for another shot of epinephrine, quickly reviving his victim for more torture. Benny then reached for his old fashioned camera and took a picture of Tommy who was sprawled out on the leaves, soaking in his own waste.

"You flunked the test. Not one question right. No stars for you," Benny said as he got up, putting the box of stars in his pocket and making his way to his hidden Jon boat. It was almost 10:00 p.m. with a full sky of brightly twinkling stars.

Benny placed a few more pieces of duct tape over Tommy's broken smile. Tommy was fully awake as he saw Benny hitch the boat to his car and clean up the scene, removing as much evidence as possible, dismissing a few blood droplets. Benny started his motor then got out and lifted Tommy's passive body into the boat. Benny dropped Tommy's body onto the center slat which made a loud thud, rocking the vessel for an instant. Tommy's right arm rested on the giant dog cage which was already in the boat. Benny then shot another dose of Sucostrin into Tommy's right calf muscle, covered his body with a black tarp, and got into the car.

"We're going fishing," Benny announced as he pulled onto Stagecoach Road and headed towards County Line Road then towards the Marquette Park Lagoon.

The small tires on the boat trailer wobbled as Benny drove down the gravel road and made a sharp turn. It was quiet and dark down County Line Road. No other cars in sight. Benny looked in his rearview mirror, making sure the boat was still secure and his human cargo had not fallen out. He then turned left down Oak Street. He saw another car coming his way from the other direction. But that's all it was—just another car, not a cop. He was careful not to speed or run any stop signs as he passed the Beach Pharmacy, the place where he bought Fizzies as a kid, then he continued on Oak Street. On the passenger's side he saw the white, foamy waves of a cold Lake Michigan crashing up against the night shore. Not a dog on the beach that frigid spring night. Just up ahead he saw the old, massive, gloomy Pavilion fast approaching and the lagoon's even colder cement pier on the right. He slowed to 15 mph and carefully turned into the Pavilion's parking lot then drove down another hundred feet, close to the shore. He stopped, looked in the side view mirror and to his horror he saw Tommy jump out of the boat, but with his hands still tied behind his back. The Sucostrin wore off and he somehow was able to free his legs. Benny forgot he loosened the knots to part his legs when he kicked Tommy in the balls. Benny quickly grabbed the tire iron and chased Tommy down and batted him in his left knee with three sharp blows, fracturing his femur just above the knee cap. Tommy dropped to the pavement and spun around like a wounded bird, still trying to get away. It was no use. Benny quickly went back to his car and loaded another dart then fired it at Tommy, hitting him square on his left shoulder. That's all it took to regain control.

With Tommy secured and laying on the pavement next to the car, Benny took the large metal cage, his lantern, and the rope, then set them down next to his car. He tightened his backpack buckle, unhitched the boat and dragged it to the water then came back to fetch Tommy. He pulled the once brave bully down the stubbly hill and hoisted his body into the boat. Benny went back up the hill to get the cage and the rest of his supplies, placing everything next to the motor. Benny looked around, making sure no one was in earshot, then pushed the button on the Evinrude motor. The motor quietly purred while he took an oar and stuck it in the shallow water to push himself away from the shore. He positioned the rudder and trolled slowly out to the middle of the water. Tommy's eyes were wide open, looking up, and he could see the stars above—he knew, for the last time.

Lake Street was just two hundred yards away. It was 10:23 p.m. and no one was on the bridge. The lantern was not yet lit. Lucky for Benny it was so cold that night. It was the break he needed.

The Jon boat was nearing the base of the abutment close to the shore. That's where Benny stopped and anchored. He snugly bound Tommy's legs and left him in the boat and sloshed out to tie the end of the sixty-foot rope to the bottom of the bridge, climbing ten feet up the concrete structure. He found a protruding rusty medal rod sticking out of one slab and fastened the rope, pulling hard on it twice and tightening the knot. He climbed back down to get the cage. The drug was wearing off. Tommy started to wiggle around—his last chance to save his life. Benny hurriedly tied the other end of the rope to the top of the cage and opened the three foot side door. Benny pulled out his knife.

The weak waves of the shallow water kissed the shore. There was an eerie silence. The boat was five feet from the bridge. Benny slogged to the boat through the seaweed and was overcome by a sudden flashback of his beating so long ago. The only face he saw was Tommy's. It was as clear as it was that night on June 14th, 1973, with Tommy holding him down while the others pummeling his young, innocent frame. The fear, helplessness, and horror flooded his tormented brain. Then back to the present moment, he saw Tommy's right leg move. Benny grabbed his knife and pulled Tommy out of the water by his shirt and stabbed him three times in his gut. Blood gushed out of Tommy's belly and mouth as Benny, in a maniacal act of rage, severed Tommy's penis, picked it up and forced it passed the duct tape and Tommy's broken teeth down his throat. Tommy was fully awake—blood pouring out of his severed appendage. The water and boat now crimson.

"This is for Eddy!" Benny audibly mouthed as Tommy lost consciousness.

Benny wasn't finished. He erected an oar in the boat by wedging the end in a handle slot, then hung his bright lantern on top of the paddle. He got a large sewing needle and thread out of his backpack and sewed Tommy's lips around the drained cock. The needle broke off in Tommy's cheek. Benny left it there and grabbed his knife and slit Tommy's throat until he saw the back of his vertebrae. Tommy's head fell to the side. Benny shoved the corpse in the steel cage and closed the door. He got out a marker and a piece of yellow construction paper and with huge letters wrote "THAT'S ONE!" He taped the note with duct tape to Tommy's blood soaked jacket and shoved the cage in the murky red lagoon—then took another picture with his Rolleiflex. Tommy's shocked eyes glowed in the light, like a Halloween jack-o-lantern. A snapping turtle waddled by and looked at the cage as it sank about two feet, the top still visible. Benny left it that way. He *wanted* someone to find it.

Chapter Twenty-Seven

This isn't going to be easy, Benny thought to himself, looking at the mess he made while committing the murder. His first step was to put on a new pair of latex gloves and clean everything he touched with rubbing alcohol. He wiped off the tranquilizer gun, the Sucostrin and epinephrine containers, the duct tape, knife, and some things he used previously, his pistol, for one.

It was a few minutes past eleven. Benny had to clean up the blood in the boat the best he could before hitching it back onto his car and getting the hell out of there. He took off his bomber and sport shirt, then put his bomber back on and used his shirt as a rag. He then put on another fresh pair of latex gloves. Using water from the lagoon, he wiped everything off the best he could, including his face and arms, then pulled the boat back up to his car, hitched it up and drove back to Stagecoach Road. A few disinterested cars passed, thinking nothing of someone puling a boat that late at night. While driving, Benny pushed in a cassette tape which played a loud, creepy instrumental version of the 1966 television comedy *Family Affair*. Good night Buffy. Good night Jody. See ya, Mr. French.

The rest of Benny's clothes were also covered in blood. He anticipated that by bringing an extra set of identical apparel, including the shoes and brown bomber. After driving back to the tree to ditch the boat, he changed in his car and put his dirty clothes in a large black plastic garbage bag after meticulously cleaning the pockets, then headed for his parents' house in Miller, just two miles away. On the way, he turned into the newly constructed National Shores beach house next to Lake Michigan, and stuffed the bag deep into a massive green dumpster, then pulled away.

He arrived at his parents' house on Tippecanoe Court around midnight. His mother Mildred was still up doing a crossword puzzle. Harry, his father, who recently retired from the clothing business, was fast asleep upstairs. His parents weren't expecting him.

Mildred and Harry, now in their late sixties, doted on Benny and his two children. Benny was an only child and they were happy to have grandkids. So it was never an imposition if Benny, or for that matter, Marsha, stopped by, especially with the *kinderlach* as Bubby Mildred affectionately called her grandchildren.

"My Benny!" Mildred exclaimed when seeing her son at the door. "Come in. You look tired."

Benny looked very tired, but his clothes looked as fresh as morning. His mother didn't notice.

"Do you want something to eat?" Mildred asked after giving him a hug. "I made an eggplant today and mandel bread."

"No thanks. Nothing now. I was out looking at some new therapy tables today in Michigan City. I picked up some dinner on the way. I have an early day at the office. I just want to get some sleep."

"Marsha called and I told her you would call if you stopped

by."

"Yeah, I almost forgot." Benny called home and left a message on the answering machine.

There was no hint and no way Mildred could have known what had just happened. Benny had no dark side—at least none visible to the outside world. When he was a child, Mildred used to tell him ghost stories. They used to read about murders in the Gary Post Tribune and the Chicago Papers. In 1966 they read, as did the whole world, about mass murderer Richard Speck who killed eight student nurses from South Chicago Community Hospital. Horrible stuff. The sort of thing that only happens to other people. But here, in her living room and soon to be sleeping his old childhood bedroom, a monster as big as any but not of his own making. Not a random or glory killer, but a tormented man who desperately needed therapy. There was only one elixir—revenge.

He reclined in his childhood bed for an hour with his eyes wide open, looking at the ceiling—dazed at his deed. He then drifted off to sleep. It was a sound sleep. In his dreams he planned his next move. He had work to do.

Benny woke up at 6:00 a.m. and left his parents' house a half hour later. No one else was up. He inspected his car before driving off and noticed a small blood spot on the back bumper. He saw an old McDonald's napkin in the back seat and dampened it in a rain puddle then carefully rubbed it off. Jesus, he thought to himself, I wonder how many more stains I left behind.

He got into his car and drove down Tippecanoe and headed towards County Line Road. It was about forty minutes past six. He turned right on County Line then stopped just ahead, waiting for a South Shore commuter train to pass. The morning rush hour was just beginning. A short line of cars, already in queue, were also waiting as the loud orange electric locomotive rushed by, paralleling Route 12. The train finally passed, freeing up the early risers on their way to work. Gunther Tire & Auto Supply was less than a mile up the road and wasn't due to open for another hour and change. Benny was about twelfth in line to cross the tracks and barely made the light, narrowly missing a car turning left in front of him. He shook his head at his near misfortune and continued down County Line Road. Stagecoach Road was coming up on his left, and in the distance he saw the tall Gas 'N Go sign to his right. Benny looked out the passenger's side window and didn't expect to see anything as he approached Tommy's store. Suddenly the unexpected—four squad cars in full strobe were flashing in the Gunther Tire parking lot. Several policemen with sticks were combing the grounds for something.

"Oh shit!" Benny screamed. "They discovered his body!"

Benny composed himself and stopped at the Gas 'N Go for some coffee, but mainly to get the scoop. Dozens of gawkers were already inside the gas station and talking amongst themselves. "What do you think happened?" asked a man in painter's clothes while looking out at the bevy of blues. "Don't know," said another. "Someone probably broke in during the night."

Benny nervously paid for his coffee, looked around, and almost spilled the cup while walking back to his car—his eyes fixed on the scene. It was early yet. He had planned to go home for a half hour, check on his family as they prepared for the day, then arrive at his office by eight o'clock. Instead, he doubled back down County Line Road, turned left onto Oak Street and cruised by the Pavilion. It wasn't long before he saw another group of squad cars, about seven, some in the Pavilion parking lot and a few on Lake Street Beach. There wasn't any doubt. They had found Tommy.

He was confused. His only prior offense was a speeding ticket he got during college after driving back to his apartment from a Hoosier's football game. And now murder. But in his mind it wasn't murder. It was justifiable homicide. He had waited and suffered a long time to get even. His main concern was for his family if he got caught. Yet somehow he was energized—a strange new feeling of power he never had. He liked it.

Benny only had time to drive to his office and begin seeing patients. He pushed the A.M. 74 button on his radio to get the news. "The outbound Kennedy is clear," newscaster Bart Jones belted out in his smooth, deep bass voice. "Watch out for Loop construction between Lower South Water Street and Lower Wacker Drive. From Higgins and 53 it's about 15 minutes to the airport. At O'Hare, the temperature is thirty-three degrees. Midway, thirty-four. Thirty-three at the lake. In local news we have a report of a gruesome killing in Miller Beach, Indiana. Officers on the scene said they recovered the body of a thirty-seven-year-old Caucasian male under the Lake Street Bridge who was beheaded and his genitalia mutilated. According to observers, the dead man's body was stuffed in what appears to be a dog cage. Police said they spotted a rope dangling from the bridge sometime this morning and thought it was left behind by workers repairing the bridge earlier this month. The victim's identity was not released. We'll keep you updated on this story later in the day. In national news, President Bush arrived............"

OK, Benny thought to himself, turning off the radio, I've got to think. I've got to stay calm. No one in a million years would suspect me. Not me.

Benny pulled up in front of his office, taking his coffee with him even though he knew Tracey always made a fresh pot in the morning.

"Scary, isn't it?" Tracey remarked as she greeted her boss that crisp Wednesday morning.

Dr. Weinstein grunted while hanging his new but identical brown bomber on a coat hook, not realizing at first she was talking about the murder in Miller.

"Sorry, I was thinking about something," Dr. Weinstein said, his mind elsewhere. "What did you say?"

Tracey handed Dr. Weinstein the morning edition of the Post Tribune. Benny's hand shook as he read the huge headline: BEHEADING AT LAKE. The large dark picture underneath showed two policemen hoisting up the cage by the rope. Only a faint image of the body was visible. But a separate picture showed a close-up of the yellow card taped to Tommy's chest that read "THAT'S ONE."

Benny scanned the article, marveling at the stealth of the story. The cops must have arrived just minutes after I left, he thought. I have to be more careful next time, he contemplated, nonchalantly plunking the paper on the magazine table in his waiting room.

"I'm frightened," Tracey said, somewhat sarcastically. "I hope I never cross paths with the lunatic who did this."

"Me too," said Dr. Weinstein. "Is Carla coming in today?"

Chapter Twenty-Eight

Benny knew he had to keep a low profile for at least a few days. Not that this thing was going to blow over any time soon, rather, to conspire a less messy modus operandi. The exact same method of execution could not be repeated for the remaining three. And the alibi, if needed, had to be the same. This is something he didn't plan until after he left work on Wednesday. So after work he drove to Balmoral Race Track in Crete, Illinois and rummaged through their garbage bin for discarded betting slips from the night before. Luckily the second bag he pulled out from the huge green bin contained hundreds of tickets from Tuesday night's simulcast. He brushed away a myriad of old disgusting cigarette butts and pop cups and got about six hundred dollars worth of losing tickets plus that night's racing form. He sorted them to make sure they displayed the right times, and not for earlier races. He hid the tickets in his Camry's sunglass compartment. If anyone asked, they were for 'tax purposes'.

It was 8:30 p.m. Thursday evening, May 14th, 1992. Benny had just arrived home from the office and Marsha was out with the kids. He was clutching a standard sized manila envelope containing two pictures. Earlier in the day he went to his clinic's x-ray room and developed the two black and white pictures he took of Tommy. Photography was one of Benny's childhood hobbies and it came in handy. He knew exactly which developer and fixer to use. Then he got the shock of his life.

There, blinking on the kitchen counter, was the new beige and yellow answering machine Marsha bought at Sears a week before. As Benny was making a peanut butter sandwich he went over to the counter and pushed the play button. It rewound for almost thirty seconds. Someone just left a hell of a long message, he thought. It wasn't a message. It started in the middle of a conversation between Marsha's friend Stephanie and Marsha, who apparently didn't realize their exchange was being recorded.

"Yeah," Stephanie said. "I just heard on the news the murdered guy's name was Tommy Gunther!"

Marsha inhaled deeply. This was quite a shock for her.

"You never told Benny what happened, did you?" Stephanie continued.

There was a long pause. It was all Marsha could do to digest what she just heard.

"No, no, no, I didn't," Marsha confided. "That affair was over five years ago and it just lasted a month."

"A month?" Stephanie knowingly said. "More like three."

Benny listened another minute and found out plenty.

* * * * *

Marsha met Tommy quite by accident while taking an evening accounting course at the I.U. extension in Gary one summer. By that time, Tommy's tire business was taking off and he took the course just so he would understand his own accountant. Marsha already knew a lot about bookkeeping and wanted a refresher for when she did work for her husband. Benny and Marsha were having some marital problems then, mostly over her lack of personal time and the stresses of raising two small children. Benny didn't think it was anything serious, but it was a difficult time for Marsha who was very pretty and attracted a lot of male attention. Marsha was thinking divorce or at the least, having an affair—which she did. But Benny didn't know all the sordid details. If he had he would have killed Tommy sooner.

Late one Thursday evening at the I.U. accounting class, Tommy walked up to Marsha, not knowing she was the wife of the man he tormented in high school. Both had just completed a particularly strenuous test. Tommy recognized the name Weinstein when the instructor asked Marsha a question, but didn't put it together right away.

"My name's Tommy Gunther," he said, introducing himself to his potential conquest. "I know your name is Marsha Weinstein. I heard when the teacher called you. I own a small tire store on County Line Road. I'm glad I'm taking this course. Lots of stuff my accountant didn't tell me."

Marsha glanced at Tommy and smiled, then walked down the hall on her way to her car.

Tommy was 32 years old and looked a whole lot better than he did in high school. Very fit and wore nice clothes. He cleaned up his act big time after his sentence was up and decided to make something of his life. He worked at another tire center before he saved enough money to buy his own. He wasn't married, but he fathered a son with a stripper he met shortly after his release. His son's mother moved to California with the kid. He rarely saw them. At the time he was taking the course he just ended a three-year relationship with a woman he had intended to marry. Just before Benny killed Tommy, he got back with his ex-fiancé and they had planned a

June wedding.

Tommy followed Marsha down the hall.

"If you're not too much in a hurry, would you like to go out for a drink?" Tommy asked in a lost *Who's On Third* puppy-dog, sort of begging way.

Marsha stopped to answer.

"I'm married."

That didn't deter Tommy.

"Oh, I don't mean anything by it," he said. "There's a place just two blocks from here. Come on. You can follow me in your car."

Marsha liked Tommy's charm. And really liked the attention. She was extremely pissed at Benny and was sure the big D was imminent. And she looked really good that night. Her long brown hair was pulled back in a ponytail. She wore the sexiest lavender lipstick and tight fitting jeans and a yellow blouse that accentuated her large breasts, with no bra. She had on Estee Lauder's Pleasures perfume. Her figure was perfect, even after having two kids. She worked out a lot. Tommy noticed.

"Okay," said Marsha. "I don't see how one drink can hurt. But just one. Benny's expecting me home by eleven.

Tommy stopped in his tracks. It can't be! he thought to himself. This is fucking perfect!

"Fine. Good," he eagerly agreed, suppressing his excitement. "One drink and I'm gone. I have to be at the store early tomorrow anyway."

Who's On Third was a new sports bar but already had a decent following. For that part of town it was fairly up to date, with a large screen TV and several smaller sets every five feet hanging from the ceiling.

Tommy slowly drove his cargo van out of the school's parking lot, waiting for Marsha to catch up to him. It was two blocks away just like he said. They parked their cars and walked into the place.

"Pretty nice," Marsha said, looking around as Tommy pulled out a bar stool for her as she sat down.

"I like it," Tommy said. "This place has only been open a couple of months, but I've been here at least a half dozen times."

They talked about their class for a few minutes as Marsha sipped a margarita. Tommy had a rum and coke, served up by Curly, the balding twenty-something-year-old bartender. Tommy ordered two more drinks in spite of Marsha's half hearted protests, but she drank another anyway. All the televisions flickered with the White Sox-Angel's night game as some of the other patrons talked about the Sox's chances that year.

An hour went by with Marsha having four drinks in all to Tommy's five.

"I better get going," Marsha said as she held her head, looking a little woozy.

Tommy got up to hold the chair for her. Marsha grabbed her purse and headed towards the exit. Tommy threw seventy bucks on the counter for a fifty dollar tab then winked at the bartender. "Keep it!"

"Thanks," said Curly.

Marsha, not used to drinking, staggered to her car, fumbling with her keys, and made five or six unsuccessful stabs at the lock.

"You're in no shape to drive home," said a somewhat inebriated Tommy as he put his hand on her shoulder. "And neither am I. You wouldn't want to get stopped by a cop this late at night with four drinks in you. Better lay down in my van for a while."

Marsha agreed and walked with Tommy to his cargo van

and lay down in the back next to three tires stacked to the side. Tommy sat beside her and put his hand on her stomach, waiting for some sort of response.

"I don't know, Tommy," said Marsha, who was aware but very tipsy, her breath scented with alcohol.

"But I do," Tommy said as he took both his hands and boldly unbuttoned her jeans in front and stuck his hand through the opening, pulling down her skimpy, white laced Victoria Secret's panties and slowly worked his middle finger past her coarse pubic hair and into her hot squishy pussy. "Who's on third now?" Tommy joked, as his finger went in deeper and deeper.

Marsha pretended to resist, but then caressed Tommy's balls through his Khakis. Tommy got hard instantly as he put his mouth on hers while grabbing her ponytail with his other hand. Marsha passionately kissed him as he continued fingering her steamy box. Her top was still on.

"Ohhh, ohhhhh," Marsha moaned as Tommy's curious digit probed and found her clitoris while Marsha peeled off his pants, unleashing his rigid organ. Marsha unsnapped the top of her jeans so Tommy could get in there better. He pulled her jeans all the way down and flung them to the side. He then pulled one of her legs out from her skimpy panties, letting them lay next to her amber bush. Tommy parted her thighs and stuck his tongue inside her waiting snatch. She moaned even louder as Tommy's tongue glided up and down her pink slit. Then he stuck his tongue deep in her pussy. Marsha got feverishly horny and returned the favor by putting Tommy's hot cock in her mouth while Tommy slid it in between her full, red lips. Marsha sucked even harder which almost made Tommy cum too soon.

"Not yet," Tommy said as he pulled his rod out of her mouth and placed it next to her inviting crack. Marsha grabbed the base of his unyielding meat and worked it inside of her until she was fully penetrated. Tommy steadily pumped in and out of Benny's wife and watched her reaction while she climaxed.

"I've got to see those gorgeous huge tits of yours," Tommy said as he ripped her blouse away, the buttons pinging against the metal door, as he put his mouth on her stiff nipples then sucked each of her plump, white, soft mountains as his cock pumped inside of her powerless beaver.

"Do you get it this good at home?" Tommy asked as Marsha shivered with ecstasy.

"Oh Tommy! Oh Tommy. Keep fucking me. Don't stop. Don't stop!"

It was almost impossible for Tommy to hold back. He was never so horny in his life—nailing the pretty wife of the guy who sent him to jail.

"Don't cum in me Tommy," Marsha pleaded during one of her climaxes. "Don't cum in me. Ohhhhhhhhhhh!"

Tommy didn't say anything as he kept pumping and watching Marsha moan as her head rocked back and forth on his van's floor with each plunge. "Don't cum in me," she repeated. "Don't cum in me. Don't cum in me. Don't cum in me" After ten minutes of reddening her squishy pussy, Tommy put his hand over Marsha's mouth, muffling her protests as his beast erupted, dumping a load of hot jizz deep into her accommodating pussy. He slid in and out of her a few more times until the last of his goo was inside her. He drilled her but good. Take that, motherfucker, Tommy silently thought while remembering Benny. Afterwards they both passed out from booze and exhaustion but woke up when they heard a loud muffler from the last car screeching out of the parking lot at 2:00 a.m., closing time.

Benny didn't ask any questions the next morning, even

though he knew his wife didn't get home until almost 3:00 a.m. He figured she was due for a ladies' night out after class. Little did he know.

Chapter Twenty-Nine

"Now I see," Benny said to himself after learning the truth about his wife from the answering machine. "Marsha had an affair with that piece of shit? I can't believe it. That sure explains a lot of things—like why she acted so anxious when we stopped by the Gas 'N Go. And why she never questions my whereabouts. And why Tommy's last words to me were, "It was her idea."

This was one bit of information he had to keep to himself, at least for now. But he did have the presence of mind to make a copy of the message with an old portable tape recorder. That little piece of tape, which he stored in his glove compartment, gave him a sense of power. It also gave him an astonishing amount of freedom he hadn't experienced since he got married. Now he could do anything. Anything! And not feel guilty.

One thing Benny had going for him was Tommy's past. Tommy was in jail a few times, the longest was in Michigan City after the beating. Anybody could have killed him. This comforted Benny. Tommy must have acquired other enemies along the way.

By Saturday, May 16th, the national media picked up this gruesome story. Everyone in the country knew about it, including Gerald, Frank, and Murphy. Benny figured they must have at least called each other or talked about it at work. Did they suspect Benny?

For a few days the Lake Street Bridge was lined with television crews and onlookers. The weather warmed up to the 70s during the day and 45 degrees in the evening, a vast improvement for the early season beach goers. But not good for Benny. I've got to change a few plans. Too many eyes outside when it's warm, he thought to himself.

For years Gary, Indiana was right up there in the top five for the highest number of murders per capita in the United States—most of which went unnoticed. Gang and drug related murders were commonplace. Like breathing. No one cared much except the families of the victims. But this was different. Tommy was murdered for no obvious motive. Who would have done this? If someone just wanted him dead, they would have shot him and that would have been the end. Instead there was a sadistic killer on the loose who wanted him dead. And not just dead—butchered. There was no question the killing was personal. Tommy's wallet was found on his body and nothing was missing—ID, money, all there. So it wasn't robbery. It was clear to the police there would be more killings. THAT'S ONE!, the note read. Who was two? Or three? Where would it end?

The autopsy report was released Monday, May 18th, 1992. The Post Tribune demoted the story to page two but it was still a hot topic: MURDER VICTIM DRUGGED, TORTURED. The article went on to describe the large amounts of succinylcholine chloride and epinephrine in Tommy's blood, what was left of it. The story also noted the numerous puncture marks on the body, entry points for the drugs.

That Monday evening, Marsha came home from the supermarket while Benny was still at work. The kids were at

Hebrew school and weren't expected back until 8:00 p.m. While putting her groceries away she gave a cursory glance at her new answering machine and noticed it blinking. There were two messages. She pressed 'play'.

"Oh my God! Oh my God!" Marsha screeched, almost fainting. "That's me! I forgot to turn off the machine when Stephanie called. Oh my God! I wonder if Benny heard it."

On to message two: "Hi Marsha, it's me," said Benny. "Listen, I'll be really late coming home. Don't wait up. I'm taking an injury lawyer to Balmoral Park tonight to bet a few ponies. I think he'll be a good source of patients."

Marsha was relieved to hear that. It sure didn't sound like Benny knew. But she wasn't satisfied. She called Stephanie and asked if Steve knew anything about the affair. Stephanie assured her he didn't. "He never mentioned anything to me," Stephanie said, trying to quell Marsha's anxiety. "It's been five years," Stephanie continued. "If he knew, it would have come out by now."

Benny did plan a late night out, but not at the track. He was running low on Sucostrin and needed more. There was plenty for one more job, but that was it. So he drove over to J.J.'s after work. He parked about a block away next to an expired meter then got out to walk to the shop, quickly glancing inside his car. "Shit, the newspaper," he said to himself, realizing he left it on the front seat. "I'm taking that with me." He entered the shop about a quarter to eight.

"Hey Sox!" Rings enthusiastically said as he saw Benny come in. Neither Rings nor J.J. knew Benny's real name. "You got something to hock this time?" he joked.

Benny looked around and didn't see anyone else in the shop. By this time he was such a good customer that he merited a more neighborly greeting. Rings went around the counter, opened the secured door and welcomed him with the 'dap' handshake—a light slap on the palms, gladiator grip, and a big finger-snapping finish. Like a bro. Benny clumsily went along with it.

"What's all this?" Benny asked Rings as they finished the shake.

"Noth'n," said Rings. "Just glad to see you. Business has been a little slow."

"Slow? Slow?" Benny said in disbelief. "I didn't think there was such a thing in your line of work—not here anyway."

"Oh, it'll pick up," said Rings, twirling a gold bracelet around his thin wrist. "That sick murder near the lake has everyone edgy. The police think the guy who did it lives near here so they doubled up their patrols. People are afraid to be seen."

"Yeah," said Benny, shaking his head. "A lot of whackos out there."

"What did you come in for?" Rings asked.

"I need some more Sucostrin. When you see J.J. tell him to get me another five hundred dollars worth. I've got a big rat problem near my house and the city won't take care of it. Around all the drainage pipes. My wife's scared of those critters."

Rings didn't ask any questions and took the five C-notes from Benny and promised the stuff in a week.

"Sure glad you stopped by, Sox," said Rings as he started walking back around the counter. "This is the first real money we made all night. J.J. isn't here and I'm minding the store. He's at home fumigating our place. We got a varmint problem, too. Good thing it's slow today. I've got momma here. Tak'n care of her here today until we can go back in the house."

"Hey Bo!" boomed a woman's voice from the back of the store. "I need a push to the toilet."

"Yo, Sox," yelled Rings. "That's momma. I'll be back in a

minute."

Benny bided his time by looking at all the goods. There must have been two hundred gold wedding bands just in the front case. And a couple hundred expensive watches next to them—Rolex, Cartier, Omega—all the top brands.

His momma? Benny thought. Sounds like she's in a wheelchair. I wonder how old she is. Rings can't be more than twenty-two.

About ten minutes later Benny heard the sound of wheels squeaking against the floor, along with Rings' footsteps. Rings was whistling *Hot Fun In The Summertime* by Sly & The Family Stone. He was pushing a white woman who looked about forty-five or fifty. She was very fat and wore a cheap K-Mart red wig with dirty curls and uneven bangs. Her legs were covered by a torn but thick blue blanket. Her face was caked with unevenly applied rouge. She wasn't self conscious in the least.

"We haven't had many visitors today and momma wanted to meet you," said Rings. "She's at home by herself most of the time. I hope you don't mind, but momma likes to hear stories about the shop when I get home. I told her about you. I didn't see the harm since I don't know your name or where you live."

"That's enough, Bo!" said his mother in a harsh tone. "I don't like when you talk for me when I'm sitt'n right here next to you."

"Oh, that's okay," said Benny, feeling very uncomfortable. "Rings here calls me Sox," deferring to his White Sox cap, attempting to change the subject.

"Rings?" exclaimed his mother. "I'm the only one who doesn't call him that—seeing he's my only kid. His name is Bo."

"Rings. Call me Rings," Rings said to Benny. "Momma is

the only one who calls me Bo."

"Fine, Rings," said Benny. "Well, it was nice meeting you, um, um….." Benny hesitated, not knowing if he should address her as momma.

"Twila," the woman interjected. "My name is Twila."

It took a few seconds for that to register. Not many named Twila. Benny's jaw dropped as he stared deeply into her craggy face. She looked much older than her 37 years.

"Oh my! Oh my!" cried Benny. "Oh my. I know you!"

Rings looked at Benny then looked at his mother, who was now scrutinizing Benny's face. His momma's eyes were weak but she could still see the specter. She gasped then asked for a glass of water. Her son had a bottle of water handy on the counter.

"Benny? Benny? Benny Weinstein? Is that you?" Twila asked like she had just seen a ghost.

Benny didn't move. He just stood there—shaking.

"Yes, yes, it's me," said Benny, reaching for her shoulder with his right hand, and squeezing her arm with his left.

"It's been over twenty years since I saw you last," Twila said as she shimmied closer and started crying. "Closer to twenty-three."

"Momma, what's the matter?" asked Rings, comforting her with a hug as he handed her the bottle. "You know Sox?"

The moment was briefly interrupted when another customer walked in, setting off the bell above the door. The man sniffed around for a minute then left.

"Yes," Twila sobbed. "I knew Benny from junior high. He was a dear friend of mine. He was good friends with your father, too—God rest his soul."

Benny thought he was dreaming. His father? Who was his father? Oh no, Benny thought. This can't be happening.

"Y-y-your father?" Benny stammered as he turned towards

Rings. "Who was your father?" Benny had a good idea.

"Bo never knew his father," Twila answered. "Eddy died shortly after he was born. Remember Eddy Moss?"

"Do I remember Eddy?" Benny repeated, his voice cracking. "Do I remember him? I'll never forget Eddy. I loved him. He was a true, dear friend of mine."

"I loved him too," said Twila. "He's why we're all here today, and why I'm the way I am."

Rings knew some things about his father Eddy, but not everything. Rings regarded J.J. as his father, but he was really his great uncle on Eddy's mother's side. Twila's parents were too poor to care for the baby so J.J. stepped in after Twila moved back from Kentucky. Everyone who knew Twila from Wirt thought she permanently moved to Louisville. But she came back to Gary when Bo was just six months old.

Benny whispered something in Twila's ear.

"Yes, yes, Bo knows all about the attack," said Twila. "I made sure he knew when he was old enough."

"But I never found out what happened to Eddy afterwards," said Benny. "He just disappeared."

Rings couldn't bear to hear anymore and went behind the counter to get the broom and clean up for the night. He was going to close early anyway.

"I'll tell you what happened," Twila said as she pointed to a chair for Benny to sit in. "You know what those delinquents did to him, don't you? And me?"

"Yes, vividly," Benny answered.

"I was already pregnant with Bo at the time of the attack. Eddy didn't want me to get an abortion and I didn't want one either. He was working at the beach to get some extra money so we both could get out of there and start a new life in another town." Twila took a long swig of water, swallowed hard, then wiped her mouth with the blanket. "Then Eddy was attacked and I was raped. They cut Eddy real bad. Real, real bad. He was in St. Mary's Hospital for a month, but he survived. Then our families thought it better for me and Eddy to move to Louisville. We stayed at my aunt's small farm and I had the baby. I liked it a lot on that farm. Gave me a lot of peace. I thought we'd settle there, you know, and get jobs and everything. Then Eddy's pain got so bad and he started having nightmares. He started drinking a lot and taking painkillers. One day he took too many and never woke up."

Benny scooted his chair closer to Twila and put his hand on her arm.

"Those pieces of shit are responsible for Eddy's death," Benny said angrily. "He never would have died if it weren't for those cowards. I miss him now more than ever."

"Eddy loved you too," said Twila. "He always told me how nice you treated him—with respect, and how you were such good buddies."

Rings finished sweeping the floor then took out the trash and started to lock up.

"Well," Benny said to Twila and Rings, who was in earshot, "I'll be back to pick up the stuff next week. And oh," Benny continued, pulling out the newspaper from inside his bomber, "you might be interested in this," as he dropped the newspaper on Twila's lap. "One of Eddy's attackers is dead."

Twila squinted to read the headline. A big smile crossed her face.

"Holy mother of God!" Twila shouted. "I saw this on the TV, but I didn't pay much attention to the name. Shit, it is one of them! I hope whoever did this gets the others, too."

Benny smiled as he opened the door to leave. "Wouldn't that be nice!"

Chapter Thirty

Tuesday, May 19th, 1992. There were still no leads on the Lake Street Bridge murder. A week passed since Tommy's mutilated body was found. The police were still scratching their heads. The weather was getting nicer and that meant kids at the beach. Pete's hotdog and root beer restaurant, directly across from the bridge, was now open for the year. Pete's was the place to be. Pete Esposito, the affable, plump Italian owner with a *Chef Boyardee* mustache, started out in the mid 60s with a corner hotdog pushcart at the end of Lake Street. His good humor and excellent fare, along with the ice cold root beer, made him a hit. By the early 70s he had his own 1,500-square-foot restaurant, which was more like a come-as-you-are outdoor café. He also sold candy, sunglasses, hats, T-shirts, and cigarettes. "No booze, no booze," Pete used to say. "Make people crazy."

Pete's became the unofficial headquarters for the murder investigation. Two plainclothes cops hung around the place and kept their ears and eyes open for any clues. Maybe the murderer himself or herself would come back to the scene of the crime.

Nine o'clock that evening, Benny was supposed to be off to

chess club, but he had other plans. Marsha and the kids were at home working on school projects. Benny's next target was Murphy Spevacek on Grand Boulevard. Yes, Murphy. He was the one who covered Benny's mouth so he couldn't scream the night of the attack. Benny was unable to scream. He was unable to scream. This was his mantra. He was unable to scream. And Benny never forgot it. His plan was to make Murphy want to scream. Benny knew how.

At 9:10 p.m. that evening, Benny parked his car on the side of the road about two hundred yards from the corner of Grand Boulevard and Hickory, approximately two blocks from Murphy's house. This particular spot was void of any street lights, with scant traffic. Benny had already loaded a potent dart. Much more potent than the ones before. He didn't care if it killed Murphy, but hoped it wouldn't. At 9:17 p.m. Benny saw a set of headlights in his rearview mirror. He put his car in drive, with his foot still on the brake and waited quietly. The headlights got closer. He could see it was a Ford pickup truck. Murphy's Ford pickup truck. Murphy was on his way to the mill. It was him. There was no mistake about that. Even from fifty feet Benny recognized the shape of that scum's skull and the way he smoked a cigarette. The truck was almost even with Benny's car, then passed as Benny lifted his foot off the brake and put his foot to the gas pedal, gunning the motor. He quickly caught up with the truck and bumped it hard from behind. BOOM! It was a solid jolt, but not enough to cause any real damage on Benny's bumper—just a scratch. Murphy was pissed as hell and started yelling even before he got out of his truck. Murphy mashed on his brakes, with plans of beating the shit out of the driver who hit him. Benny was ready.

"GET THE FUCK OUT OF THE CAR!" Murphy yelled as he got out of his truck and slammed the door behind him, running briskly towards Benny, like a charging rhinoceros.

"You did that on purpose!" Murphy exclaimed with venom in his voice.

Murphy was about fifteen feet away when Benny suddenly bolted from his car and pointed the tranquilizer gun directly at Murphy's head. Murphy froze for a second, then Benny, knowing bigger muscles absorbed drugs better, lowered the gun and fired the dart, point blank into Murphy's left thigh. Murphy hit the ground but didn't have enough breath to scream. The drug took effect immediately. Benny quickly dragged Murphy's limp body along the pavement and hoisted him onto the back seat of his car, then bound his hands and legs with rope, already cut to size. He made three loops and five knots around each limb. Benny sped off, admiring his catch in the rearview mirror and watching Murphy's truck, sitting there with the headlights still glowing as it disappeared in the distance.

Not wanting to attract attention, Benny slowed as he drove down Grand Boulevard. He then made a soft left onto Pine Street, then Oak Street, then County Line Road, snaking his way to Stagecoach Road. He could hear Murphy struggling to breathe. For a moment it sounded like he stopped. But then Benny heard a long, labored inhalation and knew he captured his prize alive. Satisfied, Benny pushed a cassette tape into his player. *American Pie*, again, and set to his favorite lyric.

Don McClean was in rare form that night, as he was every night. Benny turned up the volume and sang along.

"Don't you want to sing along too?" Benny asked as he smiled back at Murphy, who was starting to recover by now and was able to make short guttural sounds but no words.

Benny turned left onto Stagecoach Road and drove leisurely down the dark street. He kept looking in his rearview mirror to monitor Murphy's recovery, then stopped about a block from the tree, parking at the side of the road. He grabbed his tranquilizer gun from the front seat, leaning it against the car while he pulled out his thick black marker and a sheet of yellow card stock from the sun visor. He opened the back door and saw Murphy, fully awake, and screaming for help.

"HEEEEEYYYY," shouted Murphy. "ANYONE! HELP! HEEEEEEELLLLLLLP!

No one heard him. Benny knew no one could.

"WHO THE FUCK ARE YOU?"

Benny shook his head, yellow card stock in hand.

"I'm deeply, deeply, deeply, offended," Benny said while carefully snapping the head of the cap in the back of the marker. "Deeply, deeply, deeply offended."

"WHAT THE FUCK DO YOU WANT?"

Benny sniffed the head of the marker. "Hmmm," he said. "I just love that smell!"

"WHAT THE FUCK ARE YOU DOING?"

"Don't worry, Mr. Spevacek," Benny said patronizingly, "this won't take but a minute," as he scribbled something on the card.

"THAT'S TWO!" Benny wrote in big letters, then grabbing his terrified and helpless victim by the scruff of his neck, forced his eyes to read it. "Now all I have to do is keep my promise," Benny said while raising his tranquilizer rifle and shooting another dose of Sucrostrin into Murphy. Phoooooot! That shut him up. Murphy was paralyzed within seconds.

Benny closed the back door and drove to the tree, parking his car way off to the side, closer to the woods. He figured he already had enough fun torturing Tommy and just wanted Murphy dead—quickly. So he dragged Murphy out of the car, into the woods, bringing his lantern, a roll of duct tape, the tranquilizer rifle, the yellow card, one shot of epinephrine, his Rolleiflex camera, and the pictures of Tommy's mutilated body.

About forty feet into the woods, Benny stopped and raised the lantern to his own face. Murphy was on his back, unable to move, but had a full view of Benny's face.

"Take a good look," demanded Benny, his vengeful eyes glowing like orange coals. "Take a good hard look. See anyone familiar?" Benny smiled widely.

It was obvious from Murphy's eyes that he recognized Benny. Then Benny showed him the ghastly pictures of Tommy's throat cut to the core. Murphy knew it was the end for him. Benny pulled off a four-foot strip of duct tape then wrapped it around Murphy's mouth and the back of his neck three times. Good and tight. Then he taped the yellow card reading "THAT'S TWO!" to the front of Murphy's jacket.

"My name is Benjamin Arnold Weinstein," Benny said after inspecting the ropes binding Murphy's hands and legs. "The Jew!" continued Benny. "The Jew! And the nigga lover! Yes, it's me?" Benny said angrily as he swiftly kicked Murphy in the balls eight times, splitting Murphy's scrotum, Benny's favorite revenge act.

Saliva dribbled through the tape as Benny prepared to assault him again.

"Now I know it's been a few years since last we met. I'd say about nineteen," Benny continued. "And I'll understand— oh, believe me I'll understand if you don't fully remember me. But as I recall, you were once a brave soldier with three other friends, one dead now. Did you see that word 'TWO' I wrote on that card? Well, that's for you my good dead fellow. That's for you." Then Benny lifted up the lantern to illuminate Murphy's face, then snapped a couple of black and whites with the 1940's style camera. "Smile, you son of a bitch," Benny commanded. Click. Click.

Benny viciously kicked his helpless captive in the head once, and twice in his mouth, breaking his teeth, and then five more times in his balls until Murphy passed out. Benny took two more pictures from different angles— like a professional newspaper photographer.

Murphy regained consciousness but wasn't as coherent as Benny liked. Benny walked back to his car and got a bottle of water and splashed Murphy's eyes.

"Oh no you don't," shouted Benny while putting the camera down and taking out the epinephrine shot, sticking the needle in Murphy's left bicep. "I'll decide when it's time for you to die."

"Understand me now?" Benny tersely asked while capping the bottle. "I hope so because you know that pretty lady you have at home? You know who I mean—the one with the pointy tits. Yeah, that one. Even at a distance I can see how pointy her tits are. Did I mention she had pointy tits? Don't know her name, but after I'm done with you I'm going back to fuck her then put her out of her misery along with that kid of yours. I think he'd like the feel of duct tape around his mouth, too! Slicing off his balls wouldn't be bad either."

Benny had no intention of harming either one. He just wanted to see more drool dripping down Murphy's chin through the duct tape. He wasn't disappointed.

It was now 10:12 p.m. Benny was through messing around. He shot Murphy with another dose of Sucostrin then dragged the Jon boat and trailer out from its hiding place in the woods. He hitched the boat to his bumper then slid Murphy across the brush and hoisted him to the back of the boat and covered his gangly body with the black tarp. He was just about to turn right onto County Line Road when he saw two cop cars, in full pursuit with their lights flashing, driving down County Line Road the opposite way. Benny hit his brakes and watched them pass to his left. Satisfied they were out of sight and not after him, he turned right onto County Line Road, driving the speed limit and nervously looking in his side view mirrors. As he reached the top of the hill before turning left onto Oak Street, he saw the cops again. This time it did look like they were coming after him—at full speed and strobe.

"Holy fuck!" shouted Benny. "How could they know?"

The cops were gaining on him, fast. Benny cut his lights and made a sharp right turn off the side street before Oak. But that street dead-ended a hundred yards down. He had no choice but to stop his car at the end and wait for the cops to pass. He turned off the engine and glanced back at Murphy, who was still inside the boat but beginning to stir. Benny got out of the car and knelt beside the boat.

"Hold still you motherfucker," Benny whispered to Murphy. "Hold the fuck still."

Benny grabbed the tranquilizer rifle and quickly loaded another dart. He pointed the rifle at the back end of the tarp, guessing he would hit some part of Murphy's leg. He didn't fire. He waited another five seconds then he saw both squad cars rush by, turning left onto Oak Street. OK, he thought. They didn't see me.

Benny couldn't chance missing Murphy with the dart. So he climbed into the boat and took off the tarp. He saw Murphy lying there—dead.

Holy shit, thought Benny. He must have had a heart attack from all the drugs.

But he didn't have a heart attack. And he wasn't dead. Benny bent down to listen to Murphy's heart. When his ear touched his chest, Murphy woke up with a surge and wrapped his bound wrists around Benny's neck, squeezing as hard as he could, with Benny lying face up. Benny started choking and couldn't get away. Murphy was too strong, and kept squeezing as Benny tried to pry Murphy's wrist away. Benny had only one chance: He let go of Murphy's wrists, and with his right thumb Benny reached back and found Murphy's right eye and viciously pushed it in until it burst out of the socket, blood spurting everywhere. Murphy, disabled by the pain, loosened his grip and Benny was able to free himself. Benny grabbed the rifle and quickly shot Murphy with a dose, then loaded again and shot him with another until he succumbed. That ought to keep the piece of shit quiet for a while, he thought.

Benny got back into his car, swung around, and doubled back to County Line Road. Do I go back down Oak? he thought to himself. After contemplating for a few seconds, he saw a number of squad cars blinking in the distance, about five blocks down Oak Street. They weren't after me, he deduced. I think they got their man.

Benny turned right onto County Line Road, then a few feet later, left onto Oak Street. He guardedly drove down Oak towards the cops and saw they did in fact pull over not one but three cars. Four guys were already handcuffed with their hands behind their backs being booked for something. Who knows what. Benny decided to turn around and wait at the dead end road until the cops left.

At about 10:45 p.m., the cops dispersed and drove away in a convoy. Benny had given Murphy three more doses of Sucostrin during this time. It was very dark, a comfortable 50 degrees, but the wind was kicking up. The Great Lake to his right looked menacing with roaring three-foot waves crashing onto the shore every few seconds. The tarp hiding Murphy almost flew off. Benny started the car then got out to check on his passenger in the boat. He picked up the spool of twine next to the oar and cut off a long piece to secure the tarp to the oar slot. He lifted up the tarp to get more slack and noticed Murphy wasn't moving—at all. Not this time, Benny thought to himself. Fool me once. Instead of listening to Murphy's heart, Benny took his epinephrine syringe and poked Murphy everywhere, about ten times. No response. Benny grabbed Murphy's left wrist and felt for a pulse. Nothing. He then got his lantern and cautiously approached the tethered former high school bully, lifted up his already half opened left eyelid then tested his remaining pupil for a reaction. There was none. Murphy was dead. He was really dead this time. The cause of death, suffocation. His lungs just couldn't expand due to his paralyzed diaphragm. OK, OK, thought Benny while covering up the corpse in the howling wind. Let's just do this thing.

Benny got into his car and drove down Oak Street to the Pavilion. It was about 11:00 p.m. There was no one in sight. He parked in his usual spot as close as possible to the water, and slid the boat down from the trailer without first removing Murphy, who weighed almost 200 pounds. THUD! The boat landed hard on the pavement, but Benny was in a hurry. He pushed the boat down to the water as fast as he could, then went back to his car and got a twenty-foot length of rope, and his knife. He got in the boat and checked the gas supply in the motor, which was about half full. He had second thoughts. He wasn't going to start the motor. As quiet as the motor was, it still made some noise. Instead, he mounted both oars and rowed in the other direction, away from the Lake Street Bridge towards the fifty-foot Chinese bridge, a wooden walkway with oriental motifs connecting the two shallow ends of the lagoon to the east.

The waves were choppy in the usually tranquil lagoon which made the boat rock. Benny did all he could to keep the boat steady as he neared the Chinese bridge. As he approached the small structure, he lifted up one oar then stuck it into the three-foot deep water until he felt bottom. The boat came to an abrupt stop. He grabbed a wooden pole near the side of the bridge and tied a loose knot, temporarily securing the boat. Benny then pulled the tarp off Murphy, his cold body already stiffened with rigor mortis and his gray, lifeless remaining left eye wide open, like a dead carp. Benny lifted Murphy's rigid body, preparing to dump it into the water. Suddenly he saw a light across the water, about a football field away. A car pulled over and a couple of teens got out and threw something at the pier. Probably beer cans. Benny didn't move, clutching Murphy's unyielding torso, just staring at the kids. One of the young men pulled his pants down and urinated in the water. The other one got out and joined him. They were laughing loudly and yelling profanities. Then another car pulled up next to them. More teens. This time four of them. They all got out of the car to join the fracas. A few seconds later Benny heard a siren coming down Oak Street. The teens scrambled to their cars and sped off. The cops saw the two cars and went after them, leaving the area.

I don't fucking need this, Benny thought to himself as he watched the cops speed away while he tied a hangman's noose around Murphy's neck, making three loops. What was I thinking? The cops might have this place staked out. I've got to finish this quick and get out.

Benny lifted Murphy's heavy remains and pushed him off the side, making a huge splash, wobbling the boat. Benny couldn't control it and he fell into the water with the corpse. Luckily, the boat didn't capsize which would have spilled all of his personal items. Drenched and cold, Benny reached up and looped the other end of the rope over a jutting slat under the bridge, about four feet from the water. He took out his knife and stabbed the dead jerk in the belly nineteen times, one for each year after the attack. Benny swished the knife off in the water then brought the blade up to Murphy's throat and slashed it until his head fell to the side. "Take that, fucker!" he said. Most of Murphy's body was in full view, about two feet from shore. A curious duck glided down from the sky, landing a few feet from the floating body. "You're the first witness," Benny joked to himself, and got back into the boat and paddled back to his car. He saw the muddy waves roll over Murphy's motionless flesh, receding briefly to expose the yellow card, "THAT'S TWO!"

Chapter Thirty-One

Benny had to get out of there. He knew he took quite a chance bringing the second corpse to the lagoon.

Back on shore, and soaking wet, Benny pulled his Jon boat up the hill. The cloak of night hid him from passing cars as he hitched the boat back on. He took inventory, painstakingly inspecting the boat and surroundings, making sure nothing was left behind. "Let's see, knife, excess rope, good. Nothing around the car. Nothing fell out on the way down the hill. I have my wallet here," patting his back pocket. "OK. Let's go and clean up."

It was approaching midnight. Benny was supposed to be home from chess club. Not that it mattered much anymore—after learning the truth about his "devoted" wife. Nonetheless, he was determined to sleep in his own bed next to her.

At 12:04 p.m. Benny switched on his motor, pulled out of the Pavilion parking lot and turned right onto Oak Street, heading towards Grand Boulevard. He just had to take a peek. He passed his always reliable friend, the tall bronze statue of Father Pere Marquette, standing proudly and high atop blocks of Roman granite while majestically raising a gold cross with his right arm. Benny faithfully saluted the dark monument and continued down Oak Street, then turned left onto Grand Boulevard. Curious or not, it didn't take long to realize he'd better peddle back. Just up ahead he saw flashing police lights near Murphy's house. They know he's missing, he thought. They found his empty truck. Benny abruptly turned left onto Juniper, on his way back to Stagecoach Road. He had to ditch his boat there fast and go home.

A feeling of invincibility fell over Benny as he turned onto Stagecoach Road with boat in tow. Who's afraid now? he thought. I can't wait to see the headlines tomorrow after they find his body. And right under their noses in the same lagoon! Benny hid the boat near the tree, a little deeper in the woods this time, changed his clothes, stuffed the wet ones in a black trash bag after scouring the pockets, and drove back to County Line Road. He pushed a tape into his cassette player and treated himself to his favorite victory tune, that creepy instrumental version of *Family Affair*. "Good night Buffy. Good night Jody. See ya, Mr. French."

There was light traffic on I-94 as he made his way back to his home in Hammond. He looked at his waterlogged watch which still worked. "My it's late, almost one," he murmured. "I'll get up in a few hours and scavenge Balmoral's garbage bin in the morning, but I've got to dump these wet clothes off somewhere now. No, fuck, I'll do it when I get the tickets.

Wednesday, May 20th, 1992. Benny only got four hours of sleep, leaving the house at 5:30 a.m. to get in some fishing before seeing patients at 9:00 a.m. He told Marsha, who was half asleep, that he was going to fish at the Calumet River on the shore, no boat. This made more sense to her since the river was just four miles away. Again, no questions.

In the light of day, Benny inspected his car, front and back, inside and out. What a mess. There were dried blood drops on the back and front upholstery. The interior smelled of urine. So his second stop after dumping his wet clothes, and plucking out a bunch of losing tickets from the garbage bin at Balmoral, was to make a trip to K-Mart and buy some salt, hydrogen peroxide, club soda, towels, and sponges. He got to the store by 7:30 a.m. and scrubbed his car for an hour, leaving enough time to grab some coffee and get to his office by nine. His mind was elsewhere.

Seeing patients had become an exercise in making money. Benny didn't get the joy he once did treating back pain and carpal tunnel syndrome. He hoped his enthusiasm would return once his mission was over. He didn't think what he was doing was murder. It was self-help—the only way he could clear his mind of the past. But that's not how others see murder.

It didn't take long for Murphy's body to be discovered. At 5:30 a.m. that morning, the same time Benny left his house, two teenage boys, both fourteen years old, had the same idea— to go fishing before school. These two friends were just innocent lads with bamboo poles resting on their shoulders and a can of worms in their hand. The kids, Jason Wertheimer and Dale Polumczyk knew each other from their freshman class at Wirt and often fished together in the morning. Jason was short and chubby with sandy brown hair, a small nose, and wore wire rimmed glasses. Dale was taller, with dark brown hair, a long face, and exuded a pleasing Midwest charm. They were just out to have fun.

The two buddies had less than an hour to fish. It was Dale's idea to fish under the Chinese bridge since he heard big bluegills were biting there. It didn't make any sense to Jason why the bluegills would be bigger under the bridge, but it didn't matter. The two walked down from Oak Street to the water then towards the bridge. Dale spotted something in the distance, a thicket of moving black objects.

"Look Jason, it looks like something beat us to the fish."

The two lurched a little closer.

"HOLY SHIT!" Jason screamed. "Look at all the crows? Hundreds of 'em!"

"JESUS!" Dale yelled. "WHAT IS THAT?"

The two-hundred bird flock swooshed up and scattered in a deafening flutter when they heard Dale shriek.

Murphy's swollen legs were bobbing up as the birds picked at the carcass under his clothes. His face was blue and pruned. His left eye was plucked out. The muscles around his neck had been eaten away, the rope, dangling from his neck bones. Had this happened a few months earlier it would have been mistaken for a morbid Halloween prank. But it was real.

"Let's get the hell out of here and call the police," Dale gasped, retching in his worm can.

It didn't take long for the cops to arrive. By 6:00 a.m. there were about fifteen squad cars from all over, two fire trucks, and an ambulance. Newspaper and television reporters from every surrounding city and state converged on the scene as did a thousand or more curiosity seekers. Word quickly spread. Wirt and the surrounding elementary schools cancelled classes for the day due to all the absentees watching the horror unfold. Benny got the news at his office from his lawyer friend, Steve, at about 9:12 a.m.

"Hey, Benny," said Steve. "They got another one."

Benny just finished up with one of Steve's new referrals and thought he called about that.

"Who?" asked Benny. "What are you talking about?"

Tracey walked into Benny's private office with an armful of files. "Oh, doctor?" she said with the devil in her voice, and clueless about the early morning news, "Guess who just walked in? Guess whoooooooooo?" she sang.

Benny knew it was Gail, but wanted no part of her that morning. He just wanted to adjust and get out.

"I'll be with her in a minute," Benny said, covering up the receiver so Steve wouldn't hear. "What were you saying?" he asked Steve.

"I just heard on the news they murdered Murphy Spevacek. Some kids found his body not far from Tommy's in the Marquette Park lagoon—all cut up and everything. That makes two. Two of the guys who beat you up long ago, remember? My guess it's drug related."

Benny hesitated for a few seconds. "That wouldn't surprise me. Those rats were always in trouble."

"Hey," Steve continued, "how's the new injury case working out?"

"Which one? You've sent me so many this month."

"You know, the one who has the hots for you."

"Yeah, right," Benny said sarcastically. "The hots for me. Yeah, sure. She has the hots for everyone it seems."

"I don't know big boy. That's not what I heard!"

"I assure you, counselor, I have no interest in Gail other than collecting a check when her case settles."

"Okay, Benny. Gotta run. I just thought I'd tell you about the lagoon murder."

"Alright, I'll talk to you later," Benny said as he was about to put the phone onto the receiver.

"Just a second," Steve interrupted. "If I didn't know you so well, I would have thought you hired someone to kill those guys. Ha, ha, ha!"

"Ha, ha, yourself," Benny cackled. "Later, man."

"Later."

Gail did have the hots for Benny, mostly because he rebuffed her advances. That never happened to her before. He was a challenge. But Benny didn't have time. He had other things on his mind—like staying out of jail or the electric chair. He also needed to pick up his latest order of Sucostrin, but that wasn't until Monday. He had to wait at least that long.

Chapter Thirty-Two

Thursday morning, May 21st, 1992. There wasn't anyone in North America who didn't know about the murders. And it looked like all of North America was there. Throngs of reporters converged on this otherwise non-descript fishing hole. The Associated Press, UPI, and every television network were jockeying for position around the crime scenes. Not only did they bring their TV news vans complete with satellites, but campers too. Enterprising residents set up makeshift hotdog and pop stands around the perimeter of the lagoon and Pavilion. Dozens of portable toilets were donated by the city. Not that the city wanted the press, rather, they just wanted to keep the park clean. And Pete's was doing a booming business as well. "People love bad news," Pete said to a reporter during an interview. Crime, it appeared, does pay. Still, no one had any idea who did this or why. Each victim was leading a normal life, then dead, suddenly.

Thursday evening, same day. Lieutenant Ivan Mitchell just got back from a golf outing near his house in Miami Beach. Now 66 years old, he was retired from the Gary police force, and had been for seven years due to a bad heart. He walked into his small beach front home, fixed himself a Jack Daniel's on the rocks, lit a halfway smoked thick cigar, then went to the back patio and plopped himself on a well worn lounge chair. Helen, his wife of forty years, walked back to greet her relaxed husband, lovingly padded his Buddha paunch, and handed him the afternoon paper. The lakeside murders made the front page of the Miami Herald.

"Did you see this?" Helen asked while pointing to the story.

Lt. Mitchell put his drink down on the armrest and dunked his cigar in the ashtray.

"Let's see," Lt. Mitchell said, taking the paper from his wife, intently studying the newsprint.

Helen pulled up a chair next to her hubby and rubbed his arm. From the look on his face it was plain he was deeply distressed.

"What's wrong," Helen asked, reading the rest of the story over his shoulder.

Her husband shook his head. "Oh boy, ooooh boy," he uttered in concern.

"What? What?" Helen asked. "Did you know them?"

Lt. Mitchell grabbed the glass and chugged the rest of his drink, ice and all.

"I've got to make a phone call," he said while walking back into the house, setting the empty glass back on the armrest. "They might need me back in Gary for a week."

Helen followed her husband in the house as he dialed a number. "Can I go with you?" she asked.

"If you like," he said. "But it might be longer than a week."

"I don't mind," said Helen. "I'll use the time to visit our old friends."

Lt. Mitchell dialed police headquarters in Gary and asked to speak to Lt. Otis Jefferson, the new boss.

"Hello, Otis? It's me, Ivan. Fine, just fine. Yes, I'm spoiled by the weather. What? Yes, Helen's spoiled too. But she loves it. How about your wife, Florence? She doing all right? That's good." There was a two second pause. "Listen, does the name Benjamin Weinstein mean anything to you?"

Chapter Thirty-Three

Friday, May 22nd, 1992. Benny and Marsha woke up at 6:00 a.m. Marsha took a shower while Benny turned on the bedroom television to watch the network news. The kids were getting ready for school. Coverage of the lakeside murders was the story after the Indian satellite launch. Benny turned up the volume when Marsha walked into the bedroom after her shower.

"The gruesome details of the murders in Miller Beach, Indiana are still emerging," announced the voice of a regional reporter on the scene. "What we do know is the genitalia of the first victim, Tommy Gunther, was severed and sewn into his mouth. What's obvious to police is this was not some random killing. It was personal. There are still no leads, but early reports point to a drug deal gone bad. Chuck, back to you."

Benny shook his head and sighed deeply upon hearing the report.

"Wow," Benny said to his wife as she buttoned her blouse. "Isn't that amazing? Two of the guys who beat me up are now dead. And they made national news. I always knew they'd be famous."

No remark from Marsha.

"Oh, gag me," Benny groaned. "Tommy's prick was sewn in his mouth. What a sick thing to do. Imagine having that filthy cock down your throat."

Marsha's eyes widened for a second, not knowing if her husband just dropped a hint.

"I can't imagine," she said. "I'm going to 7-11 to pick up a few things. Want something for the office?"

"No, I'll grab a bite on the way," he said. "But imagine that," continuing, not letting Marsha change the subject. "Imagine having that filthy cock in your mouth."

Marsha quickly finished dressing and drove off to get some bagels. She sped down the road and sloppily parked her minivan next to a payphone in front of the crowded convenience store and called Stephanie.

"Hi Steph, Marsha," she frantically uttered, burying her mouth in her hands so no one else could hear her. "I think he knows."

"Knows what?" asked Stephanie. "Who?"

"Benny," she said. "He was watching the news about the murders and he kept on referring to Tommy's penis being stuffed down his throat. He mentioned that a couple of times."

"Well, Steve never mentioned that Benny knows anything about you and Tommy. I think this is all in your head."

"I don't know," said Marsha. "I'm worried—about a lot of things. I had a dream Benny is somehow involved in the murders."

"What?" Stephanie shouted in disbelief. "Benny? A murderer? Come on!"

"I'm not saying he did it, but maybe he knows who did. It's more than a strange coincidence that two of the guys who beat him up are dead."

"Doesn't mean a thing," Stephanie reassured. "Do you

know where he was the night of both murders?"

"I think so," Marsha said. "He was taking someone to the track—I think both times, not sure."

"Well, see if you can find out for sure," Stephanie said. "I gotta get Steve off to work and the kids ready for school. And don't worry. I won't mention anything to Steve unless you want me to."

"Thanks. See ya," Marsha said as she hung up the phone.

Benny had a lot of work to do after seeing patients that day. He sensed someone might be questioning him and had to hide everything connected to the murders. Except for his boat, everything was kept in the trunk of his car—that, and the hitch on his bumper.

At about 6:00 p.m. that evening, he drove to Stagecoach Road and gathered his pistol, tranquilizer rifle, Sucostrin, epinephrine, masking tape, scissors, everything, including the trailer hitch, and loaded them into his Jon boat which was hidden way off to one side in the woods. On the way home he stopped to have his car interior cleaned again. Okay, I think I'm covered, he thought. I wonder if Marsha has some dinner for me.

Now 7:30 p.m., it was light enough to drive with just the dimmers. As he pulled onto his street he saw a late model navy blue Lincoln Town Car with police plates parked on the street in front of his house. An officer was inside talking on his radio.

Oh shit, he thought. How do they fucking know?

Benny slowly parked in his driveway and got out of his car. He was immediately met by Lt. Otis Jefferson.

Lt. Jefferson was a large black man, about 6' 3" with a short afro, and weighed close to 250 lbs. He was all business, but had an easy smile to break the tension if necessary. He loved working for the Gary Police Department and brought compassion to his job. Not an ounce of ego in the man.

"Yes sir?" Benny uttered, clearing his throat as the bulky cop, dressed in a sharply tailored blue suit approached.

Lt. Jefferson took out a note pad. No one else was with him, so Benny didn't think he was going to be arrested. It embarrassed him, though, to see his kids peeking out the window. Marsha's car was in the drive so he knew she was home. A neighbor across the street pretended to be reading his paper on the porch.

"Mr. Weinstein?" Lt. Jefferson asked, flashing his badge as he walked up to Benny.

"Yes?" Benny said without the slightest hint of trepidation.

"Lt. Jefferson from the Gary police," he said authoritatively, extending his hand. "I suppose you heard about the two recent murders in Miller Beach."

Benny locked his car with the remote as he shook the lieutenant's hand and motioned for him to follow him into the house.

"No, thanks anyway," said Lt. Jefferson. "This won't take a minute. I'd just like to ask you a couple of questions outside if you don't mind."

"No, I don't mind," Benny said. "Sure, I heard about the murders. Who hasn't?"

Lt. Jefferson looked at his notepad, flipped over a few pages then took out a pencil.

"I understand some twenty years ago you had a run-in with the two deceased men....uh, Thomas Gunther and Murphy Spevacek. According to my notes they, along with two other men, Gerald Hill and Frank Stram, assaulted you in the spring of 1973."

"That's right," Benny said, pulling up his left shirt sleeve to show the cop a scar from that event. "That's one night I'll never forget."

Lt. Jefferson made note of that scar.

"Tell me, Mr. Weinstein, have you had any contact with these gentlemen since their release from prison in 1975?"

Benny shook his head. "No, nothing. I was lucky to escape with my life that night. But no, they never bothered me since nor have they contacted me. I want nothing to do with them. For all I knew they were already dead or had moved away."

"Okay," said Lt. Jefferson as he flipped his notepad and placed his pencil in the metal spiral ring. "That's all I wanted to know. Sorry to have caused you any concern. But we have to check all bases."

"I totally understand," Benny said, releasing his tight facial muscles.

Lt. Jefferson was about to get into his car when he remembered something. He approached Benny again.

"Just one more question. Can you verify your whereabouts for the last two Tuesday evenings?"

"My whereabouts? Yeah, sure," Benny said. "I usually go to the track after work on Tuesdays to bet the buggies."

"Was anyone with you those nights?"

"No, just myself. Sometimes I go with friends, but mostly by myself."

"Which track was that?" asked the lieutenant.

"Balmoral Park in Crete, Illinois."

"Oh, yes. Nice track. Been there myself a few times. No luck, though," Lt. Jefferson said, laughing at his last remark. "Do you ever keep the programs?"

Benny reached in his jacket for his car keys.

"Sometimes, not always. I should keep all of them for tax purposes. I've had a few signers this year—won over three grand. But I lose more than I win so sometimes I keep the losing tickets."

"I see," said Lt. Jefferson. "Do you have the tickets from the last two Tuesday nights?"

"No, I don't think I.....wait, yes I do," Benny said, mustering up his best acting skills as he unlocked his car with the remote and fished out the tickets from the sunglass compartment. "I think these are them," he said as he handed over the evidence.

Lt. Jefferson studied the time and dates on the tickets. They matched up. He handed them back to Benny.

"Good enough," said Lt. Jefferson. "Again, I apologize for the inconvenience." Then he left.

Benny put the tickets back in his car and went into his house. Josh and Rachel wanted to know what that man wanted. They already knew of the beating and Benny explained he was a man who was interested in some of the details. The kids were satisfied with that, but Marsha wasn't.

"Was he a cop?" asked Marsha, leading Benny to the kitchen away from the kids.

"Yes, a cop," Benny said as he opened the refrigerator, grabbing two ears of corn that were already cooked.

"What did he say?" Marsha asked, handing her husband a napkin.

"You know, he asked me if I still knew Tommy and Murphy. He probably looked up their files and noticed the 1973 beating. That's all."

"What did you tell him?"

"Well, I told him I never kept in touch with them, which I haven't and that was that. Oh, he did ask me where I was the last two Tuesday evenings."

"And where were you?" Marsha asked anxiously.

"I told him where I was—at the track. Balmoral," Benny said while eating off the cob like a buzz saw. "You know how I sometimes keep the losing tickets for tax purposes. I had them from both nights and I showed them to him. That was the end of it."

All of Marsha's stress drained out of her face at once. She was convinced her husband had nothing to do with the murders. But she still wasn't sure if he knew about Tommy.

Chapter Thirty-Four

Saturday, May 23rd, 1992. The weather was getting nice. The students from Wirt along with hundreds of adventure seekers swarmed around Pete's to talk about the murders. Just off Pete's property, a souvenir hawker from Chicago set up a stand selling T-shirts depicting grotesque images of a beheaded man that read "IT'S MILLER TIME!" The local politicians weren't amused.

Benny stayed away from the area that weekend and took his family to see the White Sox play the Blue Jays at U.S. Cellular Field. The Sox won, 5-2.

The "Cell" was no Comiskey Park. Even though Benny was a devout Cubs fan, he still had fond memories of going to the old south side ball park as a kid and cheering for the likes of Hoyt Wilhelm, Tommie Agee, Wilbur Wood, Bill Melton, and Carlos May. Geographically, he was a southsider and should have been a Sox fan. But the first time he set foot in Wrigley Field at age eight and saw the ivy on the outfield walls, he was hooked. This is in someone's neighborhood, he thought as a kid. It didn't matter if the Cubs won or not— mostly not. It was where Babe Ruth called the shot and pointed to the center field wall in the fifth inning of game three of the 1932 World Series and hit a home run right in that spot. Being a Cubs fan also added to his character. He learned to live with heartache, especially after that 1969 fiasco when the Cubs led the Mets by nine and a half games on August 14th then took the dive of the century, finishing eight games back and missing the playoffs. It is safe to assume that all Cubs fans are at least eighty-five percent scar tissue.

The next morning, Sunday, May 24th, 1992, Lt. Jefferson decided to pay Gerald Hill and Frank Stram a surprise visit. It was Lt. Jefferson's day off and he didn't live far from them— just a couple miles. He drove his blue Lincoln down Tyler Road. He thought he'd stop at Frank's house first. God, look at this shit hole, Lt. Jefferson thought, shaking his head as he parked in front of Frank's dilapidated residence. He got out of the car and closed the door behind him. He cautiously approached the house, peering over the fence to see if anyone was in the backyard. He noticed the dog feces and the doghouse but didn't see any animals. His service revolver was in plain view as he knocked on the door. There was no answer. He knocked again, harder, still no answer. Frank's truck was parked on the curb so he assumed someone was home. After waiting a full minute he decided to take a peek in the back. He climbed over the chain link fence. His polished boot immediately sank into a pile of dog dung. Is this place filthy, he thought. I don't see how a rat could live here. All of a sudden he heard loud barking and saw three vicious Pit Bulls charging towards him, gnashing teeth and all. "HOLY FUCK!" he yelled, reflexively pulling his gun out of his shoulder holster. He managed to fire off five quick shots, instantly killing two of the dogs and wounding the third. Though injured, the wounded beast was able to leap onto the Lieutenant and latch onto his left arm with his steel jaws, pinning the officer to the ground. Lt. Jefferson valiantly fought him off by pounding the dog on the head several times with his gun until the ferocious animal retreated. Upon hearing the commotion, Frank bolted from his house carrying a loaded shotgun, and like an insane man, ran outside to help his pets, pointing the barrel directly at the Lieutenant's face.

"GET UP NIGGER!" Frank demanded, maintaining a firm grip on his weapon. "I said GET UP NIGGER!"

Lt. Jefferson's sleeve was torn to shreds and his arm bloodied as he retrieved his ID from his inside pocket.

"I'm Lt. Otis Jefferson of the Gary Police Department. Put the gun down, NOW!"

Frank didn't believe him.

"I said GET UP NIGGER. DROP THAT FUCKING PISTOL AND PUT YOUR HANDS ABOVE YOUR HEAD!"

Lt. Jefferson had no choice. He dropped his gun to the ground and did what Frank asked.

"If you would just look at my ID," Lt. Jefferson pleaded. "I am an officer of the law."

Frank looked around and saw a squad car screech up in front of his house. And then two more. Frank's neighbor across the street called the cops when he heard the shots go off. Four officers rushed to rescue Lt. Jefferson. Outnumbered, Frank lifted the butt of his shotgun and pointed the barrel to the ground, then dropped it when the other cops drew on him.

"I was just protecting my property," Frank explained, while being handcuffed.

A minute later an ambulance arrived—on their tail, a reporter and photographer from the Post Tribune. Lt. Jefferson walked to the ambulance on his own power as the paramedics tended to him.

"Let him go," Lt. Jefferson said to the other officers. "I really do believe he was protecting his property."

Frank rubbed his wrists after being released from the cuffs.

"What are you doing snooping around my yard?" Frank demanded.

Lt. Jefferson brushed off the paramedics' attempts to help and escorted Frank to his house to talk in private. The wounded Pit Bull expired.

The inside of Frank's house was worse than the outside. There was even more dog shit and an overwhelming stench of urine. Garbage everywhere and broken toilets. Lt. Jefferson pulled a handkerchief out from his back pocket and covered his mouth and nose while he talked to Frank.

"I'm here to help you," Lt. Jefferson said, almost gagging on the odor. "I knocked on your door first but you didn't answer."

Frank looked gaunt and filthy. His stubbly brown beard was sprinkled with dried food particles. His sweat shirt was stained with who knows what. Amongst the debris were dozens of empty malt liquor cans.

"Hey, my dogs are legal. I didn't do anything."

Lt. Jefferson cleared his throat, somewhat getting used to the smell.

"I'm not here about your damn dogs. I came here to ask you about the recent murders in Miller. You must have heard about them."

Frank dropped to the floor, displacing a dozen beer cans, then sat himself up on a badly worn couch.

"ME?" Frank shrieked. "ME? You think I did it?"

Lt. Jefferson, still holding his left arm from the dog bites, motioned to Frank with his right hand.

"No, we don't think you murdered anyone," he assured Frank. "We do know that you knew the two deceased men. We don't have any suspects yet, but we are pursuing a lead. We also know you know who that is—Benjamin Weinstein."

Frank pushed himself off his worn out couch and stood up

straight next to the lieutenant. The Post Tribune reporter had his ear pressed against the front window. Lt. Jefferson escorted Frank to the kitchen—out of the reporter's earshot.

"When was the last time you saw either one of the deceased?" Lt. Jefferson asked.

Frank opened his refrigerator door and took out an already opened can of Colt 45, offering the first sip to the officer who politely declined. He downed the rest of the can in one pull.

"Aaaarrrrrrp," Frank burped while wiping his mouth with his sleeve. "I haven't seen Tommy Gunther for quite some time," Frank said. "Ever since he got all important and rich with that tire shop of his he stopped calling me. Ten years maybe. Probably afraid I'd borrow some money."

Lt. Jefferson made a mental note of that, unable to scribble in his notebook.

"What about Murphy Spevacek?" asked the cop.

"Murphy?" Frank beamed. "I see him every day. He works at the mill with me. Good friend of mine. When I heard he was killed I figured he pissed off someone at a bar. Hell, he doesn't hang with too many people aside from Chrissy and his kid."

"Chrissy. Who's Chrissy?" Lt. Jefferson asked, suffering a brief memory lapse. He had seen her name mentioned in a report.

"The mother of his boy, Chad," said Frank. "He's a good kid. Real close to his dad.....I guess not no more."

Lt. Jefferson reached for his notepad from the inside of his torn jacket and tucked it under his armpit. He was still too lame to write.

"Okay, thanks," said the Lieutenant as he made his way out. "That'll be all for now. Sorry about your dogs, but I had no choice."

Frank was relieved he wasn't arrested for anything. Those

dogs, in fact, were illegal. He and a few other workers from the mill staged dog fights every two weeks.

"I'm going to send the city a bill for my mutts," Frank said as he saw Lt. Jefferson leave. "You think I'm joking?"

Lt. Jefferson knew Frank had to make it look good. What else would he be doing with those dogs? They were obviously trained to kill.

"Do that," Lt. Jefferson insisted as he walked out the door. "I'll send you a bill for my arm."

Frank looked out the window as the Lieutenant tried walking passed the persistent reporter, who sensed what was going on. The photographer snapped a picture of Lt. Jefferson holding his bloody arm.

"LIEUTENTENT!" the reporter shouted. "Is this man somehow connected to the lakeside murders?"

Lt. Jefferson brushed him off with "No comment." The other cops gathered the dead dogs and put their carcasses in the ambulance. They had to be tested for rabies.

"I'll drive myself to the hospital," Lt. Jefferson said, waving off the medics. "I'll be at Mercy in twenty minutes."

The scene in front of Frank's house cleared, but Frank was scared. He called Gerald as soon as the last squad car pulled away.

"Hey Skunk," Frank said, calling Gerald by his more familiar name. "I think the police are on their way to your house. Get the fucking dogs inside. Mine almost killed a nigger cop and the nigger shot 'em all."

There was a moment of hesitation.

"What do they want with me?" Gerald panicked. "Someone tip them off about this Friday's fight?"

"No, no. Don't ask too many fucking questions. The phones could be bugged. The nigger just wants to know about our murdered buddies. We're in the clear. We don't know who did this. But he mentioned our old friend Benny Weinstein. Benny! Can you fucking believe this? Benny, that wimpy piece of shit. Can you imagine him having the balls to do something like that?"

"All right. All right," Gerald yelled. "I'll put the dogs in the house. But why did the nigger tell you about Benny? Does he think we're next?"

Chapter Thirty-Five

Monday morning, May 25th, 1992. The last thing Lt. Jefferson wanted was publicity. He didn't plan on shooting Frank's dogs and alarming his neighbors. But the Post Tribune's bold headline on that day read "OFFICER MAULED WHILE INVESTIGATING MURDER LEAD." Worse, the story mentioned Frank by name and street. That's all Benny had to see. He knew he had to work fast if he were to finish off Frank and Gerald. He knew the world was looking at him. He needed help.

After seeing his last patient that day at 4:30 p.m., Benny called J.J.'s from the payphone inside Harley's Bowling Alley, which was about three miles from his office. Rings answered.

"Rings?" Benny said softly.

"Yo!"

"This is Benny. I need you to do me a favor."

"Sox? Is that you?"

"Yes, yes, Sox. It's me," Benny assured him. "Listen up. I need you to deliver the stuff I ordered last week to me. Now, if you can. I'm at a bowling alley on Cline Avenue. Harley's. You probably know where it's at."

It was hard to hear in the busy bowling facility. The senior leagues were already under way. Every few seconds the thunderous sound of pins crashing against the boards could be heard, that, along with dozens of screaming teenagers who came directly from school to chill for a spell.

"I need to talk to you too," Rings said. "About some serious shit that's going down. I can be there in forty-five minutes."

"Okay, thanks," said Benny. "I'll be sitting across from lane nineteen."

There were cops everywhere in Harley's. They had better donuts at their coffee shop than most of the donut shops around town. And it was open 24 hours. None of this bothered Benny as he casually walked up to the snack counter, past the cops, and ordered a large cup of coffee—one cream, one sugar. Why not smoke a fat cigar and have a cup a coffee while I'm waiting? he thought. He also thought he'd have a nice relaxing wait—that is until a few patrons chimed in about the murders.

"I heard it was a jealous boyfriend who killed those guys," one bowler said.

"A jealous boyfriend?" said his buddy. "His girlfriend was seeing both of them? That poor schmuck doesn't know how lucky he is. I'd give anything to dump my old lady."

Benny tried not to smile and puffed on his cigar a little more ambitiously.

"I wonder if the guy who did it also kills women," said the buddy. "I could give him a lot of referrals."

The first bowler laughed like he could relate. Benny could relate, too. His sweet, devoted wife, the wonderful Marsha, the mother of his two darlings, as it turned out, had two-timed him—with his sworn enemy no less. For the first time during his marriage he felt like a free man. Even freer since he was ridding himself of almost twenty years of angst. His mind had been constipated for nearly two decades and he finally found a laxative.

Benny sipped his coffee and savored his thick Punch cigar for almost forty minutes. There he was, just sitting, puffing, and relaxing while watching the amateur bowlers gyrate, and using body English in an effort to make a spare. A predictable high pitched shrill always followed a successful roll. Suddenly, there was a hard rap on his shoulder.

"Sox!" said Rings. "Wake up!"

Benny's eyes shot open.

"Oh, fuck, Rings. You scared me."

Rings took off his cap and wiped his eyes. He was carrying a wrinkled brown lunch bag—Benny's stash.

"Jesus, man," Rings said. "You seem a little jumpy."

Benny regained his composure then tapped the thick ash off his stogie. He drank the last of his coffee and motioned for Rings to follow him. Rings put his cap back on and followed Benny outside.

"What's going on Sox? Are you in trouble too?"

Benny didn't expect that.

"What do you mean, 'too'?"

Rings looked both ways then handed Benny the bag.

"Look, Sox," Rings continued as they walked to Benny's car, "J.J. said he can't get this stuff anymore."

Benny unlocked his car. Rings got in the passenger side. Benny buckled up and asked Rings to do the same.

"Why not?" Benny asked as he started the motor and pulled out of the parking lot.

"The guy J.J. is gett'n this from is worried. He read in the newspaper about the murders down by the lake and this guy's afraid we're the ones supplying him."

Benny pulled off to the side of the road next to a laundromat. He plucked his half smoked cigar from the ashtray and lit it with his Cub's lighter then took a few hard pulls, quickly clouding up the interior.

"You are!" Benny revealed.

Rings just sat there with his mouth open. Benny had just confessed that he was the murderer everyone was looking for.

"Give that to me again," Rings nervously said while tightening his cap on his head.

Benny didn't hesitate.

"I did it," Benny confessed. "And I've got two more to go."

Rings wiped his face with his right hand and held onto the dashboard with his left as Benny peeled onto the street, making his way to Balmoral Park for the evening.

"Why did you tell me?" Rings nervously asked, not knowing for sure if he could trust this white guy he met not long before.

"Because I need your help," Benny said. "I know I'm being followed. I know they already suspect me. A cop came to my house the other day then paid a visit to one of the other guys who's gonna get it soon. I need your help."

"Whoa, man! Whoa. I don't know about this. J.J. and me are in deep enough as it is."

Benny looked at Rings and read the terror on his young face.

"You don't have to worry about me," Benny said while giving Rings a fatherly pat on the arm. "I wouldn't hurt you any more than I would hurt your dear mother or your deceased father. Eddy was a dear, dear friend of mine. I'm doing this just as much for him as for me. I know Eddy wouldn't do the thing I'm doing. His heart was too good, rest his soul. These motherfuckers tormented me as well as your father all through school. They beat the shit out of me after my high school graduation. They murdered your father. They were the ones. They raped your mother. You think I can just forget it? Just like that? Eddy was great. Your mother is an angel. Eddy was the best friend I ever had. I'm doing this for him too, Rings. And for Twila. They murdered your father. They raped your mother. Do you understand? They were the ones. They murdered Eddy, Rings. They cut him bad. I'm doing it for him."

Rings immediately calmed down and felt at ease with Benny and agreed to help any way he could. He now had a second father to look after him. At that moment he could almost hear his daddy's voice he never knew. Eddy was telling him, "Everything is going to be all right." Rings felt he owed it to his late father and his disabled mother to go along with this. Nineteen years wasn't too late.

"Where are we going?" Rings asked as he helped himself to one of Benny's expensive cigars he found in the glove compartment.

"We're going to bet the ponies," Benny said as he turned onto I-94. "That is, if you want to go."

Rings bit the end off the big cigar and grabbed the Cub's lighter from Benny's front pocket, then lit the Presidente. They were buds now.

"Of course I want to go!" Rings said. "Are you buying?"

Benny took the lighter from Rings and lit the remainder of his nearly depleted heater.

"I'm buying," Benny assured as he puffed while pulling a wad of Benjies from his left pants pocket. "I got a couple of good tips tonight. We're going to make a lot of money."

There was a short period of silence, maybe a minute or two. Benny had to ask Rings to do him not one, but two big favors. This first one was to lie to the cops if he was questioned about them knowing one another. The other favor was bigger: Benny had to use Rings' car to carry out the rest of the plan. Rings was driving a later 70s model white GMC Suburban which was perfect since it featured a covered bed. He planned on asking him after the races.

It took a little over a half hour to drive the twenty miles to Balmoral Park on South Dixie Highway in Crete, Illinois. Benny and Rings talked the whole way. It was the first time they really got acquainted. Benny told Rings the story about how Eddy once got him out of a difficult situation while hustling chess one night in Chicago.

"Your father only had his driver's license a few months before his junior year at Wirt," Benny said as Rings intently listened to every word. "He borrowed his neighbor's big old beat up 1959 Pontiac Catalina. I don't know if you've ever seen one of those. It was a long coupe with really gaudy looking tail fins. This one was gray and rusty with a loud broken muffler. There was no way to roll into town unnoticed."

Rings smiled and relit his cold stogie as Benny continued with the story.

"Your father loved that car and borrowed it often. That was the year he got that lifeguard job. Those were happier times— until later that summer. And you know what happened."

"Okay," Rings interrupted, not wanting to rehash the disturbing details of his father's beating. "So where did he take you?"

"To the LaSalle Hotel in Chicago. In the Loop! What did I know? I told him I really wanted to go there. Your father was almost three years older than I was and I thought he knew what he was doing when he headed for the Dan Ryan Expressway during rush hour. He was way out of his league. He never drove past Lake Street until then."

Rings let out a little snort, laughing at the irony. This is something he himself would do.

"But I wasn't scared," Benny continued. "Eddy dodged

and wove through traffic like he was riding a bumper car at a carnival. He was fearless. And what did he care? The car was old and rusted anyway. And we managed to get there. How? I don't know. But the biggest problem we had was parking. Every metered spot was taken and the garages charged a fortune—something we weren't willing to pay for. So you know what your father did?"

"I can only imagine!" Rings exclaimed, desperately wanting to hear everything about his crazy dad.

"He parked at the police station across the street!"

"Ha! That's fucking great!" said Rings. "That took balls."

"Sure did," said Benny. "He figured no one would tow his car in a police lot. And he was right. So then we got out of the car and entered the old musty LaSalle Hotel. It's no longer there. They tore that down sometime in the mid 70s. Anyway, the Chicago chess club met at the LaSalle every Tuesday evening from 5:30 to 9:55 p.m. The management closed the playing room by 10:00 p.m. and used that extra five minutes to clear the place."

"Did my father play chess too?"

"He did," said Benny. "But he mainly was doing me a favor. I was getting pretty good, but just around school. There weren't many club players around and I wanted to really see how good I was by playing some veterans. So we sat down at a table and set up our own chess board and clock that we brought with us. There were only a dozen or so people playing that evening. No tournament. They were just playing skittles."

"What's skittles?" Rings asked.

"Casual chess, usually five minutes a game timed on the clock," explained Benny. "I heard of the club and since it was in the city I thought it was big time. It really wasn't—just ordinary people playing chess. I don't remember seeing any masters. So there we were—just playing for fun. Then I had an idea. I quietly asked Eddy if he wanted to play for ten dollars a game. Not real money. And no one had to pay if they lost. But I wanted to show off like I was some kind of hustler who just blew into town. Yes, I was a cocky kid. Eddy agreed. He and I put a ten spot under the clock like we were playing for real. The game started and I lost right away."

"My dad was better than you?" Rings asked excitedly.

"No, he wasn't a serious player. He didn't waste his life like I did playing chess all the time. We planned it that way. So after I lost I acted like your father got lucky and I put up a stink. I kept saying 'double or nothing' but he wouldn't rematch and he said, 'I don't want to take any more of your money.' I kept pleading with him and he kept refusing. But another guy in the room, a forty-something-year-old truck driver challenged me. 'I'll play you,' he said. And I said no, telling him I didn't want to take his money. This pissed him off. And he said, 'I see you can't back up your big mouth.' Eddy tried not to smile the whole time."

"So did you play him?" asked Rings.

"Yes, but wait. I finally agreed to play him, but only for a dollar a game."

"I can see what's coming, Sox," added Rings. "You're a hustler."

"Maybe, but not a good one," admitted Benny. "So I played him a game of five-minute speed chess and lost the dollar."

"On purpose?"

"Yes, on purpose! The guy was talking out of his ass. He couldn't play. So then I said 'double or nothing.' He agreed. We played. I won. So I was up a buck."

"Then what?"

"Then I said I had to go, even though we just got there. But the guy wouldn't have any of that. He wanted to play double or nothing. We did and I beat him again. And then again and again. Soon I was up a hundred and twenty-eight bucks! That was *real* money in those days. And then I really wanted to go—with the cash!"

"Did he pay you?"

"Not at first. I asked for it, but he kept wanting to play to win it back and wouldn't show me the cash. So there I was, barely fourteen years old, trying to collect a bet from a guy as old as my father."

"So tell me, did you get the money?"

"Your dad got it for me! Your father picked up the clock and tucked it under his arm. I folded up the chess set, ready to go home. Your father was wearing a light jacket and slowly slid his hand in the inside pocket, like he had a gun or something. And there was a bulge over the pocket—something big. 'ARE YOU GOING TO PAY MY FRIEND?' he shouted, keeping his hand in the jacket. Everyone in the club was scared to death. The grossly obese club director, Richard Weber, shuffled his way to the door, probably to call the cops. Then the truck driver reached in his wallet and pulled out exactly a hundred and twenty-eight bucks and set it on the table."

"My dad was the man!" Rings blurted, relishing every word.

"He was. Then after I picked up the money from the table, Eddy pulled a banana out from that pocket, peeled it and took a bite—then offered some to the truck driver who refused. 'Don't worry,' your father said. 'It isn't loaded!' I wanted to laugh but I was getting nervous myself and wanted to get the hell out of there. Richard Weber sat down and resumed his game. The truck driver stormed out of the room. Your father and I waited until the truck driver was good and gone. Then we left."

"What did you do with the money?" Rings asked.

"We split it. I kept forty bucks and gave your father the rest. He had more expenses than I did, driving and all. I also knew he had a date with your mother the next day. Plus without him I never would have collected a cent."

"I wish I had known him. He sounds like a cool dude."

"Oh, I forgot one thing: When we went to get our car there were two cops standing next to it, examining the license plates and trying to figure out who it belonged to. So without them asking, Eddy pulled out his newly minted driver's license and showed it to them. One of the officers quickly glanced at it then nodded. Then Eddy pulled out his keys and we got in the car like we belonged in the police parking lot. As we pulled out onto LaSalle Street, your father opened the window and said, 'Thanks for looking after my car,' to one of the cops. Yes, he was the best."

Benny and Rings arrived at Balmoral around 6:15 p.m. The harness track was also running live that night, not just the simulcasts from other tracks around the country. The live heats didn't begin until seven that evening. Benny was only interested in the fourth race at Balmoral which was due to go off at around 8:20 p.m. A harness trainer, Stan Gardino, was one of Benny's patients and gave him a tip: Gerald's Pal, a five-year-old Standardbred gelding out of the Mark Winters stable, which was well known in harness racing circles. Benny couldn't resist the name, Gerald. How fitting—one of the two doomed bullies left that he had to kill—his way.

The track wasn't new to Rings. J.J. took him there on a few occasions starting when Rings was about nine. But Rings never bet much. He never had extra money to gamble. Most of what he and J.J. made went to necessities like paying for Twila's medical bills including tons of medication.

It was a pleasant spring evening that night, about sixty

degrees with a soft breeze coming from the east. Benny paid four dollars for both admissions and bought a racing form. Rings was busy checking out the people at the betting windows and sucking on the remainder of his cigar.

"I wonder how many are winners," Rings said, impressed as he watched an old man stash a bunch of bills in his left front pocket.

"Not many," Benny said. "Losing is how they keep the horses fed."

"Oh shit," cried Rings. "Look!"

There was a stack of Post Tribunes next to the snack bar. The evening headline changed to: POLICE ARE CLOSING IN ON LAKESIDE MURDER SUSPECT. And there were more security officers and regular cops around the track.

"Hey Rings, let's switch hats, quick."

"But you're wearing a Sox cap. Mine says Public Enemy."

"Okay, forget the hat," Benny said. "Just stay close to me and I'll keep my head down."

"What are we going to do until the fourth race?" Rings asked like he didn't want to be bored.

"First thing I'm going to do is buy one of those papers. I wonder who they think it is."

Benny walked over to the snack bar, picked up a paper and put fifty cents on the counter, not waiting for his fifteen cents change. He scanned the story.

"Oh Jesus!" Benny exclaimed, the look of relief emanating from his face. "Fucking Jesus!"

Rings rushed to his side.

"What? What?" Rings asked. "What happened?"

"They think it's a drug dealer but they don't say who. Can you believe it?"

"Hey Sox, I hate to burst your bubble, but I think it's a trick—intended for you," Rings said, spoken like the streetwise youth he was.

"You think so? You believe that?"

"Sure I do," Rings continued. "Why would they print a story like that with no name? If they had someone, they'd say something like 'alleged drug dealer' then mention his name."

"Not necessarily," Benny said. "If they haven't charged him with anything, then he's not a suspect. It's a legal thing."

There were a lot of people at the track that night. Many were waiting to bet on the ninth race, a $50,000.00 stakes race that featured the top performers from around the country. Benny didn't plan on staying that long. He needed to talk to Rings then leave after the fourth race.

"Let's bet on that Houston track," Rings said while watching the myriad of simulcasts on the overhead monitors.

"Sure, we can do that," Benny said with the intent on teaching this kid a lesson. "That is, if you want to throw away your money and just play numbers. You have no idea what's going to happen."

Rings grabbed Benny's racing form from his hand.

"We've got it right here," said Rings, pointing to the Texas Thoroughbred card. "They list Sam Houston too."

Benny shook his head. "Yeah, and they also list every other track as well. But you've got to have inside information, man. I wouldn't come here without it. Those other tracks could be fixed."

"They still do that?" Rings asked in amazement. It was an astonishing question from someone who should know a little about bending the rules. "So you're saying this track isn't?"

Benny snatched back his program. "I'm not saying it is or isn't. But I do know one thing—you can't handicap larceny."

Benny parentally handed Rings a twenty and a five. "Here, bet a trifecta. Box four horses for twenty-four bucks. That's a one dollar box. Bet.....I don't know. Bet your birth year."

"I can't bet my birth year with four numbers. I was born in '71. I can't use two 'ones'."

"Then change the last 'one' to a 'two'," Benny suggested. "You only need to get three numbers right."

Rings happily took the bills and walked to a betting window. "Sam Houston, third race, one dollar trifecta box, 1-9-7-2," he said to the teller as he handed him the twenty-five dollars, got his one dollar change and took the ticket.

Rings hurried back to Benny who was sitting by himself at a table away from the action.

"Well, I got it!" Rings optimistically stated while showing Benny the ticket. "See? I bet 1-9-7-2. That's a winner."

Benny glanced up at the TV monitors and noticed the third race at Sam Houston was about to start.

"You may as well tear it up now," Benny said, assuring Rings he just bought a losing ticket. "The '1' horse is 5-1. The '9' horse is 15-1. And the '2' and '7' are both 30-1. Good luck!"

"Fine," Rings said. "But like you said, only three of them have to come in."

The race went off and Benny got up to pee—didn't even wait for the race to finish. When he got back he saw Rings with a shit-eating grin on his baby face.

"What now?" Benny asked. "You shit in your pants?"

"No, but you will," Rings said as he stuck the nub of his now disgusting cigar in the corner of his mouth, like a toothpick, then waved the ticket above his own head like a flag.

"What?" Benny asked. "You won? Get out!"

Rings could hardly contain his excitement as he rechecked the monitor. Plain as day it said 9-2-7. The '1' horse, which had the shortest odds, didn't even run in the money. All long shots came in.

"Let me see that," Benny demanded.

Rings handed him the ticket. He wasn't lying. Now all there was left to do was wait for the payoffs.

"No one gets this lucky!" Benny jealously remarked, handing the ticket back to Rings. "My guess is you won at least two grand." Benny was actually very happy for Rings.

Rings tucked the ticket in his front shirt pocket then sat down to wait. It seemed like forever, but the trifecta price finally appeared on the screen—$6,340.40! Rings had a one dollar ticket which meant he had half of that.

"HOLY FUCK!" Rings screamed. "HOLY, HOLY FUCK!!"

"Shhhhh—not so loud," Benny scolded. "You're attracting attention. The last thing you want to do is let others know you won. Keep it to yourself."

Rings put his hands to his face and fidgeted with his cap. "I won over thirty-one hundred bucks!"

"Yeah, you did. But not so fast," Benny said like he knew something bad would come of this.

"What do you mean?" Ring asked, smelling trouble.

"You're going to have to sign for that and fill out a tax form."

"Why?"

"Anytime you win when the odds are 300-1 or greater, they make you fill out a tax form. You have to show your driver's license and everything. Or......"

"Or what?"

"Or you can get someone else to cash your ticket who doesn't care what he declares on his taxes. There's a lot of guys out here who make a living doing that."

"I don't know anybody here," Rings said. "Do you?"

"I do, but I don't want to ask anyone I know. Not now. You're going to have to take the ticket home with you and maybe ask J.J. to cash it. Or your mother, Twila."

Rings finally composed himself long enough to think clearly.

"Momma could sure use the money," said Rings. "And I'll be glad to give it to her. But I don't think she could cash it either. It might interfere with her disability benefits."

"That's right," Benny said as he motioned for Rings to follow him outside to the grandstands where they could talk alone before the live races started.

Benny and Rings sat on a bleacher, up twenty rows in a remote corner of the stands. It was getting cooler with the wind blowing slightly harder than when they first arrived. Benny took out a small notebook and quickly jotted down his plan for the rest of the night. Rings patted his front pocket, reassuring himself his huge windfall was safe. It was.

"We still have an hour and a half wait until the fourth race," Benny said. "We can't stick around that long. I've got something to do and I'd like you to come with me."

"But what about my ticket," Rings said. "Why can't I cash it? J.J. doesn't pay me that much where it would make a difference in my taxes."

Benny lowered the bill of his Sox cap down to his eyebrows. He fished a fresh cigar from the inside pocket of his spring jacket then raised the racing form, concealing his face.

"What's going on?" Rings asked. "Someone you know?"

"Be quiet for a second," Benny said. "Just look straight ahead. I think I see someone I know. He's way on the bottom. Don't look! Is that who I think it is?"

"Who? Where?" asked Rings, looking for someone familiar.

"Please!" Benny pleaded. "Just look straight ahead and follow me."

Both of them walked along the upper part of the bleachers until they came to the end near the clubhouse. Benny looked down for a second and saw the man was gone.

The live races were about to start. Both the upper and lower levels of the track had betting windows. As long as he was closer to the upper level, Benny decided to make his fourth race bet there and leave. He and Rings walked up to the betting window. Benny took out a wad of hundreds and softly called out his bet to the teller: "Balmoral, fourth race, eight hundred to win on Gerald's Pal, number 5." The program odds on Gerald's Pal were 9-1, but that could change by post time. Benny looked at the ticket and clipped it to his billfold and put it in his left pants pocket. He and Rings made their way to the exit.

"Let's go," Benny said while pulling out his keys.

"In a few minutes," Rings said, hesitating for an instant. "I have to drop the kids off at the pool."

"Do what?" Benny asked.

"I have to take a shit!"

"Oh, okay. Why didn't you say so?

Rings headed for the nearest toilet.

"I'll be waiting in the car," Benny blurted out. "Try not to take too long."

Benny walked to his car and sat inside to wait for Rings. He took out his notepad and jotted down a few more things. Yeah, yeah, thought Benny. We have to do this tonight, sloppily scribbling with his silver steel pen.

Fifteen minutes went by as Benny patiently waited for Rings. Then he heard three loud knocks on the back window. Bang! Bang! Bang! It was Rings.

"You scared me," Benny said, catching his breath while Rings got in the passenger's side. "There's nothing subtle about you. What the hell took you so long?"

Rings buckled up and pulled a new cigar from the glove compartment.

"Hey, man—nine White Castles with cheese can plug up the plumbing."

Benny shook his head as he pulled out of the parking lot. "Oh, you pig you. You ate nine sliders with cheese today?"

"Yeah, but they gone now," Rings said, patting his intestines.

"Good. I'm glad you feel better because we got a long night ahead of us."

Chapter Thirty-Six

Monday evening, May 25th, 1992. It was approaching 9 p.m. Both Gerald and Frank took a sick day and stayed home from work. They needed time alone to talk about things—like what the Lieutenant said about Benny. Frank went to Gerald's house and sat in his unbelievably filthy living room, drinking Bud and smoking Kool 100's. It was the kind of environment Frank was used to. Gerald's four Pit Bulls were caged in the kitchen and barked like the mad dogs they were when Gerald arrived just minutes earlier. The tormented beasts calmed down when they recognized Gerald's familiar smell.

"That nigger has me worried," Frank said, referring to Lt. Jefferson. "He made a special trip to my house just to tell me. He could have easily called me up. I'm in the book."

Gerald brought another cold six pack from the refrigerator and placed it on the floor next to Frank's feet. An ashtray loaded with cigarette butts, smoked to the nub, sat on an old splintered stack of pallets, Gerald's coffee table. Though not barking, the dogs were whining plenty in the background as the two friends chatted.

"I called Chrissy earlier today," Gerald said. "She's all broken up about Murphy—said Chad hasn't said a word since the funeral."

Frank looked around the room and put his hands to his mouth.

"Man, it stinks in here more than usual," Frank said, who usually didn't complain about such things. "Have the dogs been inside all day?"

Gerald grabbed a beer and lit a cigarette.

"Yeah, they have. I was just about to let them out when you came."

"Why don't you do that," Frank said. "I'm sad about my dogs. The nigger cop killed 'em all."

Gerald opened the cages and let the dogs out through the broken back screen door. All four relished their first taste of freedom of the day and careened out all at once, scampering around the backyard like they were trying out a new set of legs. They tired after a few minutes, then settled in their dog houses for the evening.

"We've got to do something about that motherfucker," Frank said while Gerald reclined on his huge soft couch.

"If you're referring to Benny the Jew you may as well forget it," Gerald assured his anxious buddy. "That kike doesn't have the balls to kill anyone. He's a scared rabbit. Motherfucker, sending us to the pen like that. No, it's someone else. Now think, who did Tommy and Murphy piss off?"

Frank took a long drag from his menthol cigarette and chugged the rest of his beer.

"Weinstein, the Jew, that's who!" Frank exclaimed. "I don't think Tommy spoke to Murphy all that much. Ever since Tommy got all big with his shop he stopped talking to all of us. It's got to be the Jew."

"It just doesn't make sense," Gerald surmised. "What would make him do something like this after all these years? If he wanted us dead he would have done that years ago."

It was 9:17 p.m. and completely dark outside. Tyler Road had street lights but most were broken. The city didn't allocate any funds to fix them and no one complained. Everyone on the block liked it that way. The black of night also suited Benny and Rings. After leaving the track they drove back to the bowling alley so Rings could get his suburban. Benny told Rings to follow him. It was going to take a while. They drove to Stagecoach Road. Rings didn't know why but he dutifully followed his new dad to that old deserted road. Rings followed him all the way to the tree. *The* tree. Benny's tree. Benny had to show it to Rings.

Benny parked his car deep to the side, past some bushes and into the woods, where it remained out of sight. Rings parked his white GMC next to Benny's. They both got out of their vehicles and Benny touched Rings on his shoulder.

"Follow me," Benny said, escorting Rings to the Jon boat where all of the evidence was stashed.

Though nervous, Rings curiously followed Benny until they came upon the hidden boat. Benny took off the cover, revealing his pistol, tranquilizer gun, drugs, clothes, pictures—everything.

"So now you know I'm for real," Benny said while Rings gasped and adjusted his Public Enemy cap. "It's all here. Everything you sold me—the guns, Sucostrin, needles, the works."

"My God," Rings said. "Look at all this shit."

"Take a good look," said Benny, showing Rings a picture he took of Tommy shortly after decapitating him in the lagoon.

Rings grabbed the picture and studied it then gave it back to Benny.

"Jesus, he doesn't look human," Rings gasped as a bead of sweat dripped down his forehead. "Oh shit, I touched it. I've got my fingerprints on it."

Benny snickered. "Don't worry about that. I'm going to destroy everything in a few days. Here, take a look at these, too," handing Rings another set of prints. They were pictures of Tommy and Murphy being tortured.

"I took these pictures here," Benny said as he pointed to the exact spot on the ground. "Right here! Right in the spot I'm standing now. Right here!"

"What are we doing right here?" Rings pensively asked as he handed the other photos back to Benny.

Benny took a few items from the boat then went to his car and pulled out the bag of drugs Rings brought that night.

"I need your help," Benny said. "Can we use your truck?"

It was now approaching 10:45 p.m. Frank and Gerald were good and plastered and passed out—Gerald on his couch and Frank on the urine stained carpet. The dogs remained outside, drinking up the cool spring air and fast asleep.

Benny left his car on Stagecoach Road. Benny drove while Rings did his best to clean the inside of his messy GMC during the trip—mostly fast food wrappers. They were on their way to Gerald's house. Benny had no idea Gerald was home. He only had one thing in mind that night—get rid of the dogs.

"I'd like to stop and tell J.J. I'm with friends," Rings said. "He gets all worried when I don't call."

"Okay, good idea," Benny agreed. "You can make a call from the Gas 'N Go. Does J.J. know you're with me?"

"Yes, I told him I was making a delivery. Don't worry—everything's cool."

Benny pulled into the gas station and parked close to the front entrance. Rings got out.

"Be back in less than a minute," Rings said while pulling a quarter out from his pants pocket.

Benny waited. His eyes immediately fixed at the sign next door: Gunther Tire & Auto Supply. *I wonder who's minding* the store? Benny thought. Gee, I hope business is good. You know, a thing like murder can really put a damper on business. I sure hope it's going well.

Rings emerged from the store with a smile on his face.

"What's so funny?" Benny asked. "A girl make a pass at you or something?"

Rings got in the car, smiling ear to ear.

"J.J. told me he and Twila were arguing about money just now—says he needs a few thousand dollars to buy a powered wheelchair for Twila and doesn't know where he can come up with the money. I didn't tell him about the money I won. I want to surprise everyone."

"You're a fine son, Rings. Eddy would have been real proud of you. You're just like him."

Rings took that as the supreme compliment. He only heard good things about his father and wanted desperately to be like him. And what better than to hear these things from someone who knew him best.

They got back in the car and drove west down Route 12, heading towards Tyler Road. But they had to prepare.

"Rings, load up a Sucostrin dart for me please."

"Sure Sox. What do you plan on doing with it?"

"I've got to take care of a dog or two. Have a few more ready just in case."

Rings prepared half a dozen darts. He knew what he was doing and had them all ready in less than five minutes.

"I just thought of something," Rings said. "Don't you have to call your wife? Doesn't she care where you are?"

Benny tucked a cold cigar in his mouth and looked at Rings like he already should know.

"What?" Rings asked. "What did I say?"

"Nothing," said Benny. "Yes, I'm married to a pretty, smart, capable, shapely lady who gave birth to two wonderful children."

"So? Sounds like a winner."

"I thought so too. But she's also a two-timer. Do you know who she was fucking around with? Tommy, that's who. One of the guys I killed. You know that tire center next to the gas station we were just at—that was Tommy's."

"No shit!" Rings said. "How do you know she was fucking him? Tommy tell you?"

"She accidently left that information on our answering machine while she was talking to one of her girlfriends. She doesn't know I know. I don't care to call her. In fact I'm through with her, only she doesn't know it. When Frank and Gerald are dead, then I'm gone. Outta there!"

"Gee, that's too bad," Rings said. "I mean, fucking around with the guy you hated most."

"Not as bad as all that—kind of gives me the freedom I've been missing all these years," Benny added. "If you ever get married you'll see what I mean."

"Nope, not me!" Rings said, confidently confirming his bachelorhood. "I like the ladies too much and they like me. Marriage is out of the question."

"Yeah, that's right," Benny said, smiling at Rings' naivety. "You think you know women because you haven't been caught yet. Here you are, young, smart, good looking and personable. No doubt women like you. But one day you'll meet someone and say one stupid thing after another like 'I love you,' and 'I can't live without you,' and other shit like that. And before you know it she'll be making wedding plans and you'll go along with it—not knowing what you're getting into—then you'll think it's too late to back out. But it isn't—only you don't know that."

"Is that what happened to you?"

"Word for word," Benny said. "And the worst part is that

she was very pretty. And you think, 'Wow, will I ever find another girl like that!' Okay, man," Benny said to his clueless pal. "You know best. Just keep fixing those darts."

They turned down Tyler Road about 11:25 p.m. Benny stopped Rings' white suburban a block short of Gerald's house and decided to drive behind the row of houses through the narrow alley. Benny was very familiar with these types of alleys. Until he was about five, Benny's family lived near that part of Gary during the days it was still safe to walk the streets at night. He remembered how cluttered his alley was with the old fashioned metal garbage cans and tons of junk from everywhere. Neighbors discarded old swing sets and lawn furniture next to those silver but mostly rusted cans. Kids would have a time playing with that stuff like it was their own personal Adventureland—never mind the filth and the wires sticking out of old mattresses. And oh was it a thrill to see the old orange garbage truck slowly making its way down the alley once a week, and watching the rear loader swallow and compact massive amounts of multi-colored trash—like a giant mechanical elephant.

Benny slowed to 10 mph as he approached the back of Gerald's house. He knew it was Gerald's house when he saw the dog houses and mounds of trash sitting in the tall grass which was mostly weeds. He stopped behind the chain link fence but kept the motor running.

"Where are we?" Rings asked in a voice too loud for the quiet evening.

"Shhh! Not so loud," Benny whispered. "We're behind Gerald Hill's house. You know, that guy who cut your daddy's dick. He was the one. And he's next."

Rings was scared. "You gonna kill him now? Here?"

"Shhh! You're talking too loud," Benny said, scolding Rings. "He's not home. He's at work. I just have to get those damn dogs out of the way. I don't want anything in my way when I come back tomorrow night."

Benny grabbed his tranquilizer rifle and quietly got out of the car. Rings got out too, following Benny close behind with a fistful of loaded darts.

"Look at them," Benny said, pointing to the dogs. "He's got all of his mutts running loose in the yard. Great—now's the time! Hand me a dart."

Benny loaded a dart in the rifle. He knew full well almost any dose of Sucostrin would kill a mammal that small—especially a human-sized dose. One of the dogs was close to the fence and didn't hear Benny approach as he lifted the rifle and took aim from about twelve feet.

Phhhhoooooot! "Bullseye!" Benny exclaimed with delight, nailing the angry Pit Bull in the gluteus maximus.

The dog let out a weak yelp and quickly fell to the ground. "Three more," Benny said. "Give me three more darts."

Rings extended his arm, handing the darts to Benny. The remaining dogs gathered around their wounded friend.

"Good. Very good!" said Benny. "Like shooting fish in a barrel."

Benny remained behind the fence as he shot off another dart—this time hitting a dog in his side. "Hey, there's enough junk in there to kill a moose," Benny bragged to Rings. "That pooch should be dead in short order."

The first dog wasn't moving and his chest wasn't expanding. He was dead. The second one died seconds later. By this time the other two dogs were frantic and making all sorts of noise. Benny put an end to that by firing darts into them too, fumbling only slightly while loading the fourth dart. But the yelps didn't go unnoticed. All of a sudden the kitchen light went on in Gerald's house.

"FUCK!" Benny shouted. "Someone's home!"

Benny hastily tossed the rifle in the back seat while Rings did something really stupid—he jumped over the fence to collect the spent cartridges.

"WHAT THE FUCK ARE YOU DOING?" Benny yelled as he watched Rings collect the useless pieces of plastic. GET IN THE FUCKING CAR!"

"I'M PICKING UP THE EVIDENCE," Rings shouted back, thinking he was doing Benny a favor—not seeing Gerald bolt out from his back door, shotgun in hand and running towards him at full speed. Benny saw Gerald lift up the shotgun and point it at Rings.

"WHAT THE FUCK YOU DOING, NIGGER!" Gerald yelled, not seeing Benny at first. "WHAT THE FUCK YOU DO TO MY DOGS?"

Rings froze in place—the shotgun barrel pointing at his left ear. Benny jumped the fence and ran towards Gerald, tackling him from behind. The shotgun flung into the air and landed next to one of the dead dogs. The strong stench of alcohol permeated from Gerald's mouth as they fell to the ground. Though drunk, Gerald was much stronger than Benny as the two violently wrestled on the ground.

"JAB A DART IN HIM! JAB A DART IN HIM!" Benny cried out to Rings as Gerald overpowered Benny, pinning him to the nasty feces laced soil.

Rings placed a fresh Sucrostrin dart between his thumb and forefinger and jumped on Gerald's back, then, with all of his might, he stabbed the dart in the middle of Gerald's back. The sting of the dart didn't seem to faze Gerald as he punched Benny in the face three times with his hard fists. Each punch to his face brought back vivid memories of the night in '73. It was happening again.

"I knew it was you, you fucking Jew! And you brought a scared nigger along for help, didn't you, you fucking Jew! You killed my buddies, you fucking Jew. Didn't you Jew?" Gerald had both hands around Benny's neck and vigorously shook it, as Benny's helpless head bounced off the ground a dozen times. "Now you're gonna die Jew. Hitler had the right idea. He should have cut your daddy's balls off while he had the chance and put him in the oven, too."

Benny was dazed, and his face was swollen and bloodied, but was still very conscious. Rings was doing his best to pull Gerald off of his buddy but wasn't doing a very good job of it until the drug kicked in. Thankfully, it did. Gerald released Benny's neck and fell backwards. The combination of booze, Sucostrin, and fighting was too much for him. Benny seized the moment to grab the last dart from Rings and forcefully stuck it in Gerald's left thigh. Within two minutes, he was motionless but alive.

"I didn't want to do this tonight," Benny said to Rings. "I just wanted to kill his fucking dogs. I had no idea he was home. Here, help me hoist him in the back of your truck."

Rings lowered the tailgate on his suburban while Benny dragged Gerald's gangly body to the fence. Rings helped Benny lift the listless racist over the fence and into the covered back section.

"Get his shotgun," Benny said while he prepared a few more Sucostrin darts in the back seat.

Rings hurdled over the fence and grabbed Gerald's shotgun. As he picked it up he glanced at the house and saw a face peering out the kitchen window. It was Frank. The commotion woke him up.

"SHIT!" Rings shouted. "Someone else is home!"

"MOTHERFUCKER!" Benny screamed. "IT'S FRANK! HE'S COMING AT YOU!"

Rings clutched the shotgun and leapt over the fence, just making it to his car.

"You're driving," Benny yelled as he grabbed a handful of darts and Sucrostrin and climbed in the back with Gerald. "Drive to Stagecoach Road. To our spot."

The GMC was already running. Rings tossed the shotgun in the back with Benny and jumped in the driver's seat. Still inebriated, Frank reached the fence, wearing a dirty T-shirt, torn jeans and no shoes. He only saw Rings but thought he heard two voices. Rings started to pull away.

"GET BACK HERE NIGGER!" Frank shouted as he glanced at the four dead carcasses then saw the suburban pull away in the dark of night.

As Rings made his way down the alley Benny looked out the back window and saw Frank scramble back to the house— not knowing if he was going to call the cops. But he didn't care. He was all alone in the back with Gerald. Paralyzed Gerald.

It was approaching midnight. Rings mindfully drove the speed limit while driving east on U.S. 20, making his way to Stagecoach Road. Benny was preparing a few more Sucrostin darts and happily chatting with his guest.

"Nice to see you again," Benny said, controlling the conversation while watching Gerald's fearsome, helpless eyes stare at him. "Yes, you are right," Benny continued. "I killed them both. I did. Tommy's gone. Murphy, too. I'm the fucking Jew who did it. Oh, and the nigger, as you so eloquently stated—is driving. He's my friend. You insulted my friend. He's going to assist me tonight. Do you really think he's a nigger? No, I don't think so. I just may give you the benefit of the doubt."

U.S. 20 was unusually quiet for a Monday evening, even though it was past midnight. Normally there were a lot of truckers on the road making their way to the expressway. But not that night. And Rings was glad of that. He just wanted the night to end peacefully.

"Look out there," Benny patronizingly told Gerald while preparing the drug laced darts. "Look out there," Benny stated again, knowing full well his passenger couldn't move nor could see where he was pointing. "Isn't it a lovely evening?" Benny put down a set of five darts. "It's so much like an evening during a fine June evening back in 1973. Do you remember that evening? I do. I really do. Please believe me. I remember that evening. How good is your memory? Do you remember that evening? I'M ASKING YOU A QUESTION, FUCKER!"

Gerald didn't answer. He couldn't answer.

"I hate to repeat myself," Benny said. "I don't stutter as much as I used to, but I still do. When I ask you a question I expect an answer. Now—isn't it a lovely evening?"

The first two doses were slowly wearing off. Benny didn't bring any extra rope along—thinking he didn't need any. He had some in his Jon boat. Gerald was bound only by the chemicals. His right arm flinched and he let out a grunt.

"HOLD STILL, FUCKER!" Benny screamed. "Don't get me mad."

Gerald stopped moving but Benny already had a dart in his hand.

"I wish you hadn't moved just now," Benny softly said, his anger boiling over from a slow simmer, as he grabbed a dart and viciously plunged it into Gerald's right bicep and forcefully kept it there until he got a reaction. Gerald's face winced in pain—the only muscles he could move.

"Hitler had the right idea? No, *I have* the right idea," Benny declared.

Rings turned left onto County Line Road then right onto Stagecoach Road. Every squeak the old suburban made was amplified by the quiet night as the trio rolled down that old deserted road towards the tree. Rings stopped when he came to the spot and pulled off to the side. Benny got out and met Rings on the driver's side.

"Pull all the way into the woods next to my Camry," Benny ordered. "We've got to stay out of sight."

While Rings hid his vehicle, Benny walked to his covered Jon boat, sizing up the task ahead.

"That's good, that's good," Benny said as Rings came to a dead stop. Benny opened the back door and studied his doomed and powerless prey. "Here, help me lift this maggot next to the boat. I just want this over."

Gerald felt and heard everything while they dragged his body behind the Jon boat. His panicked eyes looked upward from the ground. He felt the grip of his captors release and watched while they removed the tarp from the boat. Benny pulled out a knife and his camera while handing a large roll of gray duct tape to Rings.

"Oh, nurse," Benny sarcastically said to Rings. "Before you do anything, put these on," he said, handing Rings a pair of latex gloves. "We have to clean your prints off everything you already touched." Rings' boney fingers squeezed into the stretchy gloves. "Now wrap this around his mouth three times. But make sure he can breathe through his nose."

Rings pulled three feet of tape from the roll, and cradled Gerald's head between his knees while he coiled three tight loops of tape around his victim's mouth. "You wanna suck a big black nigger dick?" Rings asked, noticing how close Gerald's mouth was to his crotch.

"That's good, now drag him here," Benny said. "I want to take some pictures first."

Benny already had a fresh roll of film loaded in his antique camera. He pulled his lantern from the boat and set it high on a branch. The bright glow of the lamp exaggerated Gerald's unfeeling shark-like eyes while Benny steadied the lens and snapped a picture.

"That's only one," Benny said while winding the film to take another black and white. "Pull his pants down. All the way down. I want to get a shot of his dick while it's still in one piece."

Rings did what Benny asked.

"Hey Sox, he's moving! What should I do?"

Benny walked over to Gerald and stuck another dart in his thigh. "Jesus, man, your metabolism must be in high gear," Benny said while looking at Gerald. "You're going through these drugs like Mickey Rooney went through wives. Don't you know these things are expensive?" And with that, Benny jabbed him twice as hard with a second dart, the needle breaking off in his leg. "NOW STAY STILL, FUCKER!" Benny shouted, then swiftly kicked Gerald in the balls three times, one kick for each punch Benny received an hour earlier.

Benny went back to the camera and snapped the picture. Rings was getting anxious to go home.

"Can we finish up now?" Rings politely asked. "It's getting late."

"Yeah," Benny said. "We'll be out of here in five minutes."

Benny got fifteen feet of rope from the boat and made a strong noose. While carrying his lantern, he walked another fifty feet into the woods and threw the end of the rope over a sturdy branch. With the help of an adjacent tree, he climbed up a few feet to tie off the rope so the noose was seven feet off the ground. He left enough slack from the noose to reach from the ground. Then he walked back to Rings.

"Here he is, Rings. This guy right here," Benny said, making sure Gerald heard every word. "This is the creep who cut your daddy. He did it, Rings. This piece of shit killed your father. He was the one, Rings. He did it."

Gerald's eyebrows lifted up as he learned who his other captor was. Eddy's son! The overdose of Sucrostrin made it difficult for him to breathe. Gerald's dark eyes were as big as silver dollars while he gazed at Rings towering over him like a big black statue.

"Give me your knife!" Rings venomously said to Benny. "I want to do the honors."

"Here," Benny said, handing rings the knife and two ghastly pictures of Gerald's mutilated buddies. "Show him these first. I think he's a man who appreciates good art!"

Rings put the pictures in front of Gerald. Benny grabbed the photos from Rings.

"I just remembered," Benny said in his usual sarcastic tone. "You forgot to apologize to my friend over here. If I heard right, it sounded like you called him a nigger. But feel free to correct me if I'm wrong."

Gerald's mouth was still hopelessly bound by the strong duct tape and couldn't answer.

"HE'S NOT A NIGGER," Benny yelled, scolding the racist. "And neither was his father, Eddy Moss. No he wasn't. Eddy was a friend of mine. He was a dear, dear friend of mine. And so was his girlfriend, Twila. You must remember them. You must remember both of them. Now, I'll give you one chance to free yourself from this horrible mess you've gotten yourself into. But you have to do me and Rings here one favor: You must apologize for calling him a nigger. YOU MUST APOLOGIZE NOW! NOW! RIGHT NOW!"

Gerald tried to close his eyes. He knew he was doomed.

"I SAID NOW! APOLOGIZE NOW! NOW! NOW! DO YOU UNDERSTAND?"

Rings looked down at Gerald.

"I don't think he wants to answer you," Rings said. "Maybe he needs some encouragement."

205

"I think you're right," Benny agreed. "But we better encourage him right away. Those drugs I just illegally administered are already starting to wear off. Here, I'll hold him down and you do whatever."

Rings stretched his right leg backward for a warm-up, then furiously kicked Gerald's scrotum five times as hard as he could.

"I'M A NIGGER, HUH?" Rings shouted after the first kick. "A NIGGER?" Another swift kick. "A NIGGER? A NIGGER? A NIGGER?" Kick! Kick! Kick!

Gerald's sac was completely split open and his balls were leaking out.

The two dragged Gerald's alive but bloodied frame fifty feet to the rope. Rings pulled Gerald's pants down the rest of the way to his feet. It took both of them to lift Gerald up and thread his head through the noose. Benny grabbed the slack and tightened the noose around Gerald's cold throat. Rings balanced Gerald on his shoulder while Benny went back to get his camera and lantern. Benny came back and placed the lantern high on a branch.

"YOU KILLED MY DADDY!" Rings yelled as he jumped away, leaving Gerald to hang by his neck. A sickening snapping sound was acutely audible after Gerald dropped—his feet just inches off the ground. The knife fell out of Rings' hand, but he picked it up and slashed Gerald's dangling cock— a geyser of blood splattered the air.

"Look, he's trying to kick," cried Rings. "He's still alive!"

Rings moved out of the way while Benny took a picture.

"Let's put everything back in the boat before we finish him off," Benny said. "He'll keep for another couple of minutes."

Benny and Rings tossed everything back in the boat except for the camera. Benny had planned on developing the film at his office. Benny then went to his Camry, opened the trunk and got out his pistol, loading three bullets. He also grabbed a small flashlight.

"Let's put him out of his misery," Benny said, switching on the light. Rings followed close behind as they walked to the suspended Nazi worshipper.

"That gun's gonna make an awful racket," Rings said. "Why not just stab him a few more times?"

"I would have if he wasn't bleeding so much. My plan was to take him to the Lagoon and finish him off. We can't do that now. I don't want to leave a longer trail."

"We can still dump him in the Lagoon," Rings bravely said. "I think that'd be a real cool thing to do—you know, so he could be like the others."

"One problem with that," Benny said.

"What's that?"

"The cops are probably there. My guess is Frank called them. The lagoon is the first place they'll look."

"You may be right," Rings said.

"After the third shot I want you to drive home—straight home. And I'll do the same. No, better yet, I'm going to my folks. They live just a couple miles away."

"Okay," said Rings. "We'll leave after the third shot."

Benny shined the light on his pistol and aimed it at Gerald's head—his eye's still flickering with life.

"Bang! Bang! Bang!" Gerald's chin slumped to his chest. The bullets left a five-inch crater in his skull. Most of his cerebral cortex was fertilizing the shrubs below.

Both men jogged back to their cars. Benny put the gun, camera, and flashlight back in his trunk.

"Leave his shotgun here," Benny said. "I almost forgot about that. Take the shotgun and toss it underneath his feet."

Rings did as he was told and ran swiftly back, not wanting to be alone with the corpse.

"Now let's blow," Benny said as they both got into their cars. "I'll call you early tomorrow morning."

Rings got to County Line Road first and turned left, then right on U.S. 20, heading towards downtown Gary to be safe at home with J.J. and his disabled mother. Benny turned right onto County Line Road towards his folks. He was profusely perspiring from the experience and lit a half smoked stogie he pulled from the ashtray. He was just about to turn left towards the sand dunes onto Pottawattamie Trail when he saw two flashing squad cars speeding up from behind about two blocks away. He quickly made the left and veered off the wrong way on a one way street which was about a hundred feet down. He floored the engine and peeled past the small solitary three story apartment building just to his left, then swiftly turned left again into an old abandoned lumberyard, cut his lights and turned off the engine. A few seconds later he saw the two squad cars zoom down Pottawattamie, heading towards his Nobel, his old grammar school.

Shit! They know, he thought to himself. I think they know. I think we were followed. That guy I saw at the track. I know it was him. He tipped them off.

By this time it was almost 1:00 a.m. Marsha knew he wasn't at home and the Post Tribune was sure to print headlines about a missing man the next morning—somehow associating it with the two murders. One thing was sure: Benny couldn't go to his folks. Not even to sniff around. So he waited a half hour. He left when two ferocious, loudly barking German Shepherds ran up to his car, gnashing their teeth, and waking up the neighbors. Benny had to pee but was afraid to get out of his car. Someone in a third floor apartment turned a light on and peeked out the window through the drapes. That's when Benny pulled his sun visor down and drove back towards County Line Road. He looked both ways and didn't see any cops, or for that matter, any cars. He turned right onto County Line Road. For the first time during this mission he was really scared. He knew he had his camera and gun in the trunk. He knew he still had a few darts tucked in his jacket. He also had the feeling he was being followed, but he didn't see anyone. As he drove down County Line Road his brain erupted with a vivid flashback to that night in '73. I got three of those fuckers now, he thought. He drove another mile. "Yes, three are dead," he muttered to himself. "One to go!"

It was 1:12 a.m. Stagecoach Road was coming up just to his left when he saw a pair of headlights in his rearview mirror, a block away, but gaining on him. It wasn't a squad car. He didn't know who it was. He turned sharply to his left onto Stagecoach Road, mashing the gas pedal all the way to the floor. Gravel and dirt peppered his windshield as he sped down that dark road for half a mile and didn't see lights approaching. Satisfied he wasn't followed, he drove to the tree and parked his car deep into the woods. It was pitch black. The moonlight didn't help. He got out and opened his trunk, removing his pistol and camera. He grabbed his flashlight but didn't turn it on. He was cold. Benny zipped up his jacket then took the remaining darts out of his pocket, clutching them with his left hand, and holding the other items with his arms. He looked around—all the way around and didn't see or hear anything. He switched on his flashlight and shone it towards his boat. In the distance he saw Gerald hanging by his neck and swaying with the breeze. He lifted the cover off his boat and gently placed the camera and pistol on a slat, then covered the boat again. The wind kicked up. He pointed his flashlight at Gerald and saw him swaying even more in the wind. Suddenly, a massive gust took hold of Gerald's grisly corpse and spun him around like a top, nearly breaking the branch. The body stopped spinning and came to a sudden halt—facing

Benny. Gerald's eyes and mouth were wide open as if he wanted to say something. Benny ran to his car and started the motor, still holding on to his flashlight and darts. He was about to pull onto Stagecoach Road when he saw two bright headlights quickly advancing his way. He put his car in reverse and backed into the woods, then turned off his lights and engine. He watched from a distance as he saw the strange car's lights illuminate the road in front of him, slowing to 5 mph. There was just a driver inside—no passengers. But the driver looked familiar—like the person Benny saw at the track. It just can't be him, Benny thought. How could it be? Benny remained still. Then, the car stopped. Right in front of the tree.

Shit, I'm dead, Benny thought to himself as he saw a large man get out of the car heading his way, clutching a gun. I've got one chance. I've got to make a run for the boat and get my gun.

The man had a gun and a large flashlight which he shone in the trees. The beam highlighted Gerald's mutilated body hanging from the branch.

Upon seeing the light, Benny lowered his head and shimmied over to the passenger side door and quietly opened it. He curled down the best he could then slid down to the cold dead leaves below. He measured each move in a desperate attempt to remain unnoticed. But it was impossible. He heard the man walking briskly towards him. Benny stood up and sprinted to his boat.

"STOP! I'VE GOT A GUN!" the man yelled.

Benny had nothing to lose. He hurriedly uncovered his boat and grabbed his pistol, completely forgetting he shot all three bullets.

"SO DO I!" Benny screamed back, brandishing his weapon, directly pointing it at the man.

"PUT YOURS DOWN, NOW!" the man demanded. "I'M A COP!"

Benny didn't obey. "No!" Benny said, moving closer, within talking distance—his steady hand still holding his depleted weapon. "You'll have to shoot, and so will I."

The man took one step closer, gun still pointing at Benny.

"I know who you are," the man said, recognizing Benny after all these years. "And you know me. I'm Lieutenant Mitchell. When I read about the murders in the Miami Herald I knew it was you, Benjamin. Give yourself up."

Benny kept his eye on the lieutenant and refused to lower his gun.

"I can't do that, sir. I'm not going to jail."

"Give yourself up, Benjamin. It's the only way."

Benny suddenly remembered his gun was empty. The only thing he could do was become a moving target. He certainly was faster than the chubby old ex-officer. So he threw his gun at Lieutenant Mitchell, hitting him on his right shoulder, then made a dash for the woods. Lieutenant Mitchell raised his gun and fired a shot, narrowly missing Benny's head. He shot again, and again—missing each time. Then, thinking he was still a young man, the lieutenant foolishly thought he could outrun Benny and took off after him. Benny turned around and saw he was being chased. Is he kidding? Benny thought. After running only a hundred yards, Lieutenant Mitchell became winded and haphazardly fired off the rest of his rounds, each shot missing his target by a mile. He abruptly stopped and clutched his left arm and fell to the ground with a thud. He had a heart attack. Benny saw the lieutenant was on the ground and immediately rushed to his side and took his pulse. Nothing. Benny then picked up the cop's flashlight to look at his pupils. No reaction. The lieutenant was dead.

This is a lucky break, Benny thought, knowing he dodged

more than one bullet. But everyone will be looking for him and they're sure to find him. His rental is probably equipped with a Lojack. I've got to do something, fast.

Benny dragged the dead lieutenant's heavy body to the side of the road. He found the officer's car keys in his right front pants pocket and opened up the passenger's side, then, with great will, stuffed the fat cop onto the front passenger seat. He went back to the woods and retrieved the officer's gun. Benny looked back towards the trees, making sure his own car was still out of sight. He drove down Stagecoach Road, passed the houses, and turned right onto County Line Road, driving exactly one mile towards the lake. He got out of the car and shoved the blue corpse over to the driver's side, having the presence of mind to place Lieutenant Mitchell's foot on the gas pedal and the gun in his jacket holster. Benny put the car in park, but kept it running. He carefully examined the interior, making sure no personal effects were left behind. Satisfied the coast was clear, Benny ducked into the woods and jogged back to Stagecoach Road where he retrieved his own gun, placed it in his trunk and drove home—to Marsha. He pressed 'play' on his tape deck. Buffy, Jody and Mr. French were in rare form.

Chapter Thirty-Seven

Tuesday morning, 6:00 a.m., May 26th, 1992. Benny woke up after three hours of broken sleep. Marsha woke up at 6:02 a.m. Benny took a shower before he went to bed, but his face was still swollen from Gerald's punches. Marsha sat up in bed and saw that Benny was already awake.

"You were out late last night," Marsha said. "I woke up when you turned on the shower—it was way past two."

Benny didn't respond. Marsha wiped the sleep from her eyes and took a better look at her husband.

"What happened to your face?" Marsha shrieked. "Were you in an accident?"

Benny got up to dress for the office.

"It's over, Marsha. It's over," Benny stated while buttoning his shirt.

Marsha stood up and put on her robe. She walked over to the dresser to get her hairbrush.

"What's over? What are you talking about?"

Benny reached for a pair of slacks and a pair of socks. He put them on then walked into the bathroom to collect a toothbrush, toothpaste, and a disposable razor. Marsha followed close behind.

"I said, what's over? You're not answering me."

Benny put on his new loafers and grabbed the first tie he saw, then reached for the only tie clip he owned which was sitting on top of his bureau. He headed downstairs—his wife at his tail. Benny stopped at the foot of the stairs and turned towards his straying wife.

"I know about Tommy," Benny said matter-of-factly. "Let me be very clear about this: I know about *you* and Tommy. Don't ask me how I found out. I'll never tell. I just know. And don't deny it. I'm seeing a lawyer later on today."

Marsha dropped her brush to the ground and started to cry. Then she started balling.

"What did you expect me to do? Huh? Huh? Tommy was there for me when we were having a hard time. I'll bet you had your share of sluts—the way you used to stay out all night sometimes. What about that? Huh? Huh?"

Benny put on his jacket and pulled out his car keys.

"No, I haven't," Benny said. "I may have stayed out late a lot but I never cheated on you, ever, with anyone. I'll take a polygraph anytime."

Benny opened the front door of his large suburban house and looked back at Marsha who was still searching for words but couldn't find any.

"Get the kids ready for school," Benny said. "I'll call you when I find a place to stay."

And with that, Benny got in his car. He was immediately overcome with a feeling of relief. He didn't have any more explaining to do. He could just come and go as he pleased. The subtle truth was he did his family a favor. He no longer trusted his emotions and didn't know the limits of his anger. He knew he could never hurt his family. But was he sure? It was best he put them out of harm's way. He also didn't want to involve his family if things didn't go his way—like getting caught. He thought about that. He thought about that a lot.

Benny headed towards his office, but his first patient wasn't until 8:00 a.m. He had some time to kill so he stopped to have breakfast at Denny's which was about three miles from his clinic. He parked near the entrance and saw the place was packed, but decided to go in anyway, not being in a hurry. He took a seat at the counter.

"Coffee?" the cheery young waitress asked as she raised the restaurant style coffee pot.

"Yes, please," Benny said while reaching for the discarded Post Tribune left by the previous customer. The headline wasn't a surprise. "RETIRED TOP COP FOUND DEAD IN HIS CAR." A large, grainy picture of the car was just below the headline.

Benny put his coffee down for a minute to read the rest of the story: "Retired Gary officer, Lt. Ivan Mitchell, was found dead late last night in a 1991 Buick LeSabre on County Line Road in Miller. Police say they were on their way back to the station after arresting three youths who vandalized Nobel Elementary School, when they spotted Lt. Mitchell's car. Police didn't say why the retired officer was in Miller nor would they confirm reports it was related to the recent lakeside murders. Lt. Otis Jefferson of the Gary Police Department said he briefly spoke with Lt. Mitchell last week, but had no contact with him since."

Benny put the paper down and ordered an egg sandwich and got his coffee to go. He called Rings from the payphone outside the restaurant.

"Hello?" Twila answered in a weak voice. She was in the kitchen making grits when the phone rang. "Who's calling?"

"Hi, is this Twila?"

"Yes. Who is this?"

"Hi Twila, it's Sox."

"Who?"

"Benny. It's Benny. Listen, I haven't got a lot of time. Is Rings, I mean, is Bo there?"

"Yes, he's here. But he's asleep. You had him out late last night. I heard you guys had quite a time at the track."

"He told you about that?"

"Oh yes! And what a surprise! He came home with over three thousand dollars and gave it all to me and J.J.—he's asleep, too. Bo said you guys stayed until the last race. You must have been winning too."

Benny hadn't checked the fourth race results. He didn't know if Gerald's Pal won or not.

"Oh, yes," Benny said. "I had some good fortune as well. Listen, this is rather important. Can you wake him up and get him to the phone—that is, if he's nearby."

"Oh, wait," Twila said. "His ears must have been buzz'n. He's right here."

Twila handed the phone to Rings and wheeled herself out of the kitchen after turning off the stove. She knew more than she let on and wanted to give Rings some privacy.

"Yo, Sox. Whassup?"

"Plenty. Listen. I was followed last night by a cop I knew years ago. This was after you left. He followed me back to the tree and had a heart attack when he ran after me. He's dead. So when you see the news today about a cop found dead in his car, that's what happened. I'll get into the details later, but I don't think this had anything to do with Frank or the dogs last night, or Gerald. I think this cop was on his own. I can't be sure, but I don't think you were followed. Remember, you don't know anything."

"Be cool, Sox. I know. I know when to keep my mouth shut. Don't worry about me."

"Good. Now meet me at the bowling alley later on

tonight—at 5:30 if you can. We've got to talk about things. People are going ask what happened to my face. I'll say we were mugged outside the track when you walked out with your cash. By the way, who signed for you?"

"I did," Rings said. "And yes, I also had to pinch a loaf like I told you, so I wasn't lying."

"Did you keep the tax form?"

"Got it right here," Rings said, patting his front pocket. "Do you think I'll need it?"

"I think *I'll* need it," Benny said. "Hold onto it. And don't answer any questions from anyone you don't know. I'll see you later today. And oh, tell J.J. and your mother you're going meet me again tonight. I can't come by your shop for a while—if ever. Oh, and another thing—scrub out the inside of your suburban real good. Go over it twice, inside and out. Then put a lot of junk in the back where I was."

"Why the junk?"

"Just do it, please," Benny reiterated. "And tell J.J. I won't be keeping you out as late tonight."

"Yeah, okay," Rings agreed. "J.J.'s real happy with me— you know, after I gave him and my ma the money from last night. Oh, did you win?"

"I don't know. I didn't check yet. I'll see you at Harley's. Bye."

Benny bought a fresh paper from the newspaper box outside and read the rest of the story in his car. The bigger story, the one that really grabbed his attention, was on the bottom of the front page which he didn't see earlier: "MAN REPORTED MISSING AFTER DOGS WERE KILLED." The story went on: "Frank Stram, who lives in the 300 block of Tyler Road, said a black man in his early twenties abducted his neighbor and friend, Gerald Hill, after shooting and killing Mr. Hill's four Pit Bulls with a tranquilizer rifle. Mr. Stram admitted he was drunk at the time and couldn't identify the abductor's car. Police are investigating whether or not there is any connection between the disappearance of Mr. Hill and the lakeside murders."

Okay, okay. Good, Benny thought to himself. That schmuck didn't get a good look at Rings' car. Good. Oh, shit. Oh, shit. Tracey will ask a million questions about my face. And so will Carla. And so will everybody. I have to stick to the mugging story I told Rings. Everyone knows I go to the track. They'll buy it. But if I was mugged, why didn't I call the cops? Oh, because the guys took off before I could get a good look at them and they didn't get the money. Good. Okay. Calm down Benny. Think clearly. Calm down. You're going to have to be your jovial self today. Right. Don't think about Gerald hanging on the tree. Shit—I've got to go back and get the camera. Shit. Okay, I'll do that tomorrow, I hope. Oh, fuck what's this. Shit, I forgot to leave my gun in the boat. I'll have to keep this on me until I get to the office.

Benny had another forty minutes to kill before his first patient. He went to Walgreens and bought some make-up to cover up the bruises on his face. He applied the make-up in a gas station's men's room. A couple of truckers wearing the same company logo walked in and saw Benny patting his face with the flesh colored powder.

"Have a heavy date tonight, sweetie!" said one of the smart-ass middle-aged drivers. Benny smiled but should have kept his mouth shut.

"I do," Benny said. "What time should I pick you up tonight?"

"Oh, a wise guy," the trucker angrily said, landing a hard punch on Benny's arm. "Don't smart off to me!"

Big mistake on the freight trucker's part. Benny had enough of bullies and wasn't going to take it anymore, from anyone, even over-the-hill bullies. He pulled his empty gun from his jacket and pointed it right at the head of the trucker who punched him—then he pulled back the hammer which made a loud creaking noise.

"Apologize now you fucking faggot or I'll blow your cum sucking lips off your ugly face. NOW!" Benny demanded, his thumb nervously twitching on the trigger and his mouth foaming."

The trucker let out a deafening fart and shit his pants.

"Yes sir. Yes sir. I'm sorry sir. I'm sorry sir. Yes sir," the pathetic trucker cried.

"And you too!" Benny said to the trucker's buddy, now pointing the gun at him.

"I'm sorry too. It'll never happen again. Yes sir. Yes sir."

Not satisfied, Benny had one more request.

"Get on your knees and kiss your buddy's balls," Benny said to the trucker who punched him. "NOW!" Benny cocked the hammer back the whole way, ready to fire.

The trucker immediately obeyed and knelt down and kissed his co-worker's balls through his pants.

"All right, that's better," Benny said. "You tell anyone— I'll be waiting for you outside. Now git!" Spoken like the bullshit cowboy he wasn't.

The truckers bolted out of the bathroom like two scared jackrabbits and climbed into their rig. Benny gathered his make-up and casually walked out of the station like nothing happened. Both truckers watched as Benny got in his car. Benny saw them looking at him and took out his gun and flashed it out the window.

"Look you faggots," Benny shouted as he opened up the cylinder as he started to pull away, "it's empty! Take that you fucking faggots! Ha, ha, ha, ha, ha!" Then Benny screeched away and drove to his office. The haulers were too mortified to follow.

Benny arrived at his office at a quarter to nine. Tracey was already there making coffee and filling up the headrest paper bin in the adjusting rooms. He was expecting a lot of patients that day, including a few new injury cases from Steve. He hoped upon hope Carla wouldn't show, or for that matter, anyone else annoying—including Gail, the bombshell. All he wanted to do was see his patients and meet Rings later. He also had to find an apartment—some place temporary until he was ready to buy a condo. He got out of his car and took the newspaper with him. Then he walked into his office while hiding his face, said hello to Tracey, and hung his jacket on his office chair. His make-up job wasn't perfect.

"Marsha just called," Tracey loudly announced from the waiting room. "It sounded like she was really upset. Anything wrong?"

Benny milled over the files Tracey put on his desk and made a couple of notes. Mitzie was fast asleep in the hallway.

"Wrong?" Benny repeated. "Maybe just a little. We're getting divorced."

Tracey put the coffee pot down and hurried to Benny's office.

"What? What? You're getting divorced? You had a fight, right?"

"No, we didn't have a fight," Benny calmly said, jotting down a few more notes in one of the injury files. "It's been building up for a while. It's a rather personal matter. So let's just say I had no choice."

"Oh, come on," Tracey said. "Everything can be worked out. Look, you've got kids. They're in this too, you know. What about them?"

"Tracey, you're wonderful. You are the best employee anyone could ever ask for. I think the world of you. But let this one alone. I'll handle it. Is my nine o'clocker here yet?"

Tracey backed off with the questions and picked Mitzie up from the floor, bringing the tired Beagle into her office.

"No, not yet," Tracey said. "But when your nine o'clocker does arrive it's going to be Carla."

"Oh, shit. That's all I need today. Of all days."

"Why? Rough night last night?" Tracey asked while bringing Benny a cup of coffee.

Tracey walked into Benny's office and saw his face.

"What happened? What happened to your face?"

"Oh, that," Benny said. "I sort of got mugged at the track last night. I went with a friend who won a lot of money and some guys followed us out and tried to take it from him. We got into a fight and one of them punched me in the face a few times, then took off without any money. I'll be all right. It's not that bad."

Tracey wasn't buying it.

"I'll bet this has something to do with you and Marsha getting divorced, right?"

"Tracey!"

"Sorry, I'll stay out of it."

The front door opened and the delightful Carla came in, singing, making everyone nauseous.

"Oh Benjamin! Benny!" Carla sang. "I've got something here I want to show you! Dr. Weinstein!"

Benny got up from his office chair and went over to Tracey, cupping his mouth so Carla wouldn't hear.

"I hope it's a suicide note," Benny whispered to Tracey. "I can't imagine what she wants to show me."

Benny walked into the waiting room, forcing a great big smile. Tracey looked on from her receptionist window.

"What is it?" Benny asked.

Carla plucked a thick envelope from her purse and handed

it to Dr. Weinstein, astonishingly not making an immediate comment about his bruised face.

"Here, open it," Carla said. "I think you'll like it."

"I hope it wasn't expensive. You know me. I get all funny about accepting gifts."

"No, no," said Carla. "I know your fifteen-year anniversary is coming up and I wanted to get you a little something."

Tracey looked at her boss, then quickly looked down. Benny took the envelope and looked at Carla.

"Well? Well?" Carla said. "Open it!"

Dr. Weinstein unwrapped the unsealed white envelope and pulled out a cassette tape and two gift certificates to Grover's Steakhouse, Marsha's favorite restaurant.

"Thank you, Carla," Dr. Weinstein said, glancing only at the gift certificate and giving Carla an uninspired hug.

"You're welcome, Dr. Weinstein. Do you like the tape?"

"Oh, the tape," Benny said, looking at the title and almost dropping it to the floor after he read it: *Sonny and Cher's Greatest Hits* featuring *All I Ever Need Is You*.

There wasn't anything shy about Carla. She was a huge Sonny and Cher fan and saw fit to give a performance right in the waiting room. Hair, hips and all. Carla sang the first verse as she gyrated around the room then said, "Verse two!"

"No, please!" Benny blurted out, trying to make a joke out of it. "That was good. Thank you."

Dr. Weinstein motioned his exuberant patient to follow him into an exam room and thought how creepy it was Carla chose that song to sing. Like she knew something. But she wasn't that smart.

"Well, you're going to find out sooner or later," Dr. Weinstein said to his grateful and adoring patient while positioning her on the adjusting table. "Marsha and I are getting divorced."

To Carla, there was nothing better than juicy gossip. It was like talking dirty to her. She especially perked up hearing this news, and connected the dots her way. In some other universe, in some twisted, imaginary, delusional way, she thought her fantasy was now coming true—that Dr. Weinstein was leaving his wife for her. Like this was going to happen. Benny may have been a cold blooded murderer, but he wasn't crazy.

"Give that to me again," Carla said, trying in vain to hold back a smile. "Did big bad Marsha beat you up?" she said, finally acknowledging the bruises.

"It's true," Dr. Weinstein said. "I'll be looking for an apartment later today. And no, Marsha didn't beat me up. I got into a scuffle at the track last night when someone tried to rob me, but everything's OK. My mind is now on getting an apartment."

This was Carla's chance. She didn't want to blow it.

"It just so happens Alex is out of town and won't be back for another five days. He's fishing in Ontario with his boss and a few others. You can stay with me!"

"Thanks, but no," Dr. Weinstein said. "The Indiana licensing board wouldn't allow it, you know, it looks bad going home with a patient. I'll be staying with my folks in Miller."

Carla looked dejected, but she bought it. At least he wasn't staying with another woman. There was still hope.

"Good idea," Carla said, accepting the minor consolation. "You're going to keep this a family affair."

Benny's eyes widened when he heard her remark about 'family affair.' The irony was uncanny.

Dr. Weinstein treated a dozen patients that morning and finally, by noon, had a chance to relax in his office. Tracey had already left for lunch and wasn't due back until a quarter of one. He had a few minutes to himself so he thought he'd finally look at the race results from the previous night's Balmoral card. He turned to the last page of the Post Tribune's sports section.

"Let's see….Balmoral results. Hah. Here they are. Okay, fourth race. Here it is," Benny muttered to himself. "YES! YES! YES!" he shouted. Gerald's Pal won by a nose and paid $16.40 to win. That was for a $2.00 bet. Benny bet $800.00 and won over sixty-five hundred smackeroos!

Okay, good, thought Benny. Things are breaking my way. I feel lucky. I feel like I can get away with anything now. How can I lose?

Chapter Thirty-Eight

May 26th, 1992. Tuesday afternoon around 1:00 p.m.

"I'm telling you, I know there was someone with him," Frank Stram emphatically said to Lt. Jefferson, finally getting a hold of the cop. "I told you, it wasn't just the nigger I saw," Frank said, forgetting Lt. Jefferson was black. "Sorry, I mean the colored guy."

There was a short pause. Lt. Jefferson jotted something down in his notebook.

"We went through this last night," Lt. Jefferson said. "A hundred times. You said you were drunk and only *thought* you heard another voice. You never said you saw anyone else. How do you know it wasn't the dogs barking?"

"Because that nigger, I mean colored guy couldn't possibly overpower Gerald by himself and kill all those dogs."

"But you said Mr. Hill was also drunk."

"He was, but I've seen him fight drunk before. He can take care of himself and anyone else—unless he's fighting two guys."

Lt. Jefferson was more receptive that day to listen to Frank's story. Frank called him the night before when he got in the house, but he didn't sound coherent—the officer believed

225

he was making it up. But Lt. Jefferson thought maybe Frank had something—with Lt. Mitchell dead and Gerald missing.

"I know we talked about Benjamin Weinstein before," said Lt. Jefferson. "I know you think he's involved and maybe after you, too. But I went to see Weinstein at his house and he had a pretty good alibi for the nights of the other murders. I kind of doubt he's the one. He has too much to lose. But I could be wrong. Anyone can go nuts."

"Yeah, well I think he has," Frank maintained. "I think he has a good motive. I don't have to tell you. You saw my record, and the others. Do me a favor and lean on him for a while. I know he's the one. And I think I can prove it!"

"Well, all right," Lt. Jefferson agreed. "We're doing the best we can with what little resources we have."

"Your best isn't making me any safer," Frank said. "Now I got a job and I'm paying taxes and I want protection. At least make him take a lie detector test."

"A polygraph would be nice, but we can't force him unless we have strong evidence. But I'll talk to him and see if he'll volunteer."

"Okay," Frank said. "You've got my number. Let me know what he says. I'm taking my sick days now and I'll be home for a week. I'll be looking out for myself as well."

"Okay. Will do, Mr. Stram."

Lt. Jefferson made some more notes and called for his secretary, a sixty-six-year-old retiree, to tape his next phone conversation.

"I'm going to call Benjamin Weinstein at his office. I don't know if he's there, but I'd like you to record the conversation once I get him on the line, okay Orlena?"

"Yes Otis," Orlena said. "I'll see if he's there now. What's his number?"

Orlena dialed Dr. Weinstein's office. Tracey answered on

the first ring. Orlena pressed the record button on the answering machine and handed the phone to her boss.

"Hello, may I speak to Benjamin Weinstein?" Lieutenant Jefferson asked.

Tracey just finished rescheduling a patient when the officer called, and was a bit distracted.

"May I tell him who's calling?"

"Yes. I'm Lieutenant Jefferson from the Gary Police Department. I'd like to speak to Benjamin Weinstein if he has a minute."

Tracey didn't know what this was about. She thought it could be one of those phony police charity scams.

"He's with a patient now," Tracey said. "Can I have him call you back?"

"He can, but this is rather important. I'd like to speak with him now if possible."

"All right," Tracey said. "I'll see if I can pull him away."

Tracey got up and hopped over Mitzie who was taking another one of her two dozen daily naps. She softly knocked on the exam room. Dr. Weinstein opened the door.

"What is it?" Benny asked. "I'm in the middle of an ultrasound treatment."

"There's a Lieutenant Jefferson on the phone. Says it's important. Do you want to take the call?"

"Oh, for the love of...." Benny softy said, not wanting to swear in front of his patient. "Yeah, tell him I'll be there in thirty seconds."

Tracey walked back to her desk and held the phone until Dr. Weinstein walked in his office. She saw the nervous bone crusher pick up the phone. He looked worried.

"Yes, this is Dr. Weinstein—just a second. Tracey, hang up the phone!"

Tracey reluctantly hung up on her end. She desperately

wanted to know what this was all about.

"What can I do for you lieutenant?"

"Hello, Dr. Weinstein?" the lieutenant said, holding the phone to his ear on his shoulder while taking notes. "Do you have a little time to talk?"

Benny's day *was* going his way but not anymore.

"Yes," Dr. Weinstein said. "I've got about three minutes. Someone's waiting for me in a treatment room."

"Thanks. This won't take long," the officer continued. "I don't know if you read about the dead cop found in Miller last night in his car—or the dead dogs and the missing man in Gary. Did you hear about that? I think you once knew the missing man, Gerald Hill?"

Benny put his elbows on his desk, resting his face in his hands.

"Yes," Dr. Weinstein answered. "I see it right here. I've got today's Tribune. But what does that have to do with me?"

"Well nothing, I hope," the officer said, offering Dr. Weinstein a window. "So if it's okay with you I'd like you to take a polygraph and erase all doubts."

Benny felt a knot build up in his stomach. He wasn't sure how to answer. Should he call Steve or a defense attorney?

"Sure!" Dr. Weinstein confidently said, thinking he just said the stupidest thing in the world. "I've got nothing to hide. When and where?"

The lieutenant didn't expect such eager cooperation, but he wasn't going to question it.

"How about later on tonight? I can arrange for an examiner to be at your office at 7:00 p.m."

"Tonight?" Dr. Weinstein said, surprised by the suddenness. "I had plans for this evening, but I don't see why I can't break them. Is it okay to meet at your office? Lots of snoops around here, you know."

"Sure, it's okay. Let me give you directions."

After getting off the phone, Dr. Weinstein went back to the treatment room to finish up with his patient. After his patient left, Dr. Weinstein had fifteen minutes until his next one. He told Tracey he needed to get some peppermint Lifesavers at the Walgreens across the street, then walked out without putting on a jacket. What he really wanted to do was call Rings from the payphone outside the drugstore. Benny looked around before putting a quarter in the phone, then dialed Rings at his house.

"Hello?" answered the female voice.

"Hi, is this Twila?"

"Yes. Benny?"

"Yes, hi Twila. I need to speak to Rings right away. It's very important."

"Oh Benny!" Twila continued, ecstatic with the cash Rings won the night before. "It's so good to hear from you. And what a surprise last night. Oh, is that money going to come in handy. I was so sore sitting on that rickety wheelchair all day and now....."

"Hold it for a second," Benny interrupted. "I'm in an awful hurry. I need to speak to Rings if he's there."

"Oh, Rings is at the store," Twila said, realizing she was rambling. "J.J.'s working him to death today. Try him there."

"Thanks," Benny said, hanging up the phone and inserting another quarter.

"J.J.'s," the youthful voice said on the other end.

"Rings?"

"Yo! Is this......?"

"Yes, this is Sox. Listen, I need for you to do me a huge, huge favor."

"Uh oh," Rings said with much apprehension. "Are you in trouble? Or me?"

"No, just listen. I need you to go back home right now and

see what kind of medication your mom is taking and give me the list of the drugs."

"My mom? Why?"

"Please. This is very urgent. I'll explain later. But go home now and I'll call you back in a half hour. Don't call me at the office. I'll call you."

"Okay, Sox. But you've got me worried."

"Don't worry. I'll call you in a half hour—later."

Benny bought the mints and walked back to his office. His 1:45 p.m. patient was already waiting for him—Gail!

"Oh, hi Gail," Dr. Weinstein said, taking the mints out of the bag. "I'll be with you in a moment."

"Can I have one?" Gail asked with Midwest southern charm. "You never know when these can come in handy!"

Dr. Weinstein opened the bag and handed Gail a few individually wrapped peppermints.

"Wow! All of these?" Gail flirtatiously said. "Did you plan a long appointment!?"

Dr. Weinstein did his best to ignore her advances—if indeed it was one. He didn't fancy himself as a lady's man and thought Gail was acting. But now that he was getting divorced he figured, "What the hell." But he was in no mood for small talk or fooling around. His mind was on calling Rings after he finished up with Gail.

"Dr. Weinstein, your wife called again," Tracey said in full voice. "She was hysterical on the phone and wants you to call her back right away."

Big mouth, Dr. Weinstein thought. Now everyone has to know my business.

"Okay, I'll call her back," Dr. Weinstein said. "I'll be back in two minutes, Gail."

Dr. Weinstein went to his office and closed the door. Gail walked to the receptionist window to chat up Tracey about Dr.

Weinstein's wife.

"What's that all about?" Gail asked like she had a right to know, pretending to be concerned. "Is there trouble in paradise?"

Tracey lowered her head and finally mustered up the fortitude to speak softly.

"They're getting divorced, shhhh," Tracey whispered. "Don't tell him I told you."

"Aw, the poor thang!" Gail said, faking pity. "That poor boy must be suffering." She sat back down and waited for Dr. Weinstein.

"I can see you now, Gail," Dr. Weinstein said. "This way."

Gail followed Dr. Weinstein to treatment room 3, the last door on the left, furthest from the receptionist room.

"Tracey told you. I can read it on your face. You know."

"Yes, and I'm so sorry. Is there anything I can do?" Gail said, continuing to feign sympathy.

"No, nothing," Dr. Weinstein said. "These things happen."

"I know how to cheer you up!" Gail said, sliding her finger between her breasts. Dr. Weinstein pretended not to notice.

"How's your neck today? Is it doing any better?" Benny asked while lowering the adjusting table.

"My neck is much better, thanks to you! And I can make you feel better too," Gail said, her lilac perfume permeating the air. "I can make you feel *real* good! Anytime—anywhere!"

At that point, Dr. Weinstein just wanted to quickly finish up the appointment so he could call Rings back. But there was no doubt—Gail was coming on to him. And he was now a free man, well, sort of.

"Maybe some other time," Dr. Weinstein said. "I'll be busy all week. But….."

"But what!" Gail said, running her finger down her stomach, past her navel. "You need to be shown a good time.

I'm going to watch Ricky play in his band this Friday at a club in Portage. My mom's coming with. Do you want to come too?"

"Your mom's coming with?" Benny asked excitedly. "Yeah, I think I will. Just to see the look on her face. Which club is it?"

"It's down Route 12. A place called the Brass Bomber. Have you ever heard of it?"

Benny sure did hear of the Brass Bomber—and the apartment complex a block away. That's where it took place that horrible night some nineteen years earlier. That's where it happened. At that apartment. That's where Laura lost her virginity to that nasty boy—Gail's father, Larry Kroll! He wouldn't miss a chance to see Laura again. I wonder how she looks after all of these years, thought Benny. Is she married? I'll bet she got fat! That's what usually happens when you start off as sexy as she was. Yep, I'll bet she looks a sight. Well, she'll see that I'm still in shape!

"Yes, I've heard of the Brass Bomber," Dr. Weinstein said. "No one's mentioned that place to me in years. It was a club way back when, though I never went there. What time Friday?"

"Ricky's band doesn't start until after ten. But mom and I will be there at eight. We can pick you up if you like. I know mom would like to see you. I know you guys used to go together. Yes, she knows I've been coming here and she's been asking all sorts of questions—hey, you never know!"

Dr. Weinstein was tempted. Very tempted. But he didn't know what the next couple of days would bring. Should he even make plans for Friday?

"Tell you what," Dr. Weinstein continued. "I'll be staying with my folks for a couple of weeks until I find an apartment. Why don't you meet me here at my office—say around sevenish. It can't take us more than forty minutes to get to Portage."

"Where do your folks live?"

"In Miller, but I'll just be finishing up with patients around seven. Then afterwards you can just take me back here and I'll drive to my folks. I know it's out of the way for me, but I don't mind. It'll give us some time to catch up."

"Then it's a date!" Gail said. "See you Friday, at seven."

Gail stopped in her tracks. "I almost forgot," she said. "My mom is a realtor in Munster. Maybe she can help you find an apartment. Here, I'll write her number down for you. Do you have a business card?"

Dr. Weinstein pulled out a card and Gail scribbled her mother's number on it.

"Thanks, I just might call her," Dr. Weinstein said as he escorted Gail out to the waiting room and went back to his office to get his jacket. It wasn't that cold, but he had things he was carrying around—like his gun and a couple of darts. He wanted to keep an eye on that stuff.

After Gail left, Dr. Weinstein told Tracey he'd be gone for about ten minutes. "I forgot to get a birthday card for a lawyer," he said. "I'm going to Walgreens. Want anything?"

"No thanks," Tracey said, not buying the birthday card bit.

As Dr. Weinstein left, Tracey looked out the window to see if he was really going to the pharmacy. Sure enough, he was. I could be wrong, Tracey thought. Maybe he is going to buy a card.

Benny got to the drugstore and saw someone was already using the payphone. Well, might as well buy a card and make it look good, he thought to himself. He walked out two minutes later with a birthday card and called Rings.

"Rings? Sox. Did you get the name of the drugs?"

Rings fumbled with the receiver for a moment.

"Yeah, Sox. I got a mess of them here. I can't pronounce half the names on these bottles. My ma is helping me sort them out. She wants to know why you want to know."

"Tell her the truth."

"Which is what?"

"Which is I need something for my nerves. I've been under a lot of stress lately and I don't feel like going to my doctor for any pills."

"Sox, ain't you a doctor?"

"I'm a chiropractor. We don't write prescriptions."

"Oh, I forgot. Okay, let's see here: Here's something I can read. It says Codeine—60 mg."

"I pop those like candy for my pain," Benny heard Twila say in the background.

"No, don't need any of that, next," Benny said.

"Here's another one," Rings said. "Pennicillin."

"No, don't need that. But possibly later this week!"

"Huh?"

"Just kidding," Benny said. "Next?"

"Here's something called Versed," Rings said, phonetically pronouncing it.

"Oh, that's good shit," said Twila. "Makes me forget my problems."

"That's it!" Benny exclaimed. "Only it's pronounced 'ver-said'. Bring me the bottle. I'll give you fifty bucks for it and you can pay back your mom. I'll explain later, but meet me at the bowling alley at 5:30 tonight like we planned. This is real important."

"I'll be there," Rings assured Benny. "Later."

Chapter Thirty-Nine

May 26th, 1992. Tuesday evening.

Benny pulled up at Harley's Bowling Alley at 5:15 p.m. He would have gotten there sooner if it weren't for rush hour traffic. He also had a brief heart to heart with his daughter Rachel before he left the office.

* * * * *

Josh called and put her on.

"Daddy, Mommy says you're not coming home anymore."

"That's not true, little doll," Benny said somberly, his voice cracking. "I'll be home soon. I wish Mommy wouldn't say those things."

"Did Mommy do a bad thing?"

"We all do bad things, including me," Benny said. "I'll explain later."

"Will I see you tonight?" Rachel innocently asked.

"Maybe. I don't know. Daddy has to work late. I'll be there tomorrow for sure."

"Bye Daddy."

"Bye sweetie."

* * * * *

Benny thought about that a lot while driving to Harley's. What about his kids? Tracey mentioned that at the office but it didn't kick in until his little girl called. How could he leave them just like that? But he wasn't really leaving. Not really. Just living apart—very close by. How could he go back to Marsha and pretend the whole incident with Tommy never happened? Benny would have nightmares about that the rest of his life. He knew himself. He knew what bothered him. No, there was no other way. It was splitsville.

Benny took a seat in front of lane nineteen, hoping Rings would remember. The bowlers were already in high gear. The earsplitting crash of the pins was comforting to Benny. It was normal. He was in a place where the people looked normal and were doing normal things. It felt good to be out of his element—whatever that was. The world he created was sick. Very sick. But maybe that sickness would soon be over. He had one more disease to cure.

"Where's my lighter," Benny said to himself, checking all his pockets after putting a thick cigar in his mouth. Oh fuck! I forgot to leave my gun in the car, he thought, discovering the hard, bulging metal in his inside pocket. How did I not know it was there? Oh well, I'll give it to Rings to put in his car until later.

"YO, SOX!" Rings yelled, sneaking up on Benny.

"Oh, Jesus, Rings! You scared me again. Why do you keep doing that? Can't you walk into a room without startling people?"

"Sorry, Sox. Old habit. Hey, but I got the stuff. The bottle is half full," Rings said, holding the small container up to the light. "Momma put her mouth on that—hope you don't mind. She drinks it straight."

Benny took the little bottle of magic syrup that was going to save his life. He handed rings a fifty.

"Naw, keep it," Rings said, handing back the Grant. "You've given me enough money. And I appreciate it."

Benny wouldn't take back the bill. "Rings—it's for Twila. She can use it. Please—take it for your ma."

Rings stuffed the money in his pocket and thanked him. They both got up to leave. Benny handed Rings a big cigar as they walked outside towards Rings' suburban.

"For the road," Benny said. "I know you like my cigars. After I take care of my last bit of business, I'll send you a box of them."

"Thanks," Rings said, putting the unwrapped stogie in his mouth.

They reached Rings' car. Benny handed him his gun.

"What's this for?" Rings asked. "Am I going to need it?"

"No, just hold it for me until I see you next. Put it in the back seat out of sight."

Benny patted his inside pocket, making sure the bottle of Versed was still there.

"I'll level with you, Rings," Benny said, moving closer to his buddy. "The cops called me today. I'm on my way downtown to take a lie test. That's what the medicine is for. You can cheat a polygraph with Versed. Works every time!"

"No shit?" Rings said, like he just discovered the Dead Sea Scrolls. "Is that for real? Man, that's good to know."

"Yeah," Benny said. "And that's why a polygraph isn't admissible in court—'cause you can beat it with stuff like this."

Rings got in his car and started the motor.

"Call me later on tonight and let me know how it went," Rings said. "But don't call too late—J.J. needs his sleep."

"I'll call you tomorrow. Oh, how do you get to Polk Street from here?"

Chapter Forty

The breeze was blowing from the west as Benny made his way to the police headquarters, located in one of the worst sections of downtown Gary. There were no good sections. Polk Street was right in the middle of the pits. You weren't any safer stepping out of your car next to the police station than you were outside the pawn shop. Even the cops, and they were armed, walked in pairs to their squad cars, especially at night.

Benny's mind was so cluttered on that Tuesday, he completely forgot or didn't care about the circus at the lagoon. The Post Tribune's story about the missing man, Gerald Hill, heightened the morbid excitement at Marquette Park. A scavenger contest was organized to see who could find the body. Everyone thought Gerald Hill was dead. Even though the water in the Lagoon wasn't swimmable, there were daredevils in bathing suits walking the circumference and prodding with bamboo fishing poles in hopes of finding a new corpse. And Pete's was doing a grand business.

Also of interest was the location of Lt. Mitchell's car. What did he know? Was he following someone? Why was he there? This is why Lt. Jefferson wanted Dr. Weinstein to take the test, not being able to question his dead colleague.

Benny pulled up to the 500 block of Polk Street about a quarter of seven. The police parking lot was well lit—over lit, like daylight. He parked his Camry as close as possible to the building, next to a service vehicle. He sat in his car and combed his hair, then took out the bottle of Versed and drank one swallow, about 30mg. He washed it down with a gulp of his morning coffee which was waiting for him in the cup holder. The cold coffee tasted worse than the drug. Before getting out of his car, he carefully hid the vile under his seat in a cigar box that was held together by a thick rubber band. The drug took effect, suppressing his autonomic nervous system, his vitals, but Benny was still in control. He walked into the station.

The warm, friendly atmosphere inside the station caught Benny by surprise. Lt. Jefferson noticed him walk in but didn't approach him right away to take the test. Instead, the officer finished what he was doing, filled out a few reports, and heartily laughed at a joke he just heard from the dispatcher. Benny felt at ease. The drug was working. Lt. Jefferson greeted him.

"How are you Dr. Weinstein. I'm glad you made it."

"Fine, just fine," Benny said. "I hope this doesn't take too long. I have to cash a ticket at Balmoral. Won big the other night!" he continued, putting his hand on his back pocket.

"Is that so?" Lt. Jefferson said. "I wish I had your 4-leaf clover."

"We'll have to go some night," Dr. Weinstein assuredly offered, while taking a paper cup from the water cooler. "I'll show you my system!"

Dr. Weinstein filled the cup with cool water and took a small swig.

"Oh, is it okay if I have this before I take the test?"

"Yes, water is fine. You can have something stronger

afterwards—that is, once you get home, he he!"

Lt. Jefferson escorted Dr. Weinstein into an office where Mr. Lloyd Campbell, the polygraph examiner, was waiting. Mr. Campbell, a rotund black man in his early sixties, had a contract with the city to perform all of the routine polygraph exams. He was busy day and night, mostly night, with gangbangers suspected of selling drugs. On the side he also did employee screenings for the mill.

"Hello, sir," Mr. Campbell said, greeting Dr. Weinstein with a reassuring smile. "Just relax the best you can and answer each question as truthfully as possible."

Dr. Weinstein sat down, passively allowing Mr. Campbell to hook up his arms and chest with the wires leading to the machine. Lt. Jefferson quietly looked on for a minute, then left the room.

One thing about taking an anti-anxiety drug before a lie detector test, you don't have to practice breathing techniques, or squeeze your anal muscles to increase your blood pressure— all common, but unreliable methods of cheating the test. You can say anything you want without detection. The autonomic nervous system acts without conscious thought and controls blood pressure, breathing, and sweating. A person is at a disadvantage if they try to manipulate this system just with thoughts. Benny couldn't trust his.

"Okay, Dr. Weinstein," Mr. Campbell said. "I'm going to ask you a series of questions. Please answer each one quickly and truthfully—a simple yes or no, nothing else. Ready?"

"Yes," said Dr. Weinstein, taking a deep breath.

"Is your name Benjamin Arnold Weinstein?"

"Yes."

"Do you live in Hammond, Indiana?"

"Yes."

"Are you a practicing chiropractor?"

"Yes."

"Are you married?"

"Yes."

"Did you at any time know a man named Tommy Gunther?"

"Yes."

"Did you kill Tommy Gunther?"

"No."

Benny answered more than three dozen questions, each with a cool yes or no answer, just like the man wanted. Aside from Tommy, he was asked questions about Murphy, Frank, and Gerald in vivid detail. After the test, Mr. Campbell unhooked the wires and ushered Dr. Weinstein to the waiting room. After ten minutes, Lt. Jefferson entered the room.

"After a preliminary evaluation of the results," Lt. Jefferson stated, "we found you to be truthful. I apologize for the inconvenience."

Benny tried not to look relieved.

"Quite all right," he said, as if he knew it all along. "I completely understand—you're just doing your job. Here's my business card. Keep it in your wallet. You never know when you'll get the urge to fire at Balmoral!"

"Ha, ha," Lt. Jefferson laughed, stuffing the card in his front pocket. "The way they pay us here, I just might take you up on that."

Dr. Weinstein walked out of the station unescorted, briskly walking to his car. Glad that's over, he thought. Now I have to take care of something.

Chapter Forty-One

Later Tuesday evening, May 26th, 1992. Benny pulled away from the police station around 8:30 p.m. He thought he would first drive to his house and pick up some clothes and a few other items. Then he figured he would just stay with his folks in Miller that night since he would be only a couple of miles away—at Stagecoach Road.

The wind died down and the sky was clear. It was a comfortable sixty-five degrees. Benny turned left off of U.S. 20, then right onto Stagecoach Road. He had only one thing in mind: get his camera from the Jon boat. His plan was to develop the pictures he took of Gerald in his office the next day.

He pulled up to the tree at about 9:35 p.m. and turned off his headlights, just keeping his parking lights on. The woods were unusually dark as his car bounced over a branch, making its way inside the timber tomb. He stopped near his boat and reached for his flashlight from the glove compartment and got out of his car. The night air was eerily still. The only noise was a muffled crunching sound his shoes made on the dead leaves below. He slowly took eight steps towards his boat. He shone the light on the tarp covering the vessel. Out of curiosity, but mostly out of pleasure and a sense of resolution, he wanted to take a look at Gerald's hanging corpse, which he figured must be half eaten by now. He took his flashlight and tilted it up towards the tree, casting a wide white beam where the body was hanging. It wasn't there. Benny pointed the flashlight down, thinking the body fell. He scanned the ground below and saw nothing. "Am I in the right spot?" he asked himself. "A dead man just can't vanish like that." He took his light and scanned the entire area. No body. Then—a piece of the rope! He saw a small length of rope, about two feet, curled up under his feet. He picked it up and shone his flashlight on it, and saw several droplets of dried blood embedded in the fibers. "Shit, what happened? Where's the rest of the rope? Where's the fucking body. Holy fuck!" He then took his flashlight and scoured the trees once more. Nothing. Shit, someone was here, he thought, fearing the worst. Someone was here and they took the body. They know it was me.

Benny was sweating. The Versed had already worn off, but he wished it hadn't. He was plenty scared. He knew he was in trouble. And he knew someone took the body. But who? And why? Without a clue, he walked to his boat. At least I'll get my camera, and maybe a few other things while I'm here, he conceded to himself. Benny looked around then grabbed the cold tarp and flung it off the boat all at once, like he was unveiling a new statue. An imaginary sound of loud church bells filled his head as if to signal eminent danger. At that moment a nesting bird flew out of the boat, loudly flapping passed his head, which frightened the already agitated murderer. "HOLY HELL!" Benny yelled. Gerald's grisly corpse was in the boat! His supine body laid out like he was in a coffin ready to be buried. His boney, bloody hands clasped at his waist. Gerald's dead eyes were open and were staring right at Benny. The corner of Gerald's blue lips turned up in a sinister smile. The shock was excruciating. "HOLY MOTHERFUCKER! HOLY FUCK! HOLY FUCK! HOLY FUCK!" Benny screeched at the top of his lungs, not thinking he could be heard. "FUCK, FUCK!" Benny hung on to his flashlight as he bolted for his car, nearly soiling his pants, his heart pounding out of his chest. He reached for his keys and started the engine. No, he thought. I've got to get my camera. He got out of his car and ran to the boat. He lifted up Gerald's ghastly remains and shined his light underneath the body and everywhere around the interior. The camera was gone, as was almost everything else. The only item remaining was a half roll of duct tape. Shit, I'm dead, Benny thought. But I can't panic. Now's not the time.

Benny pulled the stiff carcass out of the boat and dragged it further into the woods, piling a large clump of leaves over the face. He went back to the boat, which was sitting on the trailer, and pulled it to his car and hooked it up to his bumper. He put his car in drive and slowly creaked out of the woods. He turned left onto Stagecoach Road, gradually increasing his foot pressure on the gas pedal. Not wanting to fumble with the inside controls, Benny reached out the window to adjust the side mirror with his left hand. Before his hand reached the mirror, he saw Gerald's reflection, as bright as day, looking right at him from the silver glass. It was the image Benny burnt in his own mind—the haunting image of Gerald laying there in the Jon boat. Benny wiped his eyes and the image was gone. He had to get out of there.

It was 9:55 p.m. Benny changed his plan. He drove the boat to Coros RV & Boat Storage on Cline Avenue in Hammond. After unhitching it, he padlocked the garage-style door and went back to his house, arriving at 11:00 o'clock. Marsha was awake pacing in the kitchen when she heard her husband unlock the front door. Benny looked terrible. His pants were torn, his jacket was filthy and his hair was dotted with pieces of dried dirt. He immediately went to the first floor bathroom to clean up before Marsha saw him. She was standing there when he exited the lavatory.

"Don't worry," Benny said, blotting his face with a towel. "I'm not here to stay. Just tonight—on the couch. I'll be staying with my folks until I can find an apartment."

It was obvious Marsha had been crying all day. She too looked a mess.

"Do they know? Did you tell them?"

"Yes, I called my folks today. They're not taking it very well. They're worried about our kids."

"I only told Stephanie. But word must have gotten out because my mother called. She blames you."

Benny walked into the kitchen and grabbed a handle of Jim Beam from the cabinet above the refrigerator and took a pull straight from the bottle.

"Let her," Benny said. He took a saltine from the table. "I didn't get into detail. Yes, I told a few people. Tracey knows. I didn't get into any detail. None at all. No one knows why. And I intend to keep it that way. I just said we grew apart and left it at that."

Marsha sat down at the table and put her head in her hands.

"So that's it?" she asked, her voice choked with emotion. "It ends just like this. Don't I have a say?"

Benny took one more drink and capped the bottle.

"You had your say—on the answering machine. Yes, yes, that's how I found out about you and Tommy. Now you know."

Marsha cried even louder.

"That wasn't all my fault!" she shot back. "He was there for me when I needed someone to talk you. You....you... you never were."

"Yeah, when you needed someone to talk to," Benny mocked. "Did you ever hear of AIDS? Did you know who you were fucking? God only knows what I could have caught from you. Who else did you fuck without me knowing? Are those kids upstairs even mine?"

Marsha stormed out of the kitchen and ran upstairs. Benny didn't follow. All he wanted to do was go to sleep and put this very long day behind him. He knew tomorrow was going to be even longer.

Chapter Forty-Two

Wednesday, May 27th, 1992. Benny woke up on the couch at 6:30 a.m. Rachel was already awake, hovering over her daddy. She hugged his neck and he hugged her back and kissed her cheek. They were glad to see each other. Joshua walked downstairs to get some orange juice, acting like everything was normal. Benny went upstairs to take a shower and pack a few clothes. He walked into his bedroom without saying a word to Marsha who was awake but lingering in bed.

"I'll be out of here in fifteen minutes," Benny said. "If everyone acts civil, the divorce shouldn't be painful. I'll agree to give you mostly everything including the house and our savings. I just need some money to last about half a year. The office will take care of the rest. Better you have it than a divorce lawyer."

Marsha didn't say a word as her soon to be ex finished up in the bathroom and packed two large suitcases. Benny stayed long enough to see his kids off to school. Then he got into his car and drove to a Dunkin' Donuts in the next town and called Rings on an outdoor payphone.

"Yo," Rings answered, annoyed he was prematurely woken. "What time is it?"

"Rings, this is Sox. Listen, this is important. Did you go to Stagecoach Road and put Gerald's body in the boat?"

"What?" Rings asked, puzzled by the question. "Did I WHAT?"

"I went there last night to get my camera—by myself. And Gerald's body was in my boat."

Rings wiped his face with his hands, thinking he was dreaming.

"Are you for real?" Rings asked in disbelief. "He was in the boat?"

"Yes, he was in the boat," Benny repeated. "You didn't put him there, did you?"

"Fuck no!" Rings emphatically stated. "I was glad to get out of there when I did. I'm not going back to that creepy place."

"Well someone did."

"It wasn't me. I can assure you."

"I didn't think it was you, but I had to be sure. Look, I'll call you later today. I've got to go to work and take care of a few things."

"Yo, Sox. Just a second. Did you cash your ticket from the other night?"

"No, not yet. That's one of the things I have to do—but later tonight. I'll be at Balmoral at about eight—then I'm going to sleep at my folks' in Miller. My wife and I are separated."

"You're what?" Rings said with a note of enthusiasm. "You're a free man! Hey, watch out ladies!"

"Free, that's right," Benny sarcastically replied. "Yeah, I'm free. I'll talk to you later."

"Yeah man, later," Rings repeated. "Oh, do you want your gun back?"

Benny thought for a second. "My gun….ummm… yeah. I

need it. Can you be at Balmoral at half past eight? I can meet you in the parking lot—you know, by the space I parked before."

"I think so," Rings said. "I'll tell J.J. I have to leave by seven-thirty. I don't think he'll mind."

"Good," Benny said, relieved that Rings agreed. "Later."

Lt. Jefferson called Frank and 10:00 a.m.—giving him the 'good' news.

"He passed with flying colors," Lt. Jefferson matter-of-factly announced. He passed the polygraph. Mr. Weinstein had nothing to do with the murders."

"He passed?" Frank said, absorbing the shock. "How could he have passed?"

"I don't know how he could have passed, other than he is innocent. Our finest polygraph examiner administered the test. Mr. Weinstein was telling the truth. If he had done anything, it would have shown up on the test. At least something. He knows nothing about the murders."

"So you're going to let him walk free and everything?" Frank capitulated. "Not even.....not even put a tail on him? Nothing?"

"What do you want me to do?" Lt. Jefferson replied. "If some evidence comes up pointing to Mr. Weinstein then I'll let you know. Or if you find something, let us know. We're doing all we can."

"Right. Right," Frank said, reprimanding the uncooperative officer. "I *will* let you know. But I need protection— NOW!"

Lt. Jefferson was also frustrated, but funds for private citizen security just weren't there.

"I'll have a patrol car drive down your block every couple of hours," Lt. Jefferson offered, throwing Frank a bone. "That's all we can do. Call me later if you like."

"That's not enough!" Frank angrily replied.

"Okay," Lt. Jefferson said, about to offer Frank another bone. "I'll call a friend of mine at the Hammond Police Department. Maybe they can cruise by Mr. Weinstein's office for a few days. But that's all I can do. Mr. Weinstein doesn't live or work in Gary."

Chapter Forty-Three

Wednesday evening, May 27th, 1992. Dr. Weinstein left his office at 5:30 p.m. and walked directly to his Camry. He couldn't explain it, but he had a feeling he was being watched the whole day. He didn't actually see anyone following him, or park in front of his office, but a vehicle making the same distinctive engine sound kept driving by every hour or so. He shrugged it off to paranoia and drove in the direction of Balmoral Park.

If there was a time when he needed extra money, it was now. His undertaking was nearly complete, but his finances were dwindling and were about to sink to an all-time low after his divorce. The sixty-five hundred bucks he was about to collect wasn't enough to support him or his family for a month—let alone any extracurricular activities, and certainly not his overhead. But he wasn't worried about that as much as he was about killing Frank. Benny knew he was being watched in spite of passing the polygraph. He also knew Frank called the cops and they were probably providing that bastard with protection.

The expressway was impassable for almost a half hour. Only one of the three lanes was open, moving at a snail's pace.

Benny thought it was probably due to construction, but there weren't any road work signs. The cars finally began to move. Benny was able to see the trouble; a horrible accident. An eighteen wheeler tipped over, crushing two cars underneath.

Shit, if I left just a few minutes earlier, that could have been me! he thought, thanking the Gods for his good fortune. I hope my luck lasts the rest of the night.

Benny arrived at South Dixie Highway later than expected—about 7:15 p.m. But he wasn't in any hurry so he stopped to eat at The Daily Double, a popular greasy spoon across from the track. He ordered breakfast items for dinner, scrambled eggs and a side of three wheat pancakes plus coffee. He thought he'd relax a while before cashing his ticket. Plus he had some time to kill before he met Rings. The restaurant was crawling with all sorts of degenerates, but not the kind that bothered him. They were mostly washed up lonely men looking for some company before they gambled their paychecks.

The waitress came with the food. As soon as Benny started eating, he heard the familiar sound of that car or truck or whatever it was, as it drove past the diner—the same sound he heard all day in front of his office. Again, he shrugged it off as mind tricks—maybe his conscious was beginning to bother him. No, it couldn't have been that. He was delighted three of the four animals who beat him were dead—and mutilated. Gone forever.

He finished eating, left a sawbuck on the table for a seven dollar tab then sat in his car for five minutes. Benny pulled out a new cigar and lit it with his Cubs lighter. He then drove to Balmoral's parking lot in a spot where Rings would find him later. It started to drizzle as he got out of the car and walked to the gate, paying the two dollar grandstand admission. He didn't buy a program. He just needed to cash out.

The track was busy that Wednesday evening. Balmoral had a lot of big races on their card which attracted more bettors. Everyone thinks it's less likely a stake or allowance race will be rigged—somehow they'll be more honest than cheaper races. They're not. Benny didn't care about the size of the purse or who was racing. He liked the anonymity of a large crowd.

It was now approaching eight o'clock. Benny could have cashed his ticket the moment he arrived, but he wanted some quiet time to relax. He tried to relax by sitting down for a half hour with his cigar and a cup of coffee. But there was a problem: He noticed a man looking at him from the bar. Benny didn't recognize this man, but was sure this guy was following him. It wasn't a mind trick this time. It wasn't paranoia. This guy was following him! Whoever this stranger was, it looked like he was drinking Jim Beam. He can't be all bad, Benny thought, watching the bartender pour the dude another shot.

The unidentified man was well hidden in plain sight—heavily disguised. Could have been forty, maybe younger, and wore an old fashioned brown Schlitz cap with a pair of dark shades. He had two weeks worth of growth on his face. He had on faded blue jeans and a blue Notre Dame jacket.

Benny got up and walked to the other side of the grandstands, inside, near the betting windows. The unidentified man quickly left some money on the bar and also left. Benny strolled up to a betting window and handed the teller his sixty-five hundred dollar ticket.

"You're mighty lucky," the older, balding teller said while recounting the C notes and the odd change, handing Benny an envelope.

Benny thanked the clerk with a ten spot and stuffed the money in the inside pocket of his leather bomber. He slowly looked around, didn't see anyone, then tucked his Punch back into his mouth and headed for the parking lot. As he neared the exit he thought he'd look around again. No one. Good, he thought. Maybe I was imagining things. Benny poked his head outside and scanned as far as his eyes could see. It was dark, but he didn't notice anything out of the ordinary. As he walked towards his Camry, he saw Rings was already there, waiting in the now recognizable suburban. Rings got out of his car to greet him.

"Yo, Sox!" Rings blurted out with all the subtlety of a rhinoceros. "I'm here!"

Young Rings knew how to irritate Benny.

"Do you always have to do that?" Benny said, annoyed, but happy to see his friend approach.

"Do what?" Rings asked, raising his arms in the air like he didn't know.

"I'm carrying a lot of money," Benny said, scolding his accomplice. "And in a bad part of town. Why don't you think first? Attracting attention like that......I....oh, forget it."

Rings lowered his head knowing he was just taken to the woodshed. "Sorry 'bout that," Rings apologized. "Here's your gun. And yes, it's still empty."

Benny took the silver pistol and placed it in the back seat of his Camry. They both got into Rings' suburban to talk for a few minutes.

"I almost died myself," Benny said. "I went to Stagecoach Road to get my stuff out of the boat and Gerald was in it and all my stuff was gone except for some tape. I don't know what the fuck's going on. Someone knows."

Rings tried to act cool, like he handles this sort of thing every day.

"You got another cigar, Sox? I smoked the last one last night."

Benny checked his jacket and couldn't find one. "Wait, I'll

get one from my car in a minute. Listen, I want to talk to you. You have to be careful. Don't say anything to anyone. I passed the polygraph and everything is okay, for now. But someone knows. And, my good buddy, you're the only one I can talk to."

Rings was genuinely touched. Here he was, just a kid, and someone was confiding in him.

"It could be anyone," Rings said, offering some insight. "I heard one radio station is holding a contest: 'Where's Gerald?'"

Benny took a long puff on his stogie.

"You mean like 'Where's Waldo?'"

"Something like that," Rings said. "I can't be sure."

"What's the prize?"

"Don't know. Probably publicity."

"Well someone already knows," Benny said. "And we have to get rid of his body, and fast."

Rings fidgeted in his seat.

"You mean me too? I have to help you dump the body?" Rings shouted, not realizing his window was open.

"What the hell's wrong with you?" Benny screeched, noticing Rings quickly closing his window as if to apologize. "Yes, you too. I have a plan. My boat is in a storage place on Cline Avenue. I put it there last night. Now all we have to do is go there, hitch up the boat to your car, retrieve the body at Stagecoach Road then dump him in Baines Harbor. You know where that's at. The police aren't looking for anyone there."

Rings wasn't too happy with the plan but didn't want to disappoint his dad's old friend.

"Yeah, I know about Baines Harbor," Rings admitted. "But why do we have to go through all the trouble of taking the boat? There's a bridge that crosses over it just off of Route 12. Why not just dump him over the bridge?"

Benny shook his head. "That bridge, my good man, is in full view of everyone. Even if we did that it would take at least a full minute. Anyone could drive by in a minute. But there's a hidden ravine just before the bridge where we can turn off and slide the boat down. It's pretty steep. That's why I need your help."

Rings resigned himself to the inconvenient reality that he was stuck helping Benny, better judgment notwithstanding.

"Does it have to be tonight?" Rings pleaded, not being in the mood for any excitement, desperately looking for an excuse. "I was hoping to get home early and help my ma pick out a new wheelchair out of a catalogue."

"I see," Benny said, playing the martyr, at the same time feeling guilty about getting Rings involved. "No, I guess it doesn't have to be tonight. Maybe later this week"

Rings sensed Benny conceded too easily.

"Hey Sox. I know," Rings said, offering a new, safer plan. "Why don't we bet a few races as long as we're here? I have a few bucks. Come on. It'll be fun. And we might just score again."

Benny opened the passenger side and got out of the car, walked to his Camry, opened the door and reached for a cigar under the seat.

"Yeah, okay," Benny said, as he stood up, handing Rings a cigar and plucking a fifty from his jacket. "Take this and bet a number. Call me later this week," carelessly forgetting Rings wasn't allowed to call his office since that was traceable evidence.

Rings forced a smile while his large brown eyes looked away. He took the cigar and money from Benny and tucked both gifts in his front shirt pocket.

"Tomorrow would be better anyway," Benny said, not convincing the youth. "Have a good time."

Rings felt horrible.

"Sorry Sox," Rings said, knowing he let his father's best friend down. "I just can't tonight."

Benny knew he was wrong asking Rings to help him hide a murder. And knew how badly Rings must have felt at that moment. He didn't want to leave it that way.

"I really mean it," Benny said, his spirits deceptively lifting. "Really. Tomorrow would be better. Don't give it another thought. Have a good time tonight and I'll call you tomorrow," Benny continued, correcting his earlier faux pas. "I hope you win a bundle."

"Yeah? OK." Rings affirmed, hoping there was some truth in what Benny just said. "Call me in the morning. I know I'm not supposed to call your office—I know, I know."

"Tomorrow it is," Benny said as he revved his motor. "And, oh, I almost forgot. Ask your mother if she would like me to look at her back. You know, I do know something about back pain. You could drive her to my office later this week. Maybe I can help."

"That would be great!" Rings said, believing he was still in good standing. "I would love to get some help for her. We can't afford much."

"Well, the price is right for your mother—free!" Benny said as he slowly pulled away. "Free is below my cost!"

Rings smiled and looked up towards the sky as he headed towards the grandstands. I know you're watching, daddy Eddy, he somberly thought. I'll do the right thing.

Chapter Forty-Four

Benny left the track and drove back to I-94, heading towards his storage place on Cline Avenue. He was going to toss Gerald into the harbor himself. On the way to Coros RV & Boat Storage, he couldn't help but reflect on how radically things changed in his life. This had nothing to do with his impending divorce. It had everything to do with his nature. Here he was, on his way to dump a human being, like it was a piece of meat, into a cold body of water. Where in his upbringing did he get that? He never hurt anyone before no matter what they did to him.

He remembered back to when his childhood dog, Daisy, had died.

* * * * *

Daisy was a four-year-old rescue when Benny's father adopted her from the pound—literally hours before that poor sweet mutt was to be put to sleep. Benny was about five at the time. Daisy had a miserable life before the Weinsteins took her in. She was a brown, long-haired half Golden Retriever, half who knows what with sad eyes and droopy hairy ears, who was beaten, starved and left out in the cold until the dog catchers saw her roaming the streets after escaping from her cramped cage—where she was held captive twenty-three hours a day. Benny's father always knew his son wanted a dog and thought a mature dog would need less housebreaking. Benny remembered peeking out the window and seeing his father opening the family's turtle green Buick and suddenly seeing this mass of fur fly by. Daisy ran around the yard at warp speed for a full ten minutes before Harry corralled her into the house.

Daisy loved every second of the three years she lived with the Weinsteins. Man, was she spoiled! She had the run of the house and backyard, a huge delicious dinner every night, chicken soup with whole chicken on the weekends, a daily freshened water dish, and two dogs to play with next door. Benny spent hours playing with Daisy—taking her on long walks and going fishing at the lagoon. Benny would catch a fish and Daisy would go after it in the water, pretending she caught it. Benny would clap as Daisy shook herself off, soaking everyone in sight—a small price to pay for the happiness they had together. Every day when Benny got home from school, Daisy would wildly bark and jump for joy, nearly knocking Benny over each time. Her master was home. One spring day while Benny was at school, Daisy got sick and his mother, Mildred, rushed her to the vet. It was some sort of untreatable virus. Daisy was sent home to die, and waited for Benny by her water dish. She had to see him one last time. Benny got home from school at 3:34 p.m. and saw his best friend laying there on the floor, too weak to greet him in her usual exuberant manner. Daisy could only manage to twitch her ear and sniff Benny's hand as he put it to her dry nose. At 3:47 p.m. on that rainy April day, Daisy looked up at Benny's eyes, licked his fingers and said goodbye. Daisy's limp body melted on the floor and died. Benny cried uncontrollably for a week. Mildred put her son's head in her lap and rubbed his head, assuring him he would see Daisy again someday. Maybe they will.

* * * * *

It was 9:50 p.m. Coros Storage was about two miles away. Benny turned onto Cline Avenue, slowing to 20 mph on the long, curved ramp. He passed a liquor store on his right, then two blocks down, another liquor store on his left. He wasn't in the best of areas. That's why the rent was so low. He glanced at his back seat and saw his pistol waiting for him—empty as it was. Okay, he thought to himself, let's get this over and done. I don't want to be here any longer than I have to. He pulled into the storage complex, entered his security code and waited for the gait to open. Nothing happened. He entered his code again and the motorized gate finally began to hum. Good, he thought. That's all it was. I entered the wrong numbers. The heavy black iron gate started to slide. As soon as there was room, Benny drove past the gate to his storage space. He backed his car up to the garage door and got out of his car. Off to his left he noticed a large breach in the chain linked fence which surrounded the facility. That's odd, he thought. Why don't they fix that? Anyone could just come in. I've got to hurry.

Benny walked behind his car, making sure the hitch was secured. He then grabbed the garage door handle, effortlessly raising the door, revealing his Jon boat. That's very strange, he thought. Didn't I padlock this shut yesterday? I know I did. There was no padlock to be found. Maybe I only thought I locked it. I've been under a lot of stress lately. I'll bet that's it, Benny thought, trying to convince himself he wasn't going crazy.

Benny stood there for a few seconds, inspecting his boat and contemplating the task ahead. I've got to work fast. I'm doing this alone. It's not going to be easy. Maybe Baines Harbor isn't a good place to dump the body. Come on—let's not get confused. I still have to go back to Stagecoach Road to get the body.

It was dark inside the storage space. The parking lot security lights were bright, but not enough to see what he was doing. He went back to his car and took a flashlight from the glove compartment and went back inside. Suddenly, he heard the familiar sound, the motor—the same one he heard all day. He quickly lowered the door and turned on his flashlight, waiting for the car or whatever it was, to pass. It didn't. He listened as the motor drew nearer then stopped, idling just feet away. Benny got scared. It's probably another renter getting his stuff, he thought. I'm not the only one with a boat or RV.

Benny shone the light on the boat and put his hand on the tarp. The glow cast a wide shadow in the room. A large brown beetle ran passed his foot while he inspected the cold vinyl covering—the familiar idling motor, more present than before. Who the fuck is that? he thought. Why are they still outside? Benny was scared. He wished he had taken his gun from the back seat. He knew it wasn't loaded, but maybe the sight of it would deter an attacker. He stood there another minute before thinking there might be something in the boat he could use as a weapon. Maybe the culprit left a knife in there or something. That's it, he thought, allowing himself a ray of hope. Maybe the person who cleaned out my stuff overlooked a knife.

The rumbling of the motor got louder, as if the driver purposely gunned the engine so it would be heard. Benny's hand trembled as his sweaty hand gripped the tarp. He knew there probably wasn't anything of use in the boat—bugs maybe. It can't hurt to look, he thought. He heard the engine rev up a few more times. "Let's just get this over with and get out," he whispered to himself, as he forcefully yanked the tarp off the vessel. "OH GOD! OH GOD! OH GOD!" he screamed. "JESUS! MOTHER FUCKER!! FUUUCKKKK!!" Gerald was in the boat! His grisly remains were sprawled over the slats. His mouth cut into an eerie smile, like a Jack-O-Lantern. His hollow eyes staring right at Benny. "JESUS FUCKING CHRIST! FUCKING CHRIST!!"

Benny dropped his flashlight on the corpse. His only thought was to get out of there, not caring who or what awaited outside. He groped for the garage handle and lifted the door. He bolted for his car without looking over the fence. He reached in the back seat for his gun.

"HOLD IT RIGHT THERE, JEW!" the voice in an amber pickup truck yelled. It was Frank! "DROP THE FUCKING PISTOL!"

Benny tossed his gun under his Camry.

Frank rammed his truck through the fence, as he did before, and smashed into Benny's front bumper, blocking any chance of escaping. Frank got out of his truck, pointing his shotgun right at Benny's right temple.

"Did you like my little surprise, JEW?" Frank said, referring to Gerald's body in the boat.

Benny didn't move. Frank was in control.

"I know it was you, you fucking kike. I know it was you. It was you who killed Tommy. Yes, I know it was you. I'm impressed. I didn't think you had the guts, fucking coward."

Benny looked for a way out. It was obvious Frank was drunk.

"Yes, and I know about Tommy fucking that foxy wife of yours. Yes, yes I know about that. Murphy told me. Tommy said he fucked her gooooood! Raaaaaaaaaaaaaw! He came in her twat like a horse—weeeeeeee, ha ha ha," Frank laughed. "She sucked his cock too!"

Benny was more scared than angry. He knew Frank was going to kill him—and wanted to have a little fun first.

"Yeah, and poor Murphy. Well, what can you say about good old Murphy?" Frank said, consoling himself. "He probably had it coming. Did a lot of bad shit in his life. Boy, I wanted to fuck his woman. Man, Chrissy has some nice tits, doesn't she?" Frank ranted on while backing up to get a can of malt liquor from his dashboard. "Hey! Maybe now I will fuck her," remembering she was now a 'widow'. "Right after I waste your Jew ass!"

Benny didn't say a word as his eyes scanned back and forth, waiting for an opening. Frank took a long drink from his half-filled can of suds, lifting the barrel of his gun for a split second. Benny made a move to run.

"STOP RIGHT THERE, FUCKER!" Frank screamed, dropping his brew. "DON'T FUCKING MOVE!" he said, repositioning the gun at Benny's head and enjoying every second.

"Poor Skunk. Poor Skunk," Frank sobbed, referring to Gerald's more familiar name. "Poor Skunk. Why did you have to kill him?" Frank cried, the booze exaggerating is emotions. "He was my best friend. My pal. And you killed him. YOU KILLED HIM!"

Frank was rapidly losing what little control he had, and angry that he dropped his Colt 45. Benny knew he would be shot on the spot if he opened his mouth. He kept it shut.

"The money, Jew," Frank said, cocking the trigger back, the barrel just inches from Benny's skull. "I saw you cash out. Yeah that was me at the track. You scored big, didn't you Jew. DIDN'T YOU!"

Benny kept quiet.

"That guy must have counted out sixty C-notes at the window. I saw him hand you an envelope. Now where is it? COME ON—WHERE IS IT JEW?"

No response.

"ANSWER ME FUCKER!" Frank demanded. "If you want to save your miserable fucking life you'll tell me where the money is. Is it in your car? WHERE IS IT FUCKER?"

Frank was running out of patience as he bent forward, thinking he could salvage another swallow from the can. Just then, two squad cars screeched up to the fence. A trucker tipped them off about a man in an amber pickup weaving through traffic on I-94. Another trucker reported the same vehicle speeding onto Cline Avenue.

"POLICE OFFICERS. PUT THE GUN DOWN. NOW!" an officer shouted, grabbing his revolver with two hands and pointing it at Frank.

Benny stood motionless as he saw Frank jerk his head around, surprised by the abrupt turn of events.

"GUN DOWN NOW!" the officer repeated.

Frank didn't see the other cops and thought he could outgun the one he saw. In a desperate move, Frank fired his shotgun, spraying the cop's right arm with pellets. A cop from the other car got out and shot Frank in the back of his head, killing him instantly. He dropped with a hard thud. The officers, with guns still drawn, slowly approached Benny.

"Identify yourself," said one of the cops.

"Benjamin Weinstein, sir," Benny said, relieved to be rescued.

"What are you doing here?"

"I was getting my boat out of storage, sir. My kids and I are going fishing this weekend."

"This late at night? Where do you live?"

"In Hammond, sir. Not far from here. I just came back

from Balmoral Race Track and the storage is on the way home." Benny reached for something inside his jacket.

"HOLD IT!" the officer yelled. "What are you reaching for?"

"Some losing tickets, sir," Benny respectfully said as he voluntarily raised his hands above his head. "Check for yourself."

By now, four officers were outside their cars. One was radioing for an ambulance.

"That's okay," said one of the officers. "You show them to me."

Benny reached inside his jacket and pulled out a handful of tickets he fortunately picked up off the track's floor. He always did that when he won big—tax purposes. He handed a few to the cops. They examined the tickets and put their guns down. But Benny wasn't in the clear. One of the cops walked to the boat. Benny warned him what he would find.

"There's a dead body in my boat," Benny admitted. "The guy you just shot killed him and put him there. He was trying to frame me for the murders in Miller. Ask Lt. Jefferson from the Gary Police Department. I just took and passed a polygraph about that. The guy you shot killed them all. He told me so just now. He was following me—followed me to the track and saw me cash over six grand." Benny pulled the envelope out from his jacket. "Here it is."

Two cops examined Gerald's stiff body in the Jon boat.

"Get another wagon here," an officer said to one of his colleagues. "And get forensics here too."

Benny thought he might still be in trouble, but felt a little better when the officer looked inside Frank's truck.

"Look at this!" an officer said, pointing to all the stuff he found in the back of Frank's pickup. All of Benny's old stuff was there. The same things the cops knew were part of the crime scene in Miller—rope, a sewing kit, camera, tape, twine, darts, tranquilizer rifle, Sucrostrin, adrenaline, the works. It was all there—in Frank's truck!

The cops radioed Lt. Jefferson who was busy on another murder case, like he was every night in Gary. But he confirmed Benny's statements and the officers didn't even bother searching Benny. Good thing—he had a couple of darts on him too!

The ambulance arrived and removed Gerald's body from the boat. Two tow trucks were dispatched to haul away Frank's truck and Benny's boat. "Sorry," said one of the officers. "Your kids will have to wait until the lab is done with it— shouldn't be any more than a week—two, tops."

"That's all right," Benny said, agreeing with everything the officers wanted. "I know you're just doing your job."

"Follow us to the station, Mr. Weinstein. We need to get a statement."

"Sure thing."

The officers waited until the tow trucks and ambulances left, then got into their cars, waiting for Benny to get into his. Benny tossed his keys in the air, purposely letting them drop so he would have an excuse to bend down and retrieve his gun, which he did. Benny got in his car and followed the officers to the station where he was interviewed for an hour.

"Okay, thanks Mr. Weinstein," said officer Sanders, the lead interrogator. "I mean, Doctor Weinstein!"

Benny smiled, feeling even more relieved with the officer's good humor.

"Please, just Benny. Call me Benny."

"We have your office phone number. We'll call you if we need you."

"Anytime," Benny said cheerfully. "And let me know when I can pick up my boat. It's perch season, you know!"

Benny exited the police station and walked to his car. The first thing he did was stuff his gun under the front seat. I'll eventually have to put some more bullets in this thing, he thought. I sure could have used some tonight. He drove to his parents' house to spend the night, and heard Buffy and Jody say goodnight to Mr. French.

Chapter Forty-Five

Thursday morning, May 28th, 1992. Benny slept very well at his childhood home in Miller; soundly and without guilt. His aging parents, Mildred and Harry, tried to talk him out of the divorce, but to no avail. He never told them about Marsha's affair and never planned on ever telling them. "It's just one of those things," Benny explained. "Some problems are unsolvable."

It was a beautiful spring morning, 70 degrees, birds chirping, with scant wispy white clouds above. It was the first day in almost twenty years he awoke knowing his tormenters were dead. He was proud he had a hand eradicating four pieces of filth who never had any business roaming the earth in the first place. What could be better!

Benny left his parents' house at 6:30 a.m., headed down County Line Road and stopped at the Gas 'N Go for coffee and a newspaper. He sat in his car sipping away while admiring the new window sign in Tommy's old tire store; "Under New Management." I put that there! Benny thought, pleased with his deeds. Then he reveled in the Post Tribune's headline: MURDER SUSPECT SHOT, FRIEND FOUND IN TRUNK. The paper printed Frank's awful looking driver's license picture under the headline. He wasn't smiling. Benny was. This was only bad news for Pete's hotdog stand. The crowd around the lagoon disappeared now that the murders were solved. Benny was enjoying reading the article, that is, until he saw his name mentioned!

"WHAT THE HELL!" Benny spilled his coffee, scalding his thigh. "OW, FUCK," Benny screamed, pulling out a wad of Kleenex to sop up the mess while reading the part about him: "Hammond chiropractor, Dr. Benjamin Weinstein, told police he was taking his boat out of Coros RV & Boat storage late last night when Mr. Stram approached, brandishing a shotgun with the intent of robbing Dr. Weinstein of his gambling winnings. Dr. Weinstein said Mr. Stram followed him to the storage facility from Balmoral Race Track after watching him collect over six thousand dollars." The story didn't implicate Benny, rather, it portrayed him as a hero of sorts, explaining how the cops got there just before Frank could shoot him. Still, he didn't want the publicity. Business was good enough. I've got to call Rings, Benny thought. And my kids. I've got to talk to them. No wait, I better let Marsha explain. Shit, I don't want to talk to her today. Shit, I've *got* to talk to her.

Benny arrived in Hammond at 7:25 a.m. His first patient wasn't until 8:30. But he had a bad feeling. Oh, shit, he thought. I have to see for myself. His hunch was right. He drove near his office, close enough to see the front door. Dozens of people, many of them reporters, were waiting for him. I hope Tracey isn't there yet, he thought. Of all days to come early, I hope this isn't one of them. I've got to call her. Benny was all dressed up for work, wearing his 'emergency' clothes he kept at his folks'. He wasn't exactly famous, just well known around town and didn't want to be bothered. Okay, I'll stop and make some calls at the Dunkin' Donuts in

East Chicago—a good ten miles away. First on his list was Marsha.

"Yes, it's me—Benny," he said after hearing Marsha answer.

"I was wondering if you would call," she said. "The phone hasn't stopped ringing. Why didn't you tell me? You should have called last night."

"I was tired," Benny said. "You have to tell the kids everything is fine. See how they're doing in school—if anyone is bothering them. I'll be at the office later. Call me then. And I'll let you know when I find an apartment. I'm seeing a lawyer later on.

There was a five second pause.

"You could have been killed," Marsha said, acting like she was genuinely concerned. "Our kids could have lost their father."

"And what of it?" Benny replied, not wanting to endure any niceties from his unfaithful wife. "I'm insured for over two million. You could have had your pick."

"I guess there isn't anything left to say," Marsha said, sensing the edge in his voice.

"Yes there is," Benny countered. "I'm keeping the six grand I won last night. Living expenses. Our lawyers will work out the maintenance and child support. It's over."

Benny hung up and called Tracey.

"Just don't let anyone in until I get there," Dr. Weinstein said to his trustworthy employee.

"But what if I can't?" Tracey asked. "How can I keep them out?"

"Just do the best you can. I'll be there in a half hour. Later."

Then he called Rings.

"Yo, Sox! I heard," Rings exclaimed. "Man, I'm glad

you're alive. Where the fuck are you?"

Benny transferred the phone to his other ear, getting a better grip on his newspaper.

"Where am I?" Benny jokingly said. "I'm in Havana Cuba. They're after me!"

Two second silence.

"For real?" Rings asked in disbelief.

"No, not for real!" Benny said, shaking his head at the young man's gullibility. "I'm outside a donut shop in East Chicago. I see you already know."

"Yeah, man," Rings said. "You could have been laid out with a tag on your toe. You're one lucky dude."

"I know. Listen, there's a lot of people hanging around outside my office. I'll chase them away once I get there. But I was thinking, this would be a good time for me to see your mother. Ask her if she wants me to look at her back."

"I already did, Sox. She can't wait—all excited about it, you know. No one's been able to help her. You gotta have good insurance to get good help."

"Well you tell your mother the price is right at my office— free. I already told you that. Can you stop by at three?"

"Three? Yeah, I think so. We'll see you then," Rings confirmed. "Oh, and momma loves her new wheelchair. I got eighty bucks to spare after paying for it!"

"Maybe she won't need that chair after I'm through with her."

"You think so? You can cure momma?"

"I don't know. Just talking. But I'll try. See you at three."

Benny hung up the phone and drove to his office. All of the parking spots were taken by curiosity seekers and news trucks, so he had to park across the street. He saw his first patient waiting outside amongst the onlookers—it was Carla. Tracey arrived at the same time, holding on to Mitzie for dear life. That poor frightened Beagle had her tail, not tucked, but strapped underneath her belly—the hairy tip wiggling on her chest. Both Tracey and Dr. Weinstein pushed their way through the crush of humanity as they made their way to the door. Everyone was shouting questions, or shouting obscenities, maybe hoping to get on TV. Benny pulled out his key to open his door.

"HOLD IT. HOLD IT EVERYONE," Dr. Weinstein shouted, addressing the hoard like a politician. "I'M NOT ANSWERING ANY QUESTIONS NOW OR ANY OTHER TIME. GO HOME."

Dr. Weinstein hurriedly pushed his key in the door, while shielding Tracey and Mitzie from the mass of flesh. They made it in alone, and Dr. Weinstein quickly locked the door.

"Wait, Carla's still outside," Tracey said. "Don't you want to see her?

Dr. Weinstein considered that for moment.

"Oh…..oh…all right…all right," Dr. Weinstein hesitantly decided. "I suppose if I can survive a shotgun to my head, I can survive Carla, too. YOU let her in!"

Tracey knocked on the glass door and mouthed, "I'm letting you in," to Carla. Tracey unlocked the door and Carla jumped into the office. Tracey quickly locked the door behind her. The crowd was still there.

"Just my neck today," Carla said matter-of-factly as if the whole scene didn't bother her.

"That's it?" Dr. Weinstein said in amazement. "You plowed your way through for a little neck adjustment?"

"Noooo!" Carla said devilishly. "And for this!" she said, holding out a brown paper bag.

"What is it?" Dr. Weinstein asked. "Not another cake!"

Tracey stayed to watch the unveiling. Carla pulled what looked like a heavy object from the bag. It was wrapped in newspaper. She handed it to Dr. Weinstein.

"Here, take it," Carla said as Dr. Weinstein reached for the present. "You can use it."

Dr. Weinstein lifted the package up as if to weigh it.

"Oh, no!" Dr. Weinstein lamented. "It's not what I think it is?" he asked, motioning for Tracey and Carla to move out of sight into the hallway.

"But it is!" said Carla. "Alex phoned me this morning from Canada and asked me to give it to you. He read about the trouble you had last night in an Ontario paper. Take it. It's one of his old ones. He has plenty more."

Benny tore the paper from Carla's gift. It was exactly what he thought it was—a gun!

"Ooo, a gun!" Tracey said, surprised by the sight of it. "I think I'll transcribe some patient notes. Come on, Mitzie," she said while running to her office.

"Thanks," Dr. Weinstein said. "But I really don't need this. I can't have something like this in my office."

"It's a gift," said Carla. "An antique. Alex and I both want you to have it. It'll make you feel safer. I'm pretty sure you can still buy bullets for it."

Dr. Weinstein capitulated. "Okay, thanks. I'll put it in my car after the melee is over."

Benny finished up with Cara and asked Tracey to reschedule all of his appointments to the next day and Saturday. He saw just two more patients that morning—a couple of injury cases who were already on their way. He used the rest of the morning to call his lawyer and look for an apartment.

"I'll be back at three," Dr. Weinstein told Tracey. "Why don't you take the rest of the day off—on me!"

Only a few stragglers were left by eleven o'clock. Dr. Weinstein walked past them, hiding his new gun under his bomber which he was carrying on that warm spring day. He walked to his car and put his jacket with the gun in his trunk. He didn't go straight to lunch. He drove to the Walgreens across the street to use their payphone. He had to call a realtor.

"Hello, Laura? Benny Weinstein! Your daughter said I could reach you at this number. Yes, I know we have plans for tomorrow. But I'd like to see a condo now if you have time. Great! Yes, I have the address: 1114 South Calumet Avenue, number 24. Right, I know, second floor. I can be there in fifteen minutes."

Chapter Forty-Six

Benny was all nervous when he got back in his car and headed towards South Calumet Avenue in Munster to see Laura again—the first time in nineteen years. All of this time she was that close to his neighborhood, five miles away and he didn't know it. He didn't know her married name, if in fact she was married. Gail never said whether she was or wasn't. It didn't matter. He wanted to see her. What did she look like? Could she have changed all that much? He was expecting the worst. At least it wasn't a date. He was meeting her as a professional. He needed to get a condo.

It was 12:45 p.m. when Benny pulled up to the complex. Most of the tenants were at work and the parking lot was nearly empty. He cruised down the row of buildings and spotted 1114. He was a few minutes early so he waited in his car. He reached for a half smoked cigar in his ashtray but decided not to light it. I don't think she ever smoked, he thought. He looked in his side view mirror and saw a cream colored late model Cadillac approaching. That's probably her, he thought, adjusting his tie. The car pulled up next to him. Inside was a lady, about his age, very plump with died black hair. "Oh, no," he said to himself. "If that's her….. He got out of the car and was about to say "Laura" when someone from behind covered his eyes. Her fingers smelled great, like lilac perfume. Then he heard a familiar voice.

"Guess whoooooooo?" the melodic female sound of his youth rang out.

Benny opened his eyes. Her hands light on his face. He saw her perfectly manicured nails adorned with the prettiest shade of pink polish. Benny reached for her left hand and caressed one of her fingers. He turned around to take a look. It was Laura. And she looked stunning!

"Benny! Benny! Benny!" Laura exclaimed. "Is that you? You...you...my God...you look GREAT!"

Benny blinked his eyes four times fast. "I look great? Me? Look at you! You look sensational!"

They quickly embraced, holding each other for a good ten seconds. In fact, Laura did look sensational. Her face still pretty, a little more mature, but a great smile, and long hair pulled up in an attractive bun pinned up with an ivory stick. She had a gorgeous figure, nice butt, great boobs, and sexy legs. She wore the most beautiful pink lipstick and exquisite diamond earrings. She was conservatively dressed in a beige, knee length business skirt, and gray form fitting sweater.

"WOW!" Benny howled. "I can't get over how you haven't changed. Just like the day I last saw you... just like..." Benny suddenly had a flashback to that night. That awful night. And Laura knew it.

"Come on, Benjamin," Laura said, turning on her professional persona and picking up her briefcase. She knew what Benny was thinking.

Benny followed Laura into the complex. It was a modern building with all the amenities: pool, sauna, gym, a kids' playground, clubhouse, pond, everything.

"There's no elevator," Laura said. "But it's just up one

flight of stairs. You look like you can handle it!" paying her old beau a compliment.

They reached the second floor and walked down the hallway.

"Gail tells me you're getting divorced," Laura said delicately. "I think that's so sad. I know you have kids."

"Yeah, well, what can you do," Benny replied. "It happened so fast."

"It's not that terrible, though," Laura offered. "I got divorced three years ago," she said handing Benny her business card as she stopped in front of the door. "Here it is—number 24."

Laura unlocked the door with her master key. Benny glanced at the business card as they both walked in. Laura closed the door from behind.

"I see you kept your maiden name, Burns."

"Yeah, I did," said Laura. "It was Pearson. My ex's name was Warren Pearson. He owns a plumbing company in Merrillville. Maybe you've heard of it, Pearson Plumbing. They have a corny slogan: Our Prices Won't Drain You.'"

"No," Benny said, "can't say I've heard of them. I kinda like that slogan! But I don't think it's original."

"Probably not," said Laura, completely agreeing. "There wasn't much original about him—including his girlfriend."

"Oh, sorry," said Benny.

"That's okay. I'm seeing someone now—a big shot tax attorney from Chicago—Ned."

"Who?" Benny asked.

"Oh, it's not important. Let me show you around."

Benny was somewhat disheartened to learn she had a boyfriend. Though it really didn't make much difference. He wasn't looking for a new relationship this soon, anyway.

"There's furniture in here!" Benny said, like he discovered

a new thing.

"Oh, I didn't tell you. These condos come fully furnished. But you don't have to buy it furnished. You can if you like."

"No, it's fine," Benny said. "It looks better than what I would have picked out."

Laura escorted Benny to the kitchen.

"This has everything you need," Laura said, taking out a brochure from her folder. "Microwave, ice maker, electric stove, coffee maker, dishwasher, disposal—everything. And it's in your price range."

"Nice," Benny said. "What about the bedroom?"

"This way," Laura said, clutching her pen between her pearly white teeth. "There are two bedrooms. I'll show you the master first."

Benny followed Laura into the master bedroom.

"It's so big! And I like the windows," Benny said, admiring the view.

Laura stood next to Benny, both looking out the window.

"Yes, it is nice," Laura said. "It's a great view of the pond."

Benny looked directly at Laura's beautiful dark eyes. "And it's a nice view here, too," he said, putting his hand on her waist. Laura, momentarily forgetting her professional manner, put her hand on Benny's thigh. Benny raised his hands, gently cradling Laura's gorgeous face. She gazed back at him. Benny pulled the pen out of her mouth and tossed it on the nightstand. He put his hand on the back of her neck and slowly pulled her face close to his and kissed her, smudging her pink lipstick on the side of her mouth.

"Oh don't, don't," Laura pleaded as Benny planted his mouth on hers again and closed the blinds. "I'm seeing Ned. Oh, don't, don't."

Benny reached under her skirt, softly caressing her panties

near her moist slit. Laura dropped her notebook on the floor and rubbed Benny under his sac through his pants. Benny passionately kissed her, reaching his other hand up her back and unsnapping her bra.

"No, we better not. We better not," cried Laura. "I'm supposed to be working."

Benny had his mouth firmly covering hers while he pulled her bra out from under her tight sweater, letting it fall to the floor.

"Oh, Benny, Benny. I have other appointments," Laura sighed. "Later. Not now. Later."

Benny reached up her sweater and put his palm on her huge firm melons, softly feeling each erect nipple with his fingers. He lifted up her sweater and kissed each of her perfectly formed white mounds. Then he raised her sweater off around her head, exposing her succulent tits. He pulled the ivory stick out of her bun, letting her long brown hair drape down to her shoulders. He worked his finger up her hot moist pussy, squishing inside, while she reached down his Khakis and grabbed his rock hard cock. Benny reached up and pulled Laura's panties all the way down, past her thighs and knees, to her ankles. She stepped out of them while she unbuckled Benny's pants and pulled them down. All that remained was her beige skirt which Benny didn't remove as he lifted it up while she parted her sexy thighs revealing her sizzling twat. Benny lifted her up, placing her firm white buns on the side of the bed. She grabbed his throbbing organ and placed the head next to her steamy snatch. Benny had both hands on her tits as he kissed her and slowly worked all eight inches of himself into her horny box.

"Oh, Benny! Benny! Benny!" Laura moaned, hyperventilating while climaxing after a dozen pumps. "You're so stiff. Owww, OH, OH, Oh, oh, oh," she continued to moan, her head moving from side to side. "Fuck me! Fuck me! Fuck me!" she screamed.

Benny slid in and out of Laura's scorching snatch. She put both her hands around his face and lovingly kissed him while she grabbed the back of his head, pushing his mouth harder into hers. She then reached under his enormous dick and loved up is nuts, fingering his balls, her French manicured nails caressing his sac. Benny was never so horny as he kept squishing in and out of his high school sweetheart. He took his mouth off of Laura's and kissed her neck, down to her nipples, putting each one in his mouth.

"Don't cum in me!" Laura begged. Don't cum in me! Don't cum in me! OH, OH," Laura loudly moaned, Benny plunging deeper into her pussy without pulling out. He couldn't hold it any longer and sprayed a geyser of hot cream deep inside her yielding burning twat. Laura softly kissed him as he laid her down on the bed. Both exhausted.

"Oh, God," Laura said. "That was great!" She caught her breath for another ten seconds. "It should have been you."

"What?" Benny asked while blissfully recovering.

"It should have been you that night at the graduation party. Maybe that terrible thing wouldn't have happened to you. How was I to know? I was only seventeen."

Benny got up and covered his naked body with his pants.

"I guess we all live and learn," he said, realizing Laura knew about the beating. Things would have been different for a lot of people," Benny said, secretly referring to the bullies he just killed. And I totally agree. It really should have been me. I wanted you. We should have been married."

Laura's eyes lit up when she heard that.

"You know, it's never too late," she said. "We're both free now—kind of!" she blushed.

Benny really wasn't in the mood to start a serious

relationship. But the old feelings were still there, and strong. He thought he'd better change the subject.

"Where's the shower?"

Chapter Forty-Seven

Laura and Benny left the complex at 2:30 p.m. Laura was busy combing her hair out as she walked to her lavender Mercedes.

"Gee! Look at that!" Benny said. "Looks like you're doing better than me!"

Laura smiled. "I'm doing quite well, but that's a company car. My boss likes to impress."

"Well you tell your boss, whoever it is, that I was thoroughly impressed! I'll take it."

"I'll tell her," Laura said. "Gail and I are picking you up at your office tomorrow night at seven, right?"

"I was just thinking about that," Benny said. "Why don't I just meet you at the Brass Bomber at eight. That way we'll have two cars in case Gail needs to leave early or something. I'll be staying in Miller with my folks until I move into the condo."

"Oh yeah, your folks," Laura said, fondly recollecting the days she spent with Benny at his old house. "They're great people. How are they?"

"They're fine," Benny said. "A little upset about me getting divorced, but they're fine. Dad sold the store a few years ago and he's retired. Mom likes being a bubby. She's keeping busy."

"Maybe I'll stop by and say hello," Laura said, looking for an invite. "I wonder if they'll remember me."

Benny opened his car door and looked to the ground.

"Remember you!" Benny said. "They wanted you just as much as I did."

Laura walked over to Benny and hugged his neck.

"I'll meet you tomorrow at eight," Laura said, holding back a tear. "At eight."

"I'll be there. You're a great sales lady! I can't wait to move in."

"Thanks," Laura said, knowing she made a huge mistake nineteen years earlier. "I'll bring the contracts with me."

"Deal!" Benny said cheerfully. "Until then."

Benny kissed her cheek and got in his car. He put the half smoked cigar in his mouth and lit it. It was the best he felt in a long time as he drove back to his office to treat Twila.

Rings' suburban was conspicuously parked right in front of Dr. Weinstein's office at 2:50 p.m. Dr. Weinstein parked a few spaces back and got out of his car, leaving his cigar in the ashtray. Rings was sitting in the driver's seat. Twila was sprawled out in the back seat.

"Glad you made it," Dr. Weinstein said, realizing Rings had to park close to the entrance since his mother could barely walk.

"Hi ya, Benny!" Twila yelled through the glass.

Dr. Weinstein knew he had his work cut out for him. Twila must have weighed over 250 lbs and she was in a lot of pain. I wonder how Rings got her into the car, he thought.

Rings got out and opened the back passenger door.

"I'll handle this," Rings said. "I've got a system."

Rings unloaded his mother's wheelchair from the back end

of the trailer bed and wheeled it to the passenger's side.

"Here, let me help you," Dr. Weinstein offered, reaching for the chair handles.

Both men pulled Twila out of the car and placed her on the chair.

"This doesn't look new," Dr. Weinstein said after inspecting the wheelchair. "It looks like your old one."

"It is," Twila said. "I left the new one at home. Don't want noth'n bad to happen to it."

Rings rolled his mother into Dr. Weinstein's first exam room.

"Do you think you can stand and go face down on the table?" Dr. Weinstein asked.

"I don't know," Twila said. "Looks kind of narrow. Will it hold?"

"It'll hold," Dr. Weinstein assured. "Here, let me help you."

Twila waddled up from the chair, Dr. Weinstein holding one arm and Rings, the other.

"OW! OH!" Twila shrieked. "Not used to this."

Dr. Weinstein slowly lowered his fully clothed large patient into to a horizontal position on his hydraulic table. He didn't bother taking a case history—just asked her questions as they went along.

"Any pain here?" Dr. Weinstein asked while firmly palpating her first lumber vertebra.

"Not more than usual," Twila said. "But keep trying. That felt gooooooooooooood!"

"How about here?"

"No. You can press harder if you like."

Rings was intently watching as Dr. Weinstein examined his dear ol' mother.

Dr. Weinstein knew his next poke would get a much

stronger reaction. He warned her.

"What about….here!" Dr. Weinstein said, pushing on the last lumbar vertebra.

"WOE! OWWWWW! OWWWWWWW!" Twila screamed. "OWWWWWWWWWWW!"

Rings moved closer to comfort his mother.

"You OK, ma?"

Twila started to perspire. Dr. Weinstein found what is known as a 'hot lumbar' in chiropractic circles. Possibly an old ruptured disc.

"That shot right down my bad leg," Twila stated. "I haven't been able to feel anything in that leg in years. I think you're on to something."

"Maybe I am," Dr. Weinstein said. "Possibly."

"Just do what you have to do," Twila said. "Nothing could be worse than sitting in that chair all day—don't get no exercise. That's why I'm so damn fat!"

"Did you ever have your back examined? An MRI or X-ray?"

"Naw. Had my foot x-rayed once when I twisted my ankle. The state won't pay for no fancy tests."

"All right. Here, Rings—you're going to help me. Twila, we're going to put you on your side—your bad side up. Bo is going to steady you and I'm going to push on your pelvis—okay?"

"Fine, just do it," she said. "Anything is fine. I'm grateful for anything."

Twila was laying on her left side, right side up, her huge butt in the air. Man, if I can this to move, Benny thought, I could adjust a horse! Benny thought about that. I shouldn't even think that—it isn't nice.

Twila's butt was chest high to Dr. Weinstein—too high to get any leverage for a lumbar roll. So Dr. Weinstein pulled a hard back chair next to the table and stood on it.

"You're not going to jump on me, are you?" Twila asked, not knowing what to expect.

"No, I'm not going to jump on you. I'm just worried about falling!"

While Rings steadied his mother's shoulders from the back, Dr. Weinstein placed his left hand on the side of her pelvis, and his right hand in front of her right shoulder. He then pulled Twila's pelvis towards himself, and pushed her right shoulder back like a giant pretzel. Then with full force and great speed, he lunged off the chair, popping her spine. WHAM!

"OWWWWWWW! OWWWWWWWWWWWWW!" Twila screamed, falling off the table. Dr. Weinstein fell next to her, hoping he didn't break anything of his own.

"Are you all right? Are you all right?" Dr. Weinstein asked, worried about his old friend.

"I don't know," she said, breathing heavily on the floor like a wounded moose. "My leg is burning."

Dr. Weinstein and Rings watched in amazement as Twila picked herself off the ground and danced around on that leg, shaking it awake. Both Dr. Weinstein and Rings followed her out the door and into the hallway. She was dancing!

"Look at you ma!" Rings said, jumping for joy. "Look at YOU!"

Twila didn't even know she was dancing. It was just a reflex.

"I can't believe it! I can't believe it," Twila exclaimed. "I haven't walked this far so fast on my own power in ten years. Doctor—it's a miracle!"

Dr. Weinstein was happy with the outcome, but cautioned her it could only be temporary.

"Let's get you home so you can rest," Dr. Weinstein said. "I'll call you in a few days and see how you're getting along.

Now maybe you can get some exercise and sell that new wheelchair of yours!"

Rings liked that idea. He could use the money for something else—maybe college.

"Sox, how long did you have to go to school to do this," Rings asked, his interest piqued.

"Eight years total. But you can do it too. They've got loans, you know!"

Twila got back in the suburban on her own power. Rings put her wheelchair in the back.

"Bye, Benny!" Twila shouted from the car. "Thank you!"

Dr. Weinstein watched as his friends drove away.

"If you're watching, Eddy. This one was for you."

Chapter Forty-Eight

Friday, May 29th, 1992, twelve noon. The rain was coming down in buckets. Dr. Weinstein just finished up his backlog of patients from the day before. Tracey was taking an extended lunch—Mitzie needed a new prescription for worms. Man, of all days to pour, Dr. Weinstein thought while reading the Post Tribune on his desk, thunder and lightning booming outside. Let's see here. Dr. Weinstein read the forecast for the rest of the day. A ray of hope. The paper said the rain should stop later in the evening. That could be any time, maybe even tomorrow. Dr. Weinstein thought he'd wait out the worst of the storm in his office—do some pleasure reading for a change— maybe look at other sections besides the headlines. He scanned the other sections. His eyes widened. This is interesting! Yeah, I'd like to stop by—maybe Laura would like to crash that party with me for few minutes tonight—should be good.

Dr. Weinstein couldn't wait any longer. He put on his spring jacket, covered his head with the newspaper and ran to his car. He stopped at the drugstore across the street and called Rings. The overhead awning was barely wide enough to keep him dry as the thunder got louder.

"OH, HI J.J.," Benny said loudly, recognizing the older voice on the line. "IT'S SOX. WHAT'S THE GOOD WORD?"

"Hey, son," J.J. said. "Why are you yelling? My ears aren't *that* bad."

"It's thundering. Speak up. I can hardly hear you."

"You outside?" J.J. asked. "If you are, get your butt inside."

"I will in a minute," Benny said, speaking softer after the rumble faded.

"I heard you've been keeping real busy lately," J.J. said. "Rings told me all about it. Now, stay out of trouble, you here?" J.J. said, coughing up some phlegm into his handkerchief. "What can I do for you? Need more stuff? You know your next order is on me."

"Ha, ha," Benny chuckled. "No more stuff for me—at least for a while. But thanks. I'd like to ask Rings something if he's there."

"He's here," J.J. said. "And I'm working him to death. You never know when someone will call and want to take him somewhere."

Benny didn't know how J.J. felt about the friendship he had with his young nephew until that moment. It could be J.J. figured his days were numbered and wanted someone to look after Rings.

"In fact, I was going to invite Rings out tonight. Is that okay? It won't be until seven this evening."

J.J. thought about that for second.

"Well, I suppose it'll be all right. You know, that time of night we get busy. But a place like this is no place for a young man. I like seeing him have some fun for a change. He thinks the world of you."

"I like him too, J.J. I won't keep him out too long. I want

him to meet on old girlfriend of mine."

"Oh, he'd like that," J.J. said. "I'll put him on."

"Hey Rings. Sox. You free tonight?"

"Could be. What's you got in mind?" Rings asked, looking for J.J.'s approval.

"One of my old girlfriends invited me to a bar called the Brass Bomber in Portage to listen to a live band. Her daughter's going to be there—she's something else—patient of mine."

"You gonna hook me up with her?"

"Naw, she's married—a flirt, but married. Her name is Gail. She and her mother are driving down together and I thought you might want to keep her occupied for me."

"Oh, second banana!" Rings jokingly said. "Sure, I'll come. It's on Route 12, isn't it?"

"Don't worry about that. I'll pick you up at the shop at six-thirty. I got a new gun. A patient gave it to me. Got any spare bullets?"

"Bullets?" Rings said. "Yeah, we got bullets up the ass. You plan on using some tonight?"

"No, I just don't want to go to a store and buy any. People could be looking."

"Okay," Rings said. "I'll be watching for you."

Chapter Forty-Nine

Friday evening, May 29th, 1992. Benny brushed his teeth at his office and changed his clothes. He left for J.J.'s at 6:00 p.m. The rain had died down some, but it was drizzling enough to make any outdoor activity uncomfortable. He pulled up to the shop by 6:30 p.m. and parked behind the store, next to Rings' suburban. He knocked on the back door.

"Hey Sox, come in," Rings said. "You've got to see something."

Benny followed Rings to a side room off the storage area.

"What's that noise?" Benny asked. "It sounds familiar, but I can't place it."

Rings opened up the room. "Look!"

Benny's jaw dropped. "I can't believe it! That's wonderful!"

It was Twila. She was walking on a used treadmill someone had pawned the year before and never claimed.

"J.J. paid someone cash for a treadmill?" Benny asked. "I'm really surprised."

Rings laughed. "Not too much. I think he gave the poor soul twenty bucks. It's been a coat hanger for so long. I'm glad it's finally getting some use. Look at momma!"

Twila was out of breath as she waved to Benny from the exerciser.

"Hey Benny," Twila exuberantly said. "My back is feeling better. Look, I'm walking!"

"Good! Glad to see that," Benny said. "Come see me again next week for another adjustment."

Rings escorted Benny behind some boxes.

"We keep our bullets in here," Rings said, opening up a large case. "What kind do you need?"

"Not sure about my new gun," Benny said. "It's in the car. I'll go get it."

Benny brought back both guns. Rings got J.J. to look at them.

"Nice piece," J.J. said, referring to old gun. "Where did you get this?"

"A patient gave it to me. Is it worth anything?"

J.J. inspected the gun for a minute and looked down the barrel.

"I'm not exactly sure how much, but this is an 1894 Colt Bisley Single Action Revolver. I haven't seen one of these in thirty years. How much do you want for it?"

"It's yours!" Benny said, sensing the old man really wanted it. "Keep it. A small token of my appreciation for all you've done for me."

"No, I can't accept this for free," J.J. said. "It's worth at least five hundred—could be more."

"Please," Benny said. "I want you to have it. That thing is old—I'll probably kill myself with it. But I will take some bullets for this gun."

J.J. gladly handed Benny three boxes of bullets for his Colt .45.

"Here's enough to last you at least a month," J.J. chortled.

Benny took the ammo. Rings put on his public enemy hat

and followed Benny to his car.

"Do you have to wear that thing?" Benny asked.

"You're wearing your Sox cap," Rings noticed. "The ladies like me in this hat."

Benny and Rings set out for the Brass Bomber at 7:15 p.m., each driving their own vehicle.

"Got your ID?" Benny asked.

Rings patted his wallet showing Benny he had. "And a few bucks. Drinks are on me."

"I don't plan on doing any drinking," Benny said. "The last thing I need is to be pulled over and have the cops smell booze on my breath. In fact, I don't want to stay too long—not my kind of scene."

They pulled into Bomber's parking lot at five minutes to eight. It had stopped raining. Gail and her mom were already there—waiting in Laura's Mercedes. They both looked great. Benny and Rings got out of their cars and walked towards the luxury car. The ladies got out.

"You look sensational! Like movie stars," Benny said. "Both of you are just stunning—like you're going to the Academy Awards. Man, am I underdressed!"

Both Gail and Laura were wearing knee length skirts and low cut blouses—different colors, but similar styles. And they both smelled great.

"You're not so bad yourself," Gail said, winking at Benny. "Who's your friend?"

Benny motioned Rings to come closer.

"This is my good friend, Rings," Benny said.

"Rings!" Gail said, eyeing the young man up and down. "I like that name. Do you have a last name?

Benny glanced at Rings for a second—Rings glanced back.

"Moss," Rings said. "But my real first name is Bo. All my friends call me Rings."

"Well all right," Gail seductively said in her rehearsed Southern accent. "Rings it is!"

Laura smiled at Benny as Gail escorted Rings into the bar.

"Don't worry," Benny said. "Your daughter will be okay with Rings. He's a nice guy."

"But will Rings be okay?" Laura joked. "I worry about that girl. She flirts with everyone."

Benny took Laura by the arm and sat down on the wooden bench at the end of the parking lot.

"You mean she doesn't just flirt with me?" Benny laughed.

"Sorry to disappoint you—but no!" Gail sarcastically replied. "I don't know why she got married—isn't going to last, you know. She reminds me so much of her father."

Laura put her hand over her mouth, just realizing what she had said.

"Sorry, Benny. I didn't......."

"Oh, that's all right. I understand. Believe me I do," Benny said as his eyes wandered off to the distance and saw the apartment building where Laura lost her virginity that night with Larry. Laura stared at the complex too and suddenly felt uneasy. She knew Benny knew.

"Let's go in," Laura said. "We'll have a few drinks and talk over old times. Whadda ya say!"

Laura took Benny's arm and they walked into the noisy establishment. Gail's husband, Ricky, was busy setting up the instruments and sound system for the evening's performance. Gail was at the bar talking to some guy, probably one of her husband's friends. Rings was doing pretty good himself. He struck up a conversation with one of Ricky's groupies, an attractive blond girl in tight jeans, and bought her a drink. The blond was giggling and already put Rings' hat on her head.

"Let's sit here," Laura said, pointing to a booth. "It's quieter."

A perky waitress came by to take their order.

"I'm buying," Benny said. "Please!"

"Okay," Laura agreed. "But I'm not a cheap date!"

"No problem. Order anything you like."

Laura ordered a fried shrimp for her appetizer and a sirloin steak with mashed potatoes for dinner—and a grasshopper cocktail. Benny ordered grilled salmon and diet coke.

"How do you keep such a great figure?" Benny asked.

"I work out—at lot!" said Laura. "Apparently you do too!"

"I do indeed—but you look better than I do."

They didn't care that it took the waitress ten minutes to bring their drinks, or forty minutes for their food. They were having the best time catching up.

"I was on my own when Gail was born," Laura sadly recalled. "Larry dumped me right away. He just used me—a few calls after the birth, but nothing else."

"Not even child support?"

"Some, not much. But he did spend some time with Gail when she got a little older—in between traveling and gigs— when he could find them."

"What about your ex? Warren you said his name was?"

"He was great at first—treated Gail like his own. I married him when Gail was three. Then he got busy with his plumbing business and out of town suppliers and all of that. We sort of drifted apart—then I found out he had a girlfriend. That was it."

"I take it he wasn't Jewish—well, with a name like Pearson.

"Nope, not Jewish. And I missed that. I missed that a lot. Gail has no religion."

"And no other siblings?"

"No, just Gail. I have a good career now that keeps me busy—you know?"

"Yeah."

"I hear you have two kids."

"Yes, Joshua and Rachel. Josh is going to have his Bar Mitzvah soon—next year."

"Oh, that's so nice," Laura remorsefully said, knowing she would have been a better wife for Benny.

"It's getting very crowded and very loud in here," Benny said. "Do we really have to stay to watch the band? Can't we go out and do something else. I feel like taking a drive."

"That sounds good to me," Laura said. "Are you driving?"

"Sure."

"Then I better give my keys to Gail in case we get lost!"

"Good idea!" Benny said. "I'd like a repeat of yesterday!"

Gail was in a world of her own when her mother walked up to her and gave her the keys to the Mercedes.

"I'll be back at midnight or before," Laura said loudly, trying to be heard over the sound system that was spewing out canned music until Ricky was on.

"Okay, mother," Gail said. "I'll be fine here. Don't worry. Rickey's watching!"

Benny wasn't sure if he should even tell Rings he was going out for a while. He and that sexy blond were making out in the corner. Benny just yelled from a distance.

"Rings! Rings!" Benny repeated, not getting his attention at first. "I'll be back in a couple of hours."

Rings acknowledged Benny and waved him off as if to say, "Fine, bro. Don't let the door slap you on the ass on the way out."

Benny opened the door for Laura as she got in his Camry, then looked around the parking lot.

"My God, look at all the people here," Benny said as he got in the car. "Ricky must have quite the following."

"He does," Laura said. "Do you smoke cigars?"

"Sorry about that. I forgot to clean out the ashtray. Yes, I smoke cigars. My only bad habit."

"I thought I smelled it yesterday," Laura said, pretending it bothered her. "Don't worry, it isn't that bad."

"I won't light up tonight—I promise!"

Benny pulled out from the parking spot, heading towards Miller.

"I have someplace I'd like to take you," Benny said. "Someplace you haven't been, I think, in a long, long time."

"To your folks?"

"Nope, you'll see!"

They drove for twenty minutes. Laura knew which direction Benny was heading.

"You're not taking me *there*, are you?" Laura asked.

"Just to look around for five minutes—then we're out of here."

Benny pulled up to the Marquette Park Pavilion. Portage High was having their graduation party that night. That's the party Benny saw in the paper. It just happened to work out.

"We're a couple of old fogies compared to those kids," Laura said. "We don't have tickets or anything."

"Come, on," Benny insisted. "We'll tell them we're with the caterers. They won't know. And you look dressed for the part."

"Not for doing any catering work."

"Just follow me."

The night was pleasant and still with the clouds hiding the moon. The air smelled fresh from the rain, the wet bark glimmering on the thick trees. The lagoon softly rippled in the distance.

"I forgot how pretty it was here," Laura said. "You're right. I haven't been back here since graduation day."

Benny reached for Laura's hand. They walked in the huge

marble hallway liked they owned the place. No one noticed them. No one. The band was playing at ear-splitting decibels—tunes that weren't familiar to them.

"Oh no, Benny," Laura gasped, putting her hand over her face after seeing who was playing. "How did you know?"

"The paper," Benny said. "It mentioned Larry by name as the bandleader. Man, some things don't change, do they?"

Laura felt very uncomfortable.

"Let's go," Laura insisted. "I don't want to be here."

"All right," Benny said. "I'm sorry if I upset you. I didn't mean to. Just curious."

"No harm done, let's just go."

They both got in the car.

"I will say one thing for Larry—he still looks fit. Somewhat on the gaunt side, but fit."

"Well, if you must know," said Laura, "he's a druggie. That's one of the reasons I didn't mind him not spending much time with us. Gail also has at least two half sisters and one half brother from him—all living out of state. He's no good."

Benny wasn't exactly unhappy learning Larry turned out to be a louse. It restored his faith in his own instincts.

Benny started the car and turned on the oldie station. Like a ghost from the past, the first voice he heard was Bob Cheats.

"And one more for you old time Sonny and Cher fans out there," the familiar DJ said. "This one's for Frank in Merrillville. *All I Ever Need Is You!*"

Benny quickly turned the volume down. It was too painful to listen to.

"Don't!" said Laura. "I love that song. Turn it back on."

Benny's hand reluctantly reached for the knob and turned up the sound.

Laura saw Benny shaking.

"What's the matter? What happened?" she asked,

immediately clicking the knob off.

"That's—that's the same song that I heard when I left our graduation party nineteen years ago when you ran off with Larry. I'm scared. I know something bad is going to happen."

"Oh, is that all?" Laura said, doing her best to console her old boyfriend. "It's just a coincidence. It's just a song. It's just a song."

Benny calmed down and turned left onto Oak Street. He didn't speak until he turned right onto County Line Road. He changed the station only after reaching Potawatomi Trail. It was Sonny and Cher again—same song.

Benny changed it again, but the next station had the same song playing too.

Laura was getting nervous.

"What's going on? Is this a tape? What's happening?"

Benny looked at her, doing his best to ease her fear.

"This is what's bothering me," Benny started to explain. "I never told anyone—not even Marsha, my soon to be ex. There are certain things I can't tell, even you. But it's all about you, Laura. The song, the Pavilion, the lagoon, everything. I haven't been the same ever since the beating. It keeps flashing back in my mind, over and over and over again. Like a broken record I can't fix."

Benny sensed the alarm in Laura's eyes.

"No, please," Benny said softly. "Don't be afraid. Not of me. Please. I'm not unbalanced or anything. That's my tsores, as my grandmother used to say," referring to the Yiddish word for trouble.

Laura felt better after hearing that word. Her Jewish grandmother used to say that too.

"Other than that, I'm fine!"

Benny crossed the tracks at Route 12 like he was heading for U.S. 20.

"Aren't we going back to the bar?" Laura guardedly asked.

"We will," Benny said. "I just want to make one more quick stop."

Benny continued to drive down County Line Road. It was almost eleven o'clock, very dark with scant street lights. Laura was fidgeting with her purse and took out some lipstick. The Gas 'N Go sign was now visible—about three blocks up. Benny slowed to 15 mph and turned on his brights, illuminating the green street sign for Stagecoach Road. He signaled with his left blinker, then turned onto that dark, dark road.

"Why are we here?" Laura frightfully asked, dreading the worst. "Why are you taking me here?"

Benny didn't say a word as he observed the 20 mph speed limit while passing the houses, then sped up when he got to the gravel. He drove down the road, all the way down—to the tree. He stopped his car on the side of the road, still on the gravel, but next to a puddle.

"Please, don't be scared," Benny said, assuring Laura she wasn't in any danger. "I just have to see something. It'll just take two minutes then we'll leave."

Benny turned around and reached for his gun in the back seat and loaded it with seven bullets.

"MY GOD! WHAT ARE YOU GOING TO DO?" Laura screamed.

"Shhh," Benny said. "You're OK. You have nothing to worry about. I just want to look around outside for a few minutes. You see, this was the tree where the beating took place nineteen years ago. Right here. Right at this very spot. And here, look," Benny said, pointing to the gash on the tree from his car window. "That's where they crashed my car. The Mustang my folks bought me. Remember that car?"

Laura was shaking. She knew screaming for help was

futile. But then—she suddenly felt a lot better. Benny got out of the car and left the keys in the motor with the car running.

"I'll be right back," Benny said. "Just stay here. Give me two minutes, five, tops."

Benny took the gun with him and closed the door. Laura nervously waited, not knowing what to expect. Benny in fact did just want to see something. He wanted to see if his car and his boat trailer's tire tracks were adequately filled in with mud—thinking the heavy rain should have taken care of that. He walked into the woods to the spot where his trailer was parked. The tire tracks were gone. He looked for his car tracks and didn't see any. He was relieved. The only remnant of the murders was a small piece of rope Frank left behind when he stole Gerald's body. Benny left it there.

All of a sudden, he heard a loud car coming down the road—like it had a broken muffler. "Am I imaging this?" he asked himself. He wasn't. The sound of the muffler got louder and louder with each passing second. He saw the lights coming towards him. Laura's there by herself, he thought. I have to get to her. The sound of the broken muffler was now just a few yards away. It rushed passed him as he rushed out of the woods. The car stopped, screeching its brakes when the driver saw Laura sitting all by herself in the passenger's side. Four men got out—each in their early twenties and up to no good. They were dressed like skinheads and they probably were. All with Mohawks, tattoos, and pockmarked faces. And they were all holding beer cans when they got out, approaching Laura while licking their chops. Laura saw them and tried to hit the master car lock but couldn't find it. One of the men opened her door.

Laura screamed for Benny.

"There's no one else here," one of the goons fiendishly said while covering Laura's mouth. "Don't make fools out of us.

We know what we want!"

The other three were only too glad to help. They pulled Laura out of the car and pushed her to the wet ground and started ripping her clothes off. One of them already had his pants pulled down. They were drunk and whooping it up like the crazy derelicts they were. Then, it seemed out of nowhere, Benny walked up to the back of his car.

"LET HER GO!" he shouted. "LET HER GO, NOW!"

One of the men was already mocking Benny.

"Let her go, huh fucker! And what if we don't? What are you going to do?"

Benny didn't show his gun then repeated himself.

"I'M GIVING YOU A CHANCE TO GO AND GET OUT OF HERE, NOW!" he emphatically repeated. "NOW! JUST WALK AWAY!"

The thugs were laughing at Benny and getting impatient. Two of them threw their beers to the ground and headed towards him. Benny waited until they were four feet in front of him, then drew his gun, steadily pointing it with two hands directly at the first guy.

"Now wait a minute," one of them said, raising his hands in a defensive pose, but still approaching. "We were just lea......"

BOOM! Benny shot him in the head, splattering his brains in the air. The other three got up and ran for their cars. Too late.

BOOM! BOOM! BOOM! Benny shot the other three, killing two instantly, and wounding the third. He walked up to the wounded man—the one who had his pants off. BOOM! Benny shot off his stiff dick. The wounded animal tried to get up, but Benny finished him off with his second to last bullet. BOOM right in his left temple, his brains turned to crow feed.

Benny lowered his gun and ran over to help Laura.

302

"Jesus, Benny," Laura gasped, happy to be alive. "How did you know?"

Benny gently placed her in the car and grabbed his jacket from the back seat, wiping her off.

"How did I know what?"

Laura took the jacket from Benny and placed it over her legs.

"How did you know to take your gun?"

"I didn't," Benny said. "This place gives me the willies, so I thought I'd take it with me. It makes me feel safer."

"And me too!" Laura said, thankfully.

Benny looked at the blood splatter on his car, shook his head, and got a towel out of his trunk, cleaning if off the best he could. He also got a change of clothes.

"I wish I had some new clothes for you, Laura."

"Oh, that's okay—no blood on me. I'm just wet."

Benny got in the car and put his gun in the back seat, driving past the bodies and back to County Line Road.

"Do you want anything?" Benny asked Laura. "Maybe something else to eat?"

Laura smiled, and looked at Benny like he was crazy.

"No, I don't want anything to eat. In fact I shouldn't have eaten dinner tonight. I woke up feeling sick this morning—sort of nauseous."

Benny stopped his car and looked at her face.

"You mean.......OH NO!"

The End